A Scandal in Scarlet

A Scandal in Scarlet

A SHERLOCK HOLMES BOOKSHOP MYSTERY

Vicki Delany

CROOKED
LANE

NEW YORK

Copyright © 2018 by Vicki Delany

Published in the United States by Crooked Lane Books, an imprint of The Quick Brown Fox & Company LLC.

Crooked Lane Books and its logo are trademarks of The Quick Brown Fox & Company LLC.

Library of Congress Catalog-in-Publication data available upon request.

ISBN (mass market): 978-1-64385-027-6
ISBN (hardcover): 978-1-68331-790-6
ISBN (ebook): 978-1-68331-791-3

Cover illustration by Joe Burleson
Book design by Jennifer Canzone

Printed in the United States.

www.crookedlanebooks.com

Crooked Lane Books
34 West 27th St., 10th Floor
New York, NY 10001

Hardcover Edition: November 2018
Mass Market Edition: December 2019

10 9 8 7 6 5 4 3 2 1

For my marvelous daughters,
Alex, Julia, and Caroline

Chapter One

I love owning a dog. I love being owned by a dog. No matter how tough the day has been or how low my mood might be, being greeted at the door by a joyful, exuberant animal is one of life's greatest pleasures. It's hard to stay tired or grumpy or in a thoroughly foul mood in the face of those bright eyes, perky ears, lolling tongue, shivering body, and tail wagging hard enough to knock the knickknacks off side tables.

I don't, however, love having a dog when I get home late, tired and hungry, and have pet-owner duties to perform before I can look after myself. Still, you have to take the (very occasional) bad with the (almost always) good.

"You won't mind missing your walk just this once, will you?" I said to Violet, the cocker spaniel.

She lowered her head and whimpered. "Okay," I said. "You win. Give me a minute to change my shoes and we'll go out. Walk!" I was rewarded by a dance of pure joy.

I was tired. Bone tired. It had been a hard day at work. My shop assistant, Ashleigh, had come down with a dose of summer flu and I had to manage the Sherlock Holmes Bookshop and Emporium myself in the middle of the Cape Cod tourist season. Tourist season means lots of customers and long hours.

Today, the hottest new Sherlock Holmes pastiche novel had been released, and my shop's order had somehow been lost in the chaos. I'd been turning away disappointed customers all day. Some, I feared, would order online and never return to my little shop at 222 Baker Street.

Next door, at number 220, Mrs. Hudson's Tearoom, Fiona, one of the waitresses, was down with the same bug as had felled Ashleigh. There was a crisis of some sort involving blueberries, and Jayne Wilson, part owner and head baker, had burst into tears and threatened to walk out the door. Forever. All while the lineup of eager afternoon tea drinkers stretched out the door and down the sidewalk.

Shortly before nine o'clock in the evening, as I was contemplating flipping the sign on the door to "Closed" a few minutes early, a customer came in. I greeted her warmly and told her to let me know if she needed any help.

As it happened, she did need my help. She needed a full explanation of which stories were contained in which volume of the *Collected Stories of Sherlock Holmes*. She needed to know which short story collections were not too scary and which one contained a story by Hank Phillippi Ryan (*Echoes of Sherlock Holmes*). She wanted a full plot description of each of the Laurie R. King books and asked if she'd find it too unbelievable that Sherlock Holmes had been to Timbuktu, as described in *Sherlock Holmes, The Missing Years: Timbuktu* by Vasudev Murthy. Was it realistic, she asked, that Sherlock would have had children, as was the premise of several series, including *The Daughter of Sherlock Holmes* by Leonard Goldberg? I answered all her questions with a smile and tried not to glance at the clock over the sales counter. Soon the smile turned into a grimace, and I pulled out my phone to check the time. More than once. And not subtly either.

Still she chatted. She picked up and examined every book and then put them back in the wrong place. I ran after her, trying not to be too obvious about reshelving them. Eventually I didn't worry about being too obvious about it. She liked the Benedict Cumberbatch interpretation of Sherlock, she told me, but Robert Downey Jr.'s not so much. Too frivolous, she thought. Didn't I agree?

I agreed with everything. Absolutely everything.

All the time she fussed over the shop cat, Moriarty. He wound himself around her legs, he purred, he preened. He allowed her to pick him up and stroke him. Between barking out rapid-fire questions, she complimented him on his regal bearing, his sleek black coat, his friendly personality. Moriarty peered at me from under her arms. He didn't even bother to try to hide his self-satisfied smirk.

At quarter to ten, the woman put the cat down. "That was so interesting. Thank you. I'll have to think about it."

And she left. Unencumbered by any purchases.

I twisted the lock on the door behind her and glared at Moriarty. He yawned mightily and stretched every fiber of his lean body before heading off to his bed under the center table, letting me know that his work was done for the day and he was looking forward to a good night's sleep.

I, unfortunately, had things to do once I closed the shop. I'd arranged to have a drink after work with my friend Irene Talbot, a journalist with our local newspaper, the *West London Star*. I managed to send her a text saying I was delayed while the non-shopper fussed over Moriarty. I hoped Irene would tell me not to bother, but her reply said she was waiting.

Once I'd switched off the lights and locked up, I dragged myself down to the Blue Water Café. Irene, so I discovered, had been offered a position at a newspaper in St Louis. It was a good job, but, she moaned, could a Cape Cod girl ever be happy in the landlocked flatlands? She didn't really want my advice; she needed to use me as a sounding board. I had a drink I didn't want and sat in my chair on the restaurant's deck, bouncing her words back to her. It was a beautiful Cape Cod summer's night; we were sitting outside in the warm evening, looking out over the dark sea, but I could barely keep myself awake.

At long last Irene said, "Maybe I should talk to Joe McManus. He went to Chicago."

"Excellent idea," I said, having no idea who Joe McManus was or what might be wrong with Chicago. I waved for the check, said my good nights and staggered home.

I was thinking fondly of my lovely, soft, comfortable bed when I remembered Violet had been alone most of the day. I live with my great-uncle Arthur, and Violet is technically his dog. But right now Arthur was cruising somewhere in the Mediterranean. Our next-door neighbor, Mrs. Ramsbattan, has a key to the house; if I can't get away from the store during the day, she comes over to fill the water bowl and let Violet out into the enclosed yard. But Mrs. Ramsbattan is almost Uncle Arthur's age, late eighties, and she needs the assistance of a cane, so Violet doesn't get a walk.

That task is left up to me. I took the leash off the hook by the mudroom door. Beautiful liquid brown eyes stared lovingly up into mine.

It wasn't terribly late when we left the house, not much after eleven, but this is a quiet part of a quiet town. Blue Water Place, our street, is a stretch of nice houses and well- maintained gardens. Some of the homes are new, many are renovated, and a handful date from centuries past, such as the 1756 salt box in which Great-Uncle Arthur and I live.

Once I was outside, feeling the caress of warm salty air on my skin and the scent of roses and the sea in my nose, I began to enjoy the walk. Violet wandered back and forth across the sidewalk, sniffing under bushes and at patches in the grass, finding sensations only she could interpret. A startled squirrel darted up a knurly oak as old as my house.

The stretch of harbor at the foot of Blue Water Place is a family-friendly boardwalk of ice cream shops, souvenir stores, and small markets. The lights of the Blue Water Café twinkled in the distance, and lamps from small fishing boats or pleasure craft bobbed gently as the ocean rose and fell.

We turned left at Harbor Road, heading away from town. The lights from the restaurants, shops, and the fishing pier fell away. The fourth-order Fresnel lens of the West London Lighthouse flashed its rhythm of three seconds on, three seconds off, three seconds on, and twenty seconds off. We walked down the silent street, the only sounds the swish of the occasional passing car and the gentle purr of the incoming surf against the rocky shore.

Some of the houses facing out to sea along this stretch of the road are very old. Old by American standards, that is. Not so old for someone born and raised in England, as I was.

The oldest surviving house in West London is now a museum. Built in 1648 by Robert Scarlet and family, who settled in Massachusetts in 1640, it's called Scarlet House in their honor. The property consists of kitchen and herb gardens and a working barn. The home itself has been carefully restored to its original condition and furnished with authentic period furniture and household utensils. Costumed volunteers work at tending to a few sheep and goats or sharpening scythes in the barn, and baking bread or making cakes over the open kitchen fires. It's hugely popular with school groups in the spring and tourists in the summer and fall.

As we passed the museum, Violet stopped so suddenly I bumped into her. Her ears stood up, and she woofed, low in her throat. Her head turned from side to side, and her nose twitched, pulling scents out of the air. This was not the stance she used when she detected the presence of a cat or a squirrel. She barked again. I sniffed the air, and at last my feeble human senses caught up with Violet's. The slightest trace of smoke drifted on the air. Then it was gone. The breeze was blowing inland, bringing us fresh air off the sea.

"What is it?" I said to Violet. She was staring intently at the white picket fence around Scarlet House. The wind shifted slightly, bringing another trace of smoke toward me. Violet barked.

I quickly retraced my steps and peered over the gate. An out-of-place electric light burned over the front door, and a soft glow came from the barn around back. Otherwise, all was in darkness.

Then I saw it. In the front window, a flash of red and yellow. Even as I watched, not yet entirely sure of what I was seeing, the light began to move and to grow.

Fire.

I threw open the gate and ran onto the property. I fumbled in my pocket and found my phone. I dropped the leash, pressed the emergency button, and punched 9-1-1.

"Fire, police, or ambulance?" said a calm voice.

"Fire. Scarlet House, the museum on Harbor Road. I can see flames."

"Are you safe, madam? Is anyone inside the building?"

"I'm fine. I'm just passing. I'm outside. I'll check."

"Please don't—" she said. Her words were cut off as I shoved the phone back into my pocket.

Violet was barking now, the sound constant and frantic. The animals in the barn bellowed their panic. I ran toward the house. A large padlock was looped through a wooden latch. I pounded on the door. It felt warm beneath my touch.

"Fire! Fire! Is anyone in there?"

No reply.

Hardly any time at all passed before sirens could be heard coming down the street. I continued hammering on the door. It was highly unlikely someone would be inside at this time of night, but it was also highly unlikely the empty building would catch fire. The flames were building now, eagerly gobbling up the old wooden furniture and dusty rugs, biting into the ancient wooden beams. I'd read somewhere that a fire doubles in size every minute. This one was moving faster than that. The entire house would be gone soon.

"Step aside, ma'am," said a voice. A hand touched my shoulder. I turned to see a man dressed in full bunker gear. His intense dark eyes studied me. "Is anyone in there?"

"Not that I know of. I was passing and smelled smoke. I'm trying to alert them just in case."

"I need to you get out of the way. Please. You and your dog."

I looked around. In the—what, five minutes?— since I'd stepped into the yard, the scene had changed totally. Firefighters ran across the lawn, dragging hoses behind them, shouting orders. As though night had ended early, bright light flooded the yard, and red and blue emergency lights filled the street. More sirens approached. The curious were emerging from nearby houses, many dressed in pajamas.

"Is that your dog?" the firefighter said.

Violet stood in the center of the lawn, barking her head off. Her leash trailed on the ground behind her. I smiled at her. She knew better than to get too close to the burning building, but she wasn't going to run off and leave me alone.

"Yes, she is. The barn. Animals are in there."

"We'll take care of that, ma'am." His voice was polite but firm. He didn't need any help from me.

I hurried toward Violet, scooped up her leash, and led her off the museum property. There was nothing she and I could do here but get in the way. I wasn't, at the moment, particularly curious. I've been at fire scenes before, and I know how the firefighters operate.

Police were attempting to string tape around the property and keep onlookers back. I spotted a person I knew and headed toward her. "Evening, Officer Johnson."

Stella Johnson half-turned. "Gemma Doyle. Hi. Can you move away, please?"

"Happy to. I wanted to let you know that I'm the person who spotted the fire and called it in."

"Detective Estrada's on call tonight. She'll be here soon, and you can tell her what you saw."

"Uh, maybe not. She'll be busy, and I have nothing of importance to say. I smelled smoke and saw flames in the window and called nine-one-one. I knocked on the door, so it might have my fingerprints. That's all. I saw no one on the grounds or on the street in the minute or so prior to seeing the fire. I'll go down to the station in the morning and make a statement."

"She'd rather talk to you now."

"I have absolutely no doubt about that. You can tell her I was so traumatized I had to go straight home and lie down."

Johnson studied me. "A less traumatized witness I've yet to see."

"I don't display my feelings openly. You know what we English are like. Stiff upper lip and all that. Or so they say. Besides, my dog is traumatized." Johnson eyed the animal sitting calmly at my feet. Violet wagged her stubby tail. If she could have smiled, she would have.

I gave the leash a slight tug, and we set off home. I might have walked faster than I had earlier. Detective

Louise Estrada was not, shall we say, my best friend. She'd be more likely to accuse me of starting the fire in order to attract attention to myself than to hear what little I had to report.

I gave no more thought to the fire or speculated on what might have caused it. The investigators would find out soon enough.

Chapter Two

Rather than me having to go down to the police station, the police came to me the following morning, in the much more pleasant form of Detective Ryan Ashburton. I opened the back door, wiping sleep from my eyes, to find Ryan and an extra-large takeout tea waiting for me.

I took the offered mug without a word and lowered my face to it. Warm, scented steam enveloped me. "Mmm."

I stepped back and Ryan came in. He greeted Violet with as much enthusiasm as she greeted him. Mutual admiration over, she ran past him into the yard to see what the neighborhood squirrels had been up to in the night.

"To what do I owe the honor of this visit?" I sipped my tea. English breakfast, with a splash of milk, no sugar, prepared properly.

"You're the hero of the hour," he said.

"I am?" I didn't feel much like a hero with bedhead, watery eyes, wearing yellow polka-dot shorty pajamas. No doubt I still had impressions of my pillow pressed into my cheek. It was eight AM. I'd slept soundly, undisturbed by dreams of fire and smoke.

Ryan pressed a kiss onto the top of my head and then dropped into a kitchen chair. I took the other while trying, no doubt fruitlessly, to tidy my mop of wild curls.

"You called nine-one-one last night. The fire at the museum."

"Violet and I were out for our nightly walk, and I saw flames in the window. Modesty forces me to admit that Violet noticed it first. The wind was blowing inland, carrying the smoke away from me. If she hadn't alerted me, I would have walked on past. I was planning to go up the hill at the next intersection and return home that way."

"I'll get the mayor to give the medal to Violet then."

The hero of the day ran into the kitchen. Ryan gave her a scratch on the top of her head. She'd prefer that to a shiny piece of tin and a colored ribbon any day.

"Do you know what caused it?" I asked.

"The arson investigator was on site first thing this morning. Looks, he says, like a candle had been left to burn down. Louise is talking to the museum staff, and I said I'd handle you."

I grinned at him. "As if."

Ryan Ashburton was a good-looking man at any time, but never more so than when he laughed, and he laughed now. Six foot three and solidly built, he had chiseled cheekbones, short black hair and expressive blue eyes, and a strong jaw that seemed as though, no matter how recently he'd shaved, it always had a cover of stubble.

He and I had a complicated connection. We'd been in a serious relationship once, on the point of getting engaged. (Of that fiasco, all of it my fault, the less said the better.) He had moved to Boston for a few years and had come back a couple of months ago when the job of lead detective for the WLPD came open.

And we found that our feelings for each other hadn't faded.

But I'd run afoul of the West London police before, through absolutely no fault of my own. Things had not gone well for Ryan when the Chief and Detective Estrada thought that I exerted an undue influence on him. Ryan's career was important to him, and thus to me, and so we stood at a crossroads. Sort of in a relationship, but not fully.

"Were you able to . . . uh . . . deduce anything, Gemma?" he asked now.

"I smelled smoke and saw flames. I put those facts together and decided, in an instant, that the museum was on fire. Sherlock Holmes couldn't have done better."

He didn't rise to the bait. "You didn't see or hear anything else?"

"Nothing. I saw no one, I heard nothing out of place other than the fire itself. I called nine-one-one the moment I realized what was happening. I knocked on the door, in case anyone was inside, a vagrant who'd fallen asleep or something like that. The door was locked, and no one answered. The firefighters arrived and I left." I studied his face. "You don't look overly concerned about this, so I'll assume no one was inside."

He shook his head. "No. And we're pretty sure it wasn't arson."

I sipped my tea. "Have you had breakfast yet? I can do scrambled eggs, and I bought some sausage from the farmer's market on Monday."

"I'd like that," Ryan said.

Violet, who hadn't yet had her breakfast, barked in agreement.

* * *

By the time Ryan left, it was time for me to get ready for work. Ashleigh had texted to say she was feeling better and would be at work today as scheduled. I was very pleased to hear it.

At five minutes to ten, I went into Mrs. Hudson's Tearoom for a muffin and another cup of tea. Uncle Arthur and I own half of the business, and Jayne Wilson, who serves as the manager and head baker, owns the other half.

"Morning, Gemma," Fiona said from behind the counter when it was my turn to be served.

"I'm glad to see you back," I said. "Feeling better?"

"Much. Did you hear about the fire last night?"

"I did."

"If you have a minute, Jayne wants to talk to you. She told me to send you in."

"Thanks." I accepted a raspberry muffin, always my second choice. Apparently the Great Blueberry Crisis was not yet resolved. I went through the swinging doors into Jayne's domain. By now I knew the picture of total chaos that greeted me was anything but. Jayne knew what she was doing and always did it with competence and efficiency. Occasional moments of complete panic don't last long. Yesterday's near meltdown had been a rare event. I might be a partner in the business, but at this side of the counter I'm very much a silent partner. A kitchen, of any sort, is not a place in which I feel entirely comfortable.

Unless I'm eating some of Jayne's baking, that is.

"What's up?" I said.

A lock of blond hair had escaped its net, and Jayne brushed it out of her eyes with a flour-dotted hand. At the moment she was stirring pale yellow batter in the industrial-sized mixer. Jocelyn, her assistant, rolled out pastry and cut it into small circles to make the base for miniature fruit tarts. Loaves of bread for lunchtime sandwiches and trays of scones to be served at afternoon tea were cooling on racks. Something fragrant was about to come out of the oven.

Heaven, I sometimes thought, must smell like Jayne's kitchen.

"Did you hear about the fire last night at the museum down by the harbor?" Jayne asked.

"I did."

"No one was hurt, thank heavens—not even the animals—but the house suffered a lot of damage."

"Much of their fabulous old furniture was destroyed," Jocelyn said. "Some of it dated from the seventeenth century."

"I don't have much time," I said. "I have to open the store. What do you want to talk about?"

"My mom's a volunteer at the museum," Jayne said.

"Of course she is." Leslie Wilson was a West London stalwart. Any committee to do with the promotion of arts and culture in town, Leslie would be on it.

"The museum committee had an emergency conference call meeting this morning. They need to raise funds to repair the house and restock what was lost."

"They move fast."

"That they do. Mom said they're going to move the educational programs into the barn and the back fields in the meantime, but they're determined to reopen the house as soon as possible."

"Very admirable. Dare I ask why you're telling me this?"

"It'll cost money, Gemma. A lot of money. The museum's important to the town. It attracts visitors, visitors who then shop on Baker Street."

"Or have afternoon tea," Jocelyn added.

"I know that," I said. "I'd be happy to make a donation."

"Mom says they're planning an auction as a start," Jayne said. "They're going to ask all the shops to donate something."

"I can put in a basket of books."

Jayne was thirty-two, the same age as me, short and thin and extremely attractive with soft blond hair, a heart-shaped face, good cheekbones, and perfect skin and teeth. She hefted the bowl of batter in her arms. She was a lot stronger than she looked. While she talked, she scooped sticky globs of batter into prepared cake tins. "Think bigger, Gemma. Much, much bigger."

I tried to think bigger. The Emporium was primarily a bookstore. We specialized in the Sherlock Holmes canon and modern pastiche novels and story collections, as well as nonfiction about the life and times of Sir Arthur Conan Doyle and historical novels set in the gaslight era. As well as books, we sold a wide variety of Holmes-related merchandise and things to do with the many TV shows and movies about the Great Detective. I didn't deal in anything truly collectable, except the occasional second edition Holmes book or damaged first.

"Maybe Arthur can think of something," Jayne said.

"I'll ask. What are you giving?"

She turned to me with a grin. *Oh no.* "We've agreed to host the auction here, at the tearoom."

"We have, have we?"

"Yes, Gemma. We have."

Chapter Three

Before I could contact Great-Uncle Arthur for some suggestions as to what we could donate to the museum fund-raiser, he called me.

Arthur might be cruising in the Mediterranean, but his vast network of retired ladies and gentlemen kept him fully apprised of everything that went on in West London. When I say he's cruising, I don't mean he's on a giant ocean liner with a swimming pool and billiard room, linen table napkins, and crystal glasses. I mean a twenty-five- or thirty-foot sailboat controlled by him and one or two of his old navy pals. Uncle Arthur had spent his career in the Royal Navy, eventually becoming master and commander of a battleship. To say the sea was in his blood would be an understatement. More like the sea *was* Arthur Clive Doyle's blood.

"How's the weather over there?" I asked him.

"Spot of rain the other day," he replied in his deep, rolling voice, capable of issuing orders in the face of a category-five hurricane. The "spot of rain" might have been a storm of the strength that blew Odysseus off course. "We put into Palma de Majorca to fix a small problem." The "small" problem might have been a downed mast or a shredded hull. Great-Uncle Arthur typified English understatement.

"Estelle Johnson emailed to tell me the museum committee is in need of items to be donated for their fund-raiser," he said.

"That's right. I'm thinking a basket of books from the shop."

"We can do better than that, Gemma. Scarlet House is a vital component of the West London tourist business."

"What do you have in mind?" I asked.

"*The Valley of Fear.*"

"Are you sure? That's your favorite book."

"All the more reason to let it find a new home for a worthy cause. Can you take care of that, my dear? The book is on the shelf in my room."

"Will do."

"Love to Violet," he said, and hung up.

The Valley of Fear my uncle referred to was an original Sherlock Holmes story, the last of the four novels in the Holmes canon, written in 1914. His was a first edition in pristine condition. I hoped it would get what it was worth at the auction. Rare books are only of value to people who value rare books. To everyone else, they're nothing but old volumes taking up space on the shelf and gathering dust.

*   *   *

The Sherlock Holmes Bookshop and Emporium is located in a small yellow building with white trim that started life as a house. The shop itself occupies one room on the ground floor, with furniture and shelving separating the various areas: Sherlock Holmes originals, pastiche, nonfiction, gaslight, young adult, and merchandise. A reading nook with a comfortable chair, side table, and lamp has been set up next to the bay window overlooking the street. A back door tucked under the stairs leads to the alley. All the nonpublic areas of the building are located upstairs: my office, staff washroom, storage rooms. If ever we have to move, I will never again buy a place that requires carrying boxes full of books up and down seventeen steps all day.

It was the height of the tourist season, and we were satisfyingly busy. Otherwise, an uneventful week passed after the fire. On a sunny Thursday afternoon, a few people were browsing the Emporium shelves while Ashleigh helped a customer pick out a book for her granddaughter's birthday present. She held up *Rivals in the City* by Y. S. Lee, and the woman said, "That will be perfect, thank you. Plus one of those books with the illustrations done in Legos. Such a clever idea. A great way to introduce young people to classic books." She was referring to the series of original Holmes stories illustrated by P. James Macaluso.

I glanced at the clock on the wall, next to a framed reproduction of *Beeton's Christmas Annual* from December 1887, the first time Sherlock Holmes appeared in print, in *A Study in Scarlet*.

The clock said 3:38. Time for me to go. Every afternoon promptly at twenty minutes to four, I head into Mrs. Hudson's for a tea break and my daily partners' business meeting with Jayne.

"I'm popping next door. Back soon." I said.

Ashleigh gave me a nod. One of the highlights of my day is seeing what my assistant chooses to wear this time. Ashleigh does far more than change her clothes. She changes her entire persona on a daily basis. Today she'd dressed in a wide-brimmed straw hat, a T-shirt that said "Gardening IS Life" amid a riot of flowers, baggy navy blue capris, and pink-and-purple rubber boots.

She hadn't done a thing to her face, but she looked at least ten years older than she had yesterday.

I went through the sliding doors that join the Emporium to the tearoom. Jayne was arranging items on the shelves next to the kitchen, where we have a small selection of teas and tea sets and locally sourced preserves for sale. She held a length of pink rope in her hands. "What do you think of this?"

"Not much," I said. "It's ugly."

"Geez Gemma. Don't say that out loud."

"Then you shouldn't have asked me out loud. What is it?"

"A whimsy. A decoration. They're made by a woman in Brewster, and I bought a couple to see if they sell." She looped one end of the rope over a nail in the top shelf. It was about five feet long; a series of miniature teacups had been tied by their handles into the rope at regular intervals. Jayne secured a second "whimsy" to the other end of the shelf. I peered at the price tag. "Fifty dollars?"

"Handmade, Gemma. By a local artist."

"You never can tell what some people will buy," said the woman who sold "I am SHERlocked" mugs and life-sized cutouts of Benedict Cumberbatch.

"Mom's here," Jayne said. "She wants to talk to us."

Leslie Wilson sat at the table in the window alcove, the one where Jayne and I like to have our meeting, if it's free. A woman I hadn't met, but whom I recognized from around town, was with her. She wore the small scarlet badge that was the emblem of the museum pinned to her shirt. Leslie waved at me, and I headed toward them. The chimes over the door tinkled as a group left.

The tearoom closes at four. Three tables, other than ours, were still occupied. Fiona brought out a plate of scones along with tiny pots of butter, clotted cream, and strawberry jam for a table for two. A larger group of six sun-bleached, laughing women, shopping bags piled in heaps around them, poured out the last of their tea. In the back corner, a young couple gazed intently into each other's eyes while their tea went cold and their pastries remained uneaten.

Jayne and I slipped into our seats, and Jocelyn put a teapot in the center of the table. Today's choice was Darjeeling.

"Gemma," Leslie said. "I don't think you've met Kathy. Kathy Lamb, Gemma Doyle. Kathy's the chair of the Scarlet House board and is in charge of the auction."

"Pleased to meet you," we said in unison. Kathy was in late middle age and recently divorced, judging by the slight tan line on the ring finger of her left hand. Judging by the dark circles under her eyes and the angry lines radiating out from the corners of her mouth, she was also still bitter about it. I'd seen her around town a few times over the years. In the past, her hair, now a brittle blond, had been brown streaked with gray, and her makeup had been middle-class New England subdued.

Now it was what I'd call angry: lipstick a sharp red line, eyes outlined in fierce black. She had, probably to her dismay, put on a good stone, fourteen pounds, recently—another indication that the divorce had not been her idea and that a young lover, or at least a new lover for Mr. Lamb, had been responsible for the breakup of her marriage. I suspected the lawyers had been expensive, and even if the settlement had gone in her favor, it had not left her in a comfortable position. Her clothes were several years out of date, showing signs of wear, and they no longer fit properly with the weight she'd put on. She didn't have the money, or the desire, to buy anything new.

I've been learning from Jayne not to tell people what I know about them. She says they don't like that, and so I refrained from offering Kathy my sympathies. Instead, I handed her a page I'd printed from a book collector's catalog. "This will give you some idea of the potential value of the book we're contributing and should help you set the opening bid price."

"Thank you so much," Kathy said. "This is very generous of you, and it's bound to fetch a handsome sum."

"It's not mine," I said, "but a gift from my great-uncle Arthur. He's away at the moment, so he won't make the auction."

"Be sure and thank him for me. And Jayne, thank you for offering to host our little event."

"It's our pleasure. Isn't it, Gemma? Gemma?"

"What? Oh yes. It's our pleasure."

"We'll be sending everyone a tax receipt for their donation," Leslie Wilson said.

"I hope you understand," Jayne said, "that I can't manage a full afternoon tea in July for the numbers you expect. It's the height of the season." She waved her hand to indicate the tearoom. "We open at seven in the summer and by four o'clock my staff and I want to drop where we're standing."

Jocelyn brought us a selection of tea sandwiches and pastries. One of the benefits of being part owner of a tearoom is that I get to indulge in the leftovers.

"The cream tea your mother and I discussed will be fine," Kathy said.

Jayne nodded. "We can prepare scones ahead of time, right, Gemma?"

I dared, perhaps foolishly, to hope that *we* didn't include *me*. "Right," I said.

"With only two choices of tea," Jayne said. "English breakfast plus a decaffeinated option, things won't get too complicated."

"That way attendees can concentrate on what's important," Leslie Wilson said. "Bidding at auction."

"Are you getting some good things?" Jayne asked.

"Oh yes," Leslie said. "Everyone has been so generous."

"Almost everyone," Kathy muttered.

Jayne and I exchanged glances.

"People have donated what they can afford, and that's all I expect," Kathy said. "Only one person flatly said no to my face."

"Maureen won't help at all?" I asked.

Kathy gave me *that* look. The one people get when they think I've read their mind. I don't read minds. I simply observe.

And yesterday I had observed Kathy coming out of Beach Fine Arts, located across the street from me at 221 Baker Street. It had been a gorgeous Cape Cod summer day, but a personal thundercloud might have hung over Kathy's head as she marched out of the store and down the street. Maureen Macgregor, proprietor, followed her out and stood in the doorway, watching Kathy tapping her foot angrily as she waited for the light at the intersection to change. Nothing out of the normal had been visible on Maureen's face. Her expression of sneering disapproval was so fixed, it was likely Maureen slept with it. Community spirit was not her strongest point. She didn't bother to decorate the street in front of her shop with flowers or potted plants, but instead dragged them over from the adjoining properties under cover of darkness.

"She had the nerve to tell me she doesn't see why she should be out the price of one of her goods because the museum was foolish enough to try to burn itself down." Fire blazed in Kathy's eyes at the memory. "As if she and her store aren't a part of this community."

I selected a cucumber-and-cream-cheese sandwich, my favorite.

"Speak of the devil," Jayne said. "Incoming."

As if our talk had summoned her, the door swung open, the chimes tinkled, and Maureen Macgregor marched into the tearoom. She often arrives minutes before closing, expecting a discount on the last of the day's baking. Jayne had long ago told her staff Maureen was to pay full price, but Maureen never stopped asking. I suspected that when Jayne or I weren't around, the women gave in just to make her go away.

"Good afternoon, Maureen," I said cheerfully. "How nice to see you today."

She grunted in her usual manner. "Must be nice," she said, "to be able to sit around talking and having high tea in the middle of the business day."

"High tea?" I said for the umpteenth time. "We don't serve high tea here. We serve afternoon tea. High tea is a working-class evening meal, whereas afternoon tea—"

"Whatever. I'm surprised you two are still in business, the way you carry on." Jayne and I were seated at chairs pulled up to the table, facing the door. Leslie and Kathy had taken the bench seats tucked into the window alcove. Kathy snorted, and Maureen noticed her for the first time.

"Oh, look. It's the museum committee having lunch on the museum budget. And you have the nerve to ask me to pay for it."

"That is simply not true," Leslie said. "We don't use museum funds for anything but operating the museum."

"Save your breath, Leslie." Kathy poured herself another cup of tea. Her voice was calm, but her hands shook with anger. Maureen definitely got under her skin. I wondered if it was more than just the refusal to donate a plastic lighthouse or set of postcards to the museum auction.

"I would have thought," I said, "a charity auction would be the perfect way to advertise the *fine art* you sell, Maureen." Beach Fine Arts sold anything but. They stocked the same made-in-China tourist stuff you could find up and down the coast, mass-produced postcards with standard Cape images, a few good gift cards by local artists, and a selection of Maureen's own art. Jayne thought the paintings were paint by number, and I had to agree. Half the people who went into Maureen's store mistakenly thought it was the location of the Sherlock Holmes shop. Instead of thanking me for sending business her way when that happened, it simply loaded another chip onto the pile on Maureen's shoulder.

"What does that mean?" she asked me.

I sipped my tea. "The proud owner will show her new possession off to her friends. Maybe she'll pass the business card stuck to the back of the painting on to others. People who attend charity auctions tend to be quite well off, wouldn't you agree, Kathy?"

"That's true."

"And they have well-heeled friends." I selected a raspberry tart. "Up to you. The museum will be giving receipts, so the donors can get a tax deduction on their donations."

Maureen harrumphed, but I caught the flicker of interest in her eyes at the magic words *tax deduction*. She spun on her heels and walked across the room to the counter.

I didn't catch what she said, but Fiona replied. "I'm sorry, Maureen; it's not our policy to offer discounts."

"You did it the other—"

"That'll be three fifty," Fiona said quickly.

Maureen grumbled, carefully counted out three dollars and fifty cents in coins, accepted a paper bag containing a slice of strawberry cake, and left, still grumbling.

Kathy shook her head once the door had slammed shut behind Maureen. "What a miserable person she is."

"Don't take it personally," I said. "She's nasty to everyone."

"I never did hear," Jayne said. "Did they find out what caused the fire?"

I knew, because Ryan had told me over dinner the other night. "The paper's playing it down," I said, "because no one was hurt, and it was probably an accident. The volunteer who was last to leave simply forgot to blow out a candle on a table in the main room. The candle burned down, and the dying flame must have flickered and caught a piece of paper someone had left on the table too close to it."

Kathy snorted. "Pure carelessness. Stupid woman."

I looked at her, surprised at her tone.

"That's not entirely fair," Leslie said. "Accidents happen."

"That's no excuse," Kathy said. "I haven't been board chair for long, but long enough to know some changes need to be made, and soon. Robyn was sloppy and indulgent, and now that I'm in charge, I intend to sweep out all the cobwebs she left behind. I was in the process of doing so when the fire started. Once we get this auction out of the way, I have even more reason to get the necessary changes made and put the museum on a far more efficient footing."

"Robyn did a good job when she was board chair," Leslie said. "She had her own style, yes, but you can't put any blame on her for the fire. She's not even on the board anymore."

"She kept that useless woman on far longer than she should have. That's exactly what I mean about cobwebs."

"What sort of changes are you talking about?" Leslie asked.

"You'll see. Right now, I need you to concentrate on the auction." Kathy gathered up her purse. "Thanks for this, Gemma. See you both next Saturday at four thirty."

"What's happening next Saturday at four thirty?" I asked.

"Gemma!" Jayne said. "You can't have forgotten already. You're serving tea."

Chapter Four

The following Saturday at four thirty, I managed to avoid serving tea at the Scarlet House restoration fund auction.

I was pleased Jayne had told Kathy and Leslie she couldn't do a full afternoon tea. I'd been roped into helping prepare for similar events in the past, and as I might have said, a kitchen is not my natural environment.

Jayne and Jocelyn had stayed late the night before, making hundreds of scones. I'd come into the tearoom at quarter to four, as ordered, to help them get the dishes washed and the tables reset for the auction. It was an advance-tickets-only function, and an excited Leslie had called Jayne this morning to let her know every seat had been sold.

Meaning we'd have a full house. More than a full house, as extra tables and chairs had been brought in by museum volunteers.

I wasn't surprised at the news. The museum team had been out in force all week, plastering the town with posters and making phone calls. When I told Jayne I was impressed at their efficiency, she said, "Poor Kathy has to have something to do. She can be a bit over the top sometimes, with all her talk about changes and new brooms sweeping out cobwebs, but Mom's glad she has this to throw her energy into. Bad enough that her husband left her after thirty-five years of marriage and two kids, but he did it *after* she'd sent out the invitations for their wedding anniversary party."

"Tough," I said. "I assume he ran off with some sweet-faced young thing?"

"On the contrary, he dumped her for a woman he met in church at a wedding, of all things. If anything, she's older than Kathy."

"Scandal in the vicarage. The stuff of classic mystery novels. Did this wedding guest leave a cheated-on husband?"

"She's a widow. A widow who inherited a lot of money after her husband's suspicious death."

I wasn't much interested in Kathy's marital problems, but that got my attention. "Suspicious how?"

Jayne shrugged. "I don't know the details. It happened when I was living in Boston. Mom said the police spent a lot of time looking into it, but no charges were ever laid."

"Gemma," one of the museum volunteers called, "can you give us a hand with these tables, please?" I hurried to obey. In order to squeeze as many patrons as possible into Mrs. Hudson's, we were going to move our tables closer together and fill the space with card tables and plastic chairs. I helped rearrange furniture while Fiona and Jocelyn quickly and efficiently threw red tablecloths over them and laid out napkins, silverware, bone china teacups, and matching plates. The tablecloths had been supplied by the museum. In keeping with the name of the museum,

Scarlet House, they were a dark red. Each table featured a thin plastic vase holding a single red carnation, which had been provided by one of the volunteers. Guests had been asked to dress in red to show their support of the museum, and I'd obliged by finding the one red item I had in my closet: a deep red—scarlet—blouse, worn with black capris. Jayne had bought red shoelaces specifically for today, which she handed to Jocelyn and Fiona to lace through their work sneakers.

My job was to stand at the door and collect tickets. I'd managed to get out of pouring tea when Jayne remembered past disasters. Shortly before the doors opened, I nipped into the Emporium, took *The Valley of Fear* out of a drawer beneath the sales counter, and picked a basket off the floor. The book was Uncle Arthur's personal contribution, and I needed to donate something myself on behalf of the shop. I'd bought an attractive wicker basket and filled it with both volumes of *The Complete Sherlock Holmes*, *Memoirs from Mrs. Hudson's Kitchen* by Wendy Heyman-Marsaw, a copy of the anthology *In the Company of Sherlock Holmes*, *Sherlock Holmes and the Case of the Disappearing Diva* by Gemma Halliday and Kelly Rey, a *Sherlock: The Mind Palace* coloring book, an "I am SHERlocked" mug, a book of photographs from the Jeremy Brett TV show, and a DVD of *Murder by Decree*, starring Christopher Plummer as Holmes. I was pleased with the basket: something for every variation of Holmes lover.

"I have my phone on me if you need me," I told Ashleigh, dressed today in a severe black skirt suit, with her hair pulled tightly back and plain glass spectacles perched on her nose. She once told me she dressed according to her mood. Presumably, today she was in the mood of an auctioneer at Sotheby's.

"It'll be great," she said. "The auction's the talk of the town."

"I'll be back as soon as it's over. Hopefully some of the people attending will wander in here after."

I took my donation into the small storage room at the back of Mrs. Hudson's. A steady stream of visitors had been dropping off their auction contributions throughout the day. Leslie Wilson was stationed in here to accept the goods and check them off her list. The room wasn't large, and today it was packed almost to the rafters. Leslie's face peered out at me from behind a box as I put my basket and *The Valley of Fear* onto a table. She put a pair of scissors on top of the box and reached for her clipboard. "That's the last of it, Gemma," she said, making a tick with a dramatic flourish.

"What's your job during the auction?" I asked. "I hope you won't be stuck in here guarding the things?"

She smiled at me. "Fortunately, no. One of the volunteers and I will run back and forth, bringing out the items in turn. Kathy's acting as the auctioneer."

"She's done a lot for this."

"She's been an absolute marvel, Gemma. She's thrown her heart and soul into organizing this thing. It's amazing how quickly it all came together. It wouldn't have happened without her enthusiasm and drive. There's been a lot of dissent on the museum board, and it hasn't been a nice place to be lately. Some people weren't entirely happy when Kathy took over as chair, but she's won everyone over with this. In that way, although not in any other, the fire did us a favor."

"As often happens in the face of disaster," I said.

Leslie glanced at her watch. "Almost four thirty."

"Then I'd better get to work. Good luck." I left her and assumed my post by the front door. The sliding door joining the tearoom to the Emporium had been closed so no one could come in that way. All I had to do was collect tickets and hand each arrival a copy of the auction program book, which listed all the items, the donors, and the suggested opening bid for each.

A large group of people were milling about outside, in a sea of red clothing, waiting for me to unlock the door. The moment I did so, Maureen Macgregor pushed her way through the crowd, a thin, flat rectangle wrapped in beige packing paper tucked under her arm. She had not received the memo and was not dressed in red.

"Ticket please," I said.

She waved the package at me. "I don't need a ticket. I've brought something for you to auction off." Judging by the size and shape, it was a painting.

"That's nice of you, Maureen, but you still need a ticket. This is a charity event. I bought a ticket. Even Jayne bought one, and she's doing all the work."

"More fool you," she said. She attempted to push her way past me. I stood firm.

"I didn't see your painting on the list," I said.

"What list?"

"The list of items to be auctioned. People want to know ahead of time what's on offer so they can mull over what they want to buy."

"I don't need to be on any list. Where's the auctioneer going to stand? I'll put this up there so everyone can see it."

"What's the hold up here?" a man's voice called.

"Maureen, will you get the heck out of the way," a woman said. "I'm not standing in the street all day."

Maureen spun around. "Pardon me, Janet O'Leary, but I'm donating one of my own paintings to this auction, and I have business to discuss first. I intend to ensure it's handled properly."

"I also made a donation," Janet replied. The light wind made the black feather on the scarlet fascinator attached to her head dance. "But I don't discuss my business in front of half of West London."

A riot on Baker Street would not be good for the museum's image. "Fiona," I said, beckoning the passing waitress, "take over here for a minute, will you?"

"But Jayne sent me to—"

"Won't be long." I grabbed Maureen's arm. "Let's find Kathy."

I dragged Maureen through the tearoom, dodging tables and chairs and museum volunteers, to where Kathy stood at the podium we'd borrowed from the library, studying her list. She was dressed in red from top to toe. Red shirt, red jacket, red trousers, red shoes. The jacket was too large for her and the trousers too long. I wondered if she'd borrowed the clothes.

She heard Maureen order me to unhand her and looked up. Kathy's eyes widened in surprise, and then her face settled into a serious frown.

Maureen waved the package at her. "I brought something for your auction. I hope that makes you happy."

Kathy swallowed heavily and made no attempt to smile. "You should have told me before this. We've prepared an auction sheet."

"Doesn't matter," Maureen said. "We'll put my painting right here where everyone can see it. You can auction it last, as a climax to the afternoon."

"I've already determined the order of presentation," Kathy said.

"Well then you'll have to un-determine it, won't you? Do you want my contribution or not?"

"Probably not," Kathy muttered.

"What was that?" Maureen said.

"Nothing," Kathy said.

"Why don't you unwrap it," I said, "and let us have a look at it?" The room was filling as people poured through the doors and found seats. I needed to get back to my post, but I was curious as to what Maureen had brought.

She peeled away the paper.

I swallowed a bark of laughter. Kathy gasped and said, "That's absolutely hideous!"

"I'll have you know I painted it myself," Maureen said.

"Then it's even more hideous." Kathy threw up her hands.

Hideous might not be the word I would have chosen. More like childish, amateurish, tasteless. The painting showed Elvis Presley, identifiable only by his baby-blue leisure suit and a balloon over his head saying "The King," swinging his hips on a Cape Cod beach. I peered closer and could see traces of the printed outline Maureen's paintbrush hadn't completely covered up.

"Get that horrible thing out of here," Kathy said.

"What's the matter with you?" Maureen yelled. "You asked me for a donation, and now you say you don't want it. Not good enough for you and your fancy committee, is it?"

"Are you trying to make me look like a fool?"

Ears began flapping at the tables nearest us. A sudden hush settled over the tearoom.

"I wouldn't have to try very hard to do that, now would I?" Maureen said.

An onlooker gasped. Someone else chuckled.

"I'll buy it myself just to get it out of my auction." Kathy's eyes were narrow with anger, her face was threatening to match the color of her outfit, and a vein pulsed in her forehead. "One dollar and fifty cents."

"Your auction? I thought this was for the museum." Maureen made no attempt to use her indoor voice. "Who appointed you Queen of West London, anyway?"

Kathy sputtered. A man at the front table laughed. I glared at him, and the laugh turned into a cough.

"Why don't we go into the back room and discuss this?" I said, attempting to be the voice of reason.

"There's nothing to discuss. This doesn't involve you, anyway. You and your Sherlock Holmes nonsense—you think you're so important in this town." Maureen might be yelling, but she showed none of the barely pent-up rage Kathy did. If anything, she was enjoying herself.

"Calm down," I said. "Both of you. You're creating a scene."

"I don't want that piece of junk in my auction," Kathy said. "You call yourself an artist? Ha! My sister's granddaughter could do better."

"How dare you!" Maureen shouted.

"You tell 'er, Kath," someone called, to much laughter. Maureen was not a popular figure in West London.

I touched Kathy's arm. "That's enough. Accept Maureen's gift in the spirit in which it's intended." What that spirit might be, I didn't know, but this was not the time to speculate.

Kathy visibly struggled to gather herself together, and then she reached for the painting. Maureen held on, looking as though she were going to put up a fight, but eventually she released it.

"I'll take this in the back with the other items," Kathy said through gritted teeth. "It will go in the middle of the auction. Lot 34B."

"Thank you," I said.

But Kathy had to squeeze in the last word. "The opening bid will be one dollar and fifty cents." She walked away with the ghastly thing.

"Happy now?" I said to Maureen.

She threw me a smirk. "I'd love a cup of tea. If there's one thing you English people are good for, it's making tea. Get me one, Gemma. Milk, two sugars. I see the mayor has arrived. I'll join her at her table." She walked away, back straight, head high, a slight swagger to her bony hips.

I took a couple of deep, cleansing breaths. I'd been told that was relaxing. It didn't seem to be working so I gave up and made my way to the front to relieve Fiona. I arrived in time to greet Grant Thompson.

"Good afternoon," I said. "Nice to see you here."

"How could I resist? I hear a first edition Conan Doyle is on offer." He smiled warmly at me, and the green flecks in his hazel eyes sparkled. He looked very handsome in a white dress shirt accented by a red bow tie and red pocket handkerchief.

I handed him a program book in exchange for his ticket. "So rumors say."

"Catch you later, Gemma."

Grant liked me. I liked him, and we had a lot in common, including a love of books and fond memories of England. He was American, but he'd studied at Oxford, where he'd learned to love a proper pub and a mug of hearty stout. For a while, something almost lit a spark between us, but I finally realized Ryan Ashburton was the man I loved. Grant had taken the change in our relationship well, and we remained friends.

Donald Morris, prominent Sherlockian, was one of the last people to arrive. He had dressed for the occasion not in red, but in a brown suit under an Inverness cape. A gold-framed pin showing a silhouette of the Great Detective with his pipe was fastened to his chest.

"Aren't you rather warm in that get-up?" I asked him.

"A gentleman dresses for the occasion, regardless of the weather," he said.

I searched through my memory banks, trying to remember if that was a quote from Holmes. If it was, it was obscure, and my own knowledge of the canon isn't that vast or very detailed.

I handed Donald a program. "Here for *The Valley of Fear*, are you?"

His narrow eyes glimmered. "I might have a mild interest." He glanced around the room. His face fell when he spotted Grant Thompson taking his seat. Donald was a keen collector, but he didn't have enough money to properly indulge his hobby. Grant, on the other hand, was a rare book dealer. He'd be prepared to spend whatever he thought he'd be able to sell the book for.

At quarter to five, every seat was taken, and all the program books had been handed out. At a signal from Jayne, the staff began serving tea. It wasn't complicated. Each table was preset with milk and sugar for the tea, and pots of jam and clotted cream and a plate of butter for the scones. Two teapots were placed on each table: a red or pink one containing English breakfast and a green or blue with decaffeinated tea. I helped Fiona and Jocelyn serve the scones. I suffered no mishaps, and none of the precious baking hit the floor. Food served, I went into the kitchen and took off my apron, as did Jayne. Then she and I joined Leslie at the table of museum volunteers, while Fiona and Jocelyn kept an eye on the teapots. The room was fragrant with the scent of hot tea and scones warm from the oven. People laughed and chatted and served themselves food and drink. I noticed some people, with looks of intense concentration on their faces, jotting notes in the margins of their auction booklet.

Not everyone had worn scarlet but enough had, in one way or another, that the audience looked as though they were attending a Valentine's Day party. The volunteers all had handcrafted corsages, made of red ribbon, pinned to their chests next to the museum's small badge.

Jayne and I were seated at a round table that normally accommodated six. We'd been squeezed in tight to make places for eight. Some of these women were regulars to the bookshop, and I was introduced to the ones I didn't know. One chair at our table was unoccupied. I glanced around the room. "Where's Kathy?"

"She's in the back doing a last-minute check," Leslie said. "She told me to leave her alone."

One of the volunteers was short and stout, with the round cheeks of a chipmunk and the twitchy, nervous mannerisms of a small animal venturing out of her nest for the first time. "I'm not surprised Kathy doesn't want to come out," she said. "There's nothing she loves more than to be the center of attention, and that woman ruined her spotlight." As one, the table turned to glare at Maureen leaning over the person next to her and waving her finger in the mayor's face. Her Honor's smile was fixed, and her eyes might have been rolling.

"Poor Kathy. She's worked so hard for the museum," another volunteer said. "We're lucky to have her at this critical time. Can you imagine if Robyn were still in charge? She'd still be organizing committees and arguing over whether we need coffee and tea at the meeting or if coffee's enough." She put on a serious frown and a deep voice. "'The twenty-second order of business will be to decide if two spoons of sugar per person are enough or if one will do.'"

Half the women at our table laughed. The other half scowled in disapproval. "Robyn might be a micromanager," Chipmunk-woman said, "but that's only because she always wants the best. We all know she's totally devoted to the museum. Kathy's only in it for herself."

"That's unfair, Sharon," someone said. "There's not a lot of glory, and certainly no money, to be found in running a museum of our size."

"Robyn was good at managing people," said a woman with deep black hair sprayed into a stiff helmet. "Which can't be said for Kathy, who's driven many of the longtime stalwarts away."

"Oh, pooh. That bunch of old biddies haven't had a new idea in this century." One of my store regulars laughed. "Heck, some of them probably hadn't had a new idea in the last century either. Kathy brought in fresh new blood. I, for one, am glad we have her."

"Speaking of Robyn," Helmet-hair said, "she's noticeable by her absence. I thought I saw her outside when I arrived."

"You were imagining things, Barb," Sharon said. "I'm not surprised she didn't come. Robyn's too proud to take a chance of Kathy humiliating her again."

"If Robyn feels she was humiliated, it's her fault," Helmet-hair, aka Barb, said. "Kathy merely pointed out the obvious, that—"

"Let's not squabble," Leslie said. "Regardless of what you think of Kathy, she's worked hard for this event, and she didn't need a public spat with Maureen on top of all the gossip about her husband."

"I can't believe they had the nerve to show up here," Sharon said.

"Disgraceful," Helmet-hair said. The others nodded in agreement. Tea was poured.

"You mean Kathy's ex-husband came?" I whispered to Leslie.

"Yup. That's him and his paramour at the table nearest the bookshop door. Gray hair and glasses and sour faces. They do look rather alike, come to think of it."

I had a quick peek. He had a thick mane of iron-gray hair curling around his collar and wore rimless glasses. Her white hair was cut short, and she peered myopically at the world through coke-bottle-bottom spectacles. If I didn't know otherwise, I'd assume they were a many-years-married couple, judging by the way they sat in adjacent chairs but didn't look at each other or say anything more intimate than "Please pass the milk." He stared off into space, munching on a scone, and she scowled into her teacup. Neither of them had worn a drop of red, and they didn't join the conversation at their table.

I didn't recognize her, but I knew him. He was a bookshop regular, fond of Holmes pastiche novels, particularly ones that featured a twist on Holmes and Watson as we know them. His most recent purchase had been *Sherlock Holmes—The Labyrinth of Death* by James Lovegrove, but that was months ago. He hadn't been into the Emporium for quite some time. I hoped he'd drive up the bidding on my basket of books.

Once the scones were but crumbs on people's plates, and the jars of jam and Devonshire cream had been scraped clean, Jocelyn and Fiona went through the room one last time, offering fresh pots of tea. The plan was to have a short pause before the auction began. Give people a bathroom break and a chance to greet their friends or study the auction book in detail. I'd given the book a quick glance and had decided to bid on item number twenty-three, a pearl necklace. I didn't need, or particularly want, a pearl necklace, but it was one of the few items I could comfortably afford, providing the bidding didn't go too high. West Londoners had been extremely generous.

People were getting up from their seats and milling about. A few headed for the restroom, and some studied the teapots and tea paraphernalia we offered for sale. Of the two ropes decorated to make teapot chains Jayne had earlier hung on the wall, only one remained. Someone must have bought one already. Jayne would be pleased.

I leaned back in my chair and smiled at my friend. "That went well. The scones were delicious."

She lifted her teacup in a salute. "Now that part's over, I can relax and enjoy the auction. I see Rebecca Stanton and some of her crowd came—that should drive the prices up. Are you going to bid on anything, Gemma?"

"I might try for the pearl necklace. I could give it to my mother for Christmas. If I don't get that, then maybe the dinner at the Blue Water Café. Speaking of which, how's Andy?"

"He's fine, I guess."

"You guess? Don't you know?"

"It's summer, Gemma. Andy's busy with his business. I'm busy with mine."

Jayne has asked me many times not to interfere in her love life. I have no intention of following those instructions. If things weren't progressing to my satisfaction between Jayne and Andy, it was Jayne's fault. The man adored her and was perfect for her, and at the moment she wasn't seeing anyone. I decided to buy the dinner voucher and make her use it to treat Andy to a date at his own place.

The women at my table began talking about the things they hoped to get for the museum with the proceeds from the auction. Jayne excused herself to check on the kitchen. Leslie asked me if I'd heard from Arthur. After I'd given her his news, I glanced around the tearoom.

People were getting restless. More than a few had taken out their phones, and I noticed the mayor checking her watch. Fiona and Jocelyn were clearing empty teacups off the tables. Helmet-hair was tapping her teaspoon against the table in what was rapidly becoming a highly annoying rhythm. "We need to get things going," I said to Leslie, "or people are going to start leaving."

Leslie glanced around the room. "Kathy hasn't come out yet. She said wanted to be left alone until it was time to begin."

"You've left her alone for long enough. We need to get this show on the road."

"Gemma's right," Barb said. "I feel sorry for Kathy over what happened, but we shouldn't have to wait any longer for her to get out of her sulk. She can be a downright prima donna when she wants to be."

I stood up. "I'll check on her. I'll tell her five minutes."

I passed Maureen heading for her seat, and she gave me a sniff of disapproval. Then the swinging doors to the kitchen opened, and I skipped nimbly out of the way. "What's happening?" Jayne said. "Are they starting?"

"I'm getting Kathy now."

Jayne fell into step behind me. I turned the handle on the storage room and pushed it open. "Kathy, you need to get out there. People are getting restless."

I stepped into the room. I stopped so abruptly that Jayne crashed into the back of me. "What's the matter?" she said.

As well as the usual supplies for a busy bakery and restaurant, the room was full of auction items, everything from a woman's winter coat to a gold and diamond necklace, to a concrete garden statue of a resting Buddha. Kathy Lamb lay on the floor among a scattering of broken miniature teacups. The pink rope that had tied the cups together was wrapped around her neck, and she did not move.

Chapter Five

"You again!" said Detective Louise Estrada.

"Sadly, yes. Me again," I said.

"If you went back to England, the murder rate in this town would decline sharply."

"I hope you're not implying that I am personally responsible for everything that happens here. I shouldn't have to point out to you, Detective, but I will—"

"Enough." Ryan said. "Tell us everything that did happen here, Gemma."

I leaned against the counter in the kitchen and sighed. When people said they wanted to know *everything*, they rarely did. Ryan looked at me with his beautiful blue eyes, the color of the ocean on a sunny day, and Estrada watched me with her dark ones, a hurricane fast moving inland. I took a moment to gather my thoughts.

When Jayne and I had burst into the storage room, I'd dropped to my knees beside Kathy and tore at the rope wrapped tightly around her neck. I could tell by the emptiness in her eyes and the still skin beneath my fingers that we were too late, but still I shouted, "Hand me those scissors!" to Jayne.

"What scissors?" she asked.

I'd noticed them when I'd been in the room earlier. "On top of the box marked lot 67."

"Got them!" She pressed the cold steel into my hand. I cut the rope, and it fell away in a clatter of breaking china, but Kathy Lamb did not move.

"Call nine-one-one," I said to Jayne. "Then get out there and tell everyone the auction has been delayed for a medical emergency. Ask Grant to guard the door. No one in or out until the police and ambulance get here."

Jayne did as I'd asked, and I jumped to my feet and studied the room. The door to the back alley was unlocked. Interesting. Had it been left unlocked when the tea began, or had Kathy opened it to admit her killer? If the latter, it didn't necessarily mean she knew that person. Many people open doors without checking who's there, at least in the center of town in the daytime.

Although in this case thousands of dollars' worth of goods were stacked in the room.

Nothing appeared to have been moved since I'd been here earlier, except for the arrival of Maureen's painting, which stood propped against the wall next to a beautiful piece by a local artist who'd achieved some degree of international fame. The proximity did Maureen's amateur attempt no favors.

The auction items were labeled and arranged in the order in which they would be presented. Envelopes containing gift cards or experiences were mixed in with the physical goods. The one in the front had the logo of the Harbor Inn. The auction book had told me the Inn was offering a fall weekend for two in the main suite, including one night's dinner in the restaurant, for an opening bid of five hundred dollars. Next came my basket of

Holmes goods, offered at two hundred and fifty. I'd been almost embarrassed when I'd seen its listing: it was the cheapest item there. Even dinner for two at the Blue Water Café, including wine with every course, was going for upward of three hundred dollars.

Mine was cheapest, that is, other than Maureen's painting, for which Kathy herself had offered a buck fifty.

The most expensive item in the auction was the diamond necklace, opening bid fifteen thousand. It was lot number ninety, the final one. I spotted the small blue box and walked carefully through the room, trying to avoid disturbing anything, and opened it, taking care not to leave any fingerprints on the box itself. The necklace nestled within. Even in the dim light of the storage room, the jewels sparkled. In other circumstances, I'd take the time to admire it. Instead, I closed the box. The second most expensive item was lot number eighty-nine, Uncle Arthur's copy of *The Valley of Fear*, with an opening bid of twelve thousand. The book was sitting where I'd put it. I tried to remember what other small, easily portable items had been listed. There weren't many of those. Most of the expensive things were experiences, such as three days sailing offered by the West London Yacht Club for nine thousand. No thief would take a gift certificate and expect to cash it in without being caught.

Would they?

Ninety items had been listed in the auction program book; as far as I could tell with a quick look, ninety-one, including Maureen's last-minute addition, were still in this room.

As I'd been checking out my surroundings, I'd been aware of the sound of rising voices coming from the tearoom. People were questioning what was going on.

Someone knocked on the door. "Gemma. It's Jennifer Barton here. Can I be of assistance?"

I opened the door a fraction.

Jennifer stood in the doorway. More than a few curious faces attempted to peer over her shoulder.

"Come in, Doctor," I said. "Mrs. Lamb has, uh, taken ill. Has someone called nine-one-one?"

"Yes. They're on their way." She came inside, and I shut the door firmly behind her against the babble of shouted questions.

Dr. Barton looked at the body on the floor. She looked at me.

"Dead," I said.

"So it would appear." She dropped to her knees beside Kathy Lamb. I could hear sirens approaching and a renewed buzz of voices from the tearoom.

"Through there," someone shouted. Boots sounded on the floor.

"I'll let them in." I opened the door once again.

I slipped out of the storage room, past the paramedics and police officers filling the narrow hallway, and went back to the restaurant. A uniformed officer stood at the door while guests milled about. Blue and red lights flashed from the vehicles on the street outside. The curious began to gather on the sidewalk. Inside, auction guests threw questions at the emergency personal or one another. A couple of women wept. Sharon spotted me and hurried over. "Is she okay? Kathy? What's going on? I didn't mean the things I said about her—really, I didn't." She twisted her hands, and her small eyes darted about.

"I'm sorry, but I don't remember your name," I said, which wasn't entirely true.

"I'm Sharon Musgrave. I'm the bookkeeper at the museum, and I also volunteer in the kitchen. I wear a long dress and a bonnet and bake bread, and I—"

"Why don't you go back to your seat, Sharon?" I suggested.

She ducked her head and tiptoed away.

"When's the auction going to start?" The man standing in front of me was dressed in the best of Ralph Lauren summer-in-New-England wear. White trousers, navy-blue jacket with thin white stripe, blue shirt with white collar, red handkerchief in the jacket pocket, gold cuff links. Even blue canvas shoes worn without socks. "I don't have all day here. I've got an important dinner meeting tonight."

"I'm sure your dinner companions will understand that even yacht club business must wait for a medical emergency, Mr. O'Callaghan," I said.

His eyes narrowed. "How'd you know I'm from the yacht club? And how'd you know my name? Have we met?"

"No," I said. If his clothes and his attitude hadn't told me he was with a yacht club, I'd earlier observed him pointing out item number seventy-four on the auction sheet to the elderly lady with the same close-set eyes and thin lips seated next to him at tea. His expression had been boastful, not hopeful, meaning he had contributed the item, not that he intended to bid on it. His gold cufflinks were monogrammed "JOC." The commodore of the West London Yacht Club went by the name of Jock O'Callaghan. Great-Uncle Arthur, proud seaman, had been approached several times about joining the club. When he was being polite, he called the club in general, and Jock O'Callaghan in particular, "a bunch of stuck-up chinless twits."

"I suggest you cancel your dinner plans," I said. "We might be here for a while."

Jock O'Callaghan gave me a look that told me his opinion of my suggestion and went to join his mother at their table.

Ashleigh stood on the Emporium side of the glass doors, peering in, a small crowd behind her. Moriarty had his nose pressed up to the glass. I gave Ashleigh a rueful shrug and mouthed, "Sorry."

I turned back to the tearoom. Grant was standing by the door, talking to Officer Johnson. Donald remained in his chair. He'd pulled a book out of his satchel and was reading *The House of Silk* by Anthony Horowitz. I'd recently managed to convince Donald that not all the pastiche works made a mockery of the Great Detective, and I felt a small frisson of pleasure as I watched him read.

The mayor had sought some privacy and had gone to a corner, standing with her face almost pressed into the wall while she talked on her cell phone. Maureen had cornered the owner of Fun and Frolic, a dress shop on Baker Street, and was waving her finger in the woman's face. The woman looked like she was considering biting the offending appendage off.

Jayne and her mother stood close together against the windows. I could tell by the look on Leslie's face that

Jayne had given her the news. Jayne helped her mum sit on the bench in the alcove and then came to join me. "Dead?" She kept her voice low.

"Yes," I said.

"Murder?"

"Unquestionably."

"What do we do now?"

"We wait for the police to tell us we can leave, like everyone else."

"Do you have any guesses as to what might have happened?" Jayne asked.

I gave her a look. "I do not guess, Jayne. You know that. To guess would mean to theorize in advance of the facts. That would be a capital mistake."

"Oh, right. Didn't Sherlock Holmes say that?"

"Whether he did or not, Gemma Doyle is saying it now."

"It's none of your business!" a woman yelled.

I glanced over to see the man who'd been pointed out to me as Kathy Lamb's ex-husband rising to his feet. He plucked his new wife's hand off his arm. "Of course it's my business, Elizabeth. Let go of me." His face was pale, his expression stricken. He walked up to Jayne and me. "You found her, they say. Is she okay? My—I mean Kathy. The doctor and the paramedics have been in there for a long time. That's good, right? Means it's not an emergency, right?"

"I don't know, Mr. Lamb," I lied. "All we can do is wait."

"Why can't we leave?" Jock O'Callaghan demanded of Officer Johnson. "If there's not going to be an auction, I have better things to do."

"Please sit down, sir," she said.

"I'll be speaking to the chief of police about this," he said. He turned sharply, and his eyes fell on the second Mrs. Lamb. His face stiffened and he said, "Elizabeth," in a tone full of ice.

"Jock," she replied, with no greater degree of warmth.

"Still out of jail, I see," he said.

"Still pretending to be a big man around town, I see," she replied. "I notice your wife didn't come with you today. Showing the handsome young crewman you hired for the summer all the ropes, is she?"

"One of these days, Elizabeth," he said, "you'll get what's coming to you."

"One of these days, Jock," she replied, "you'll be dead."

He shoved his way past a group of onlookers who were not even pretending not to be listening, and returned to his seat.

"Was that Elizabeth Dumont?" his mother asked. "She's aged a great deal since I saw her last. What did she say? I couldn't hear."

"Never mind, Mother." Jock pulled out his phone.

"I'll make more tea," Jayne said. "I'm sure we can all do with a cup. Fiona, give me a hand."

"Can I take a peek at *The Valley of Fear*, Gemma?" Donald looked up from his book as I passed.

"I don't think this is a good time, Donald."

"I'd love to bid on it. I came hoping I'd get a bargain." He sighed heavily. "But the opening bid itself is too rich for my blood. And even if I could offer that, Grant tells me he has a buyer in mind, so he'll outbid me."

"The auction probably isn't going to go ahead today," I said, "so I'll be taking it home. Why don't you come to the house for tea one day when Uncle Arthur's back in town? He'll show it to you then."

Donald beamed. "That would be marvelous, Gemma. In the meantime, as long as we're stuck here for a while, I'll say hello to Jock and Mrs. O'Callaghan." He slipped a bookmark into the book before closing it, and then got to his feet.

"You know them?" I asked.

"Oh yes. I'm a member of the West London Yacht Club. Have been for many years."

Not a lot of things surprise me, but that one had my jaw hitting the floor. A more unnautical person than Donald Morris, I had rarely come across. "You are?" I said to his retreating back. Jock saw him coming, put his phone away, and stood up. The men shook hands, and Donald bent to speak to Mrs. O'Callaghan.

Grant was keeping Officer Johnson company as she let emergency personnel in and out, but no one else. I went to find out what was going on.

"Gemma," she said.

"Stella. How's your grandmother?"

"Doing well, thank you. What's happening back there?"

"Don't you know?"

"I was told to keep everyone here, that's all." She spoke softly. "People are saying heart attack, but it sounds like more than that to me."

Once again, I lowered my voice. "Everyone dies of heart failure eventually. It's what causes the heart to fail that's the issue."

"You mean someone caused this," Grant said.

I nodded.

The radio at Stella Johnson's shoulder crackled. I strained to hear around the static and the noise of voices, both curious and indignant, behind me. Johnson bent her head closer. I did the same. She gave me a glare and half-turned away.

Conversation over, she pivoted back to face us. "The detectives have arrived. They'll want to have a quick look at the scene and then talk to everyone. You first, Gemma."

"I'll be in the kitchen," I said. I didn't run, but I might have walked very quickly across the room.

And there I was, helping Jayne boil water, when Ryan and Estrada marched in, and Estrada implied it was all my fault.

"Kathy Lamb went into the storage room shortly before the tea was served," I explained in answer to Ryan's question. "She was expected to join us, but she didn't show up. When the tea finished, people were getting restless, so I went to get her. Jayne came with me, and we found her on the floor."

"If she didn't join you for tea, does that mean she was dead before it began?" Ryan asked.

"Not necessarily. I didn't know her," I said, "so I can't say for sure, but people said she was upset about something and wanted time in here alone before the auction began."

"What upset her?"

"I doubt it has anything to do with her death."

"Why don't you let us be the judge of that, Gemma," Estrada said.

"She had a minor disagreement with Maureen Mac-gregor shortly before we all sat down to tea."

"She of the purloined planters," Ryan said.

"The very one. Maureen's contribution to the auction was, in Kathy's opinion, too little and too late."

"But she agreed to include it," Jayne said. Fiona had been sent out of the kitchen while the detectives interviewed Jayne and me. I leaned against the counter, speaking calmly. Jayne fussed about with teapots, milk, and sugar. All the good china cups were dirty or stacked in the dishwasher, so she'd put a pile of takeout cups onto a tray.

"Did anyone go into the storage room after Kathy sought this time alone?" Estrada asked.

"Someone clearly did. The person who killed her. Other than that, I can't say. I was in the tearoom, at a table for eight, seated between Jayne and Leslie Wilson. My chair faced toward the windows, not the back of the building. You know the layout of this place, Detective. A corridor leads out of the dining room. The two restrooms are on one side, and the kitchen on the other. The storage room's at the end of the hall, and the door to the alley is accessible through there. People were getting up and moving about all the time, going to the loo, greeting friends, particularly after tea finished and we were waiting for the auction to start."

"The door leading to the alley is unlocked," Ryan said.

"I wondered if you'd noticed that," I said.

"This isn't a game, Gemma," Estrada snapped. "If you know something, tell us. Don't wait for us to tease it out as though we're on a fishing expedition here."

I had to admit that for once she was right and I was wrong. "Sorry," I said. "Leslie Wilson was in the back room most of the afternoon, accepting and cataloguing auction donations as they came in. Both doors, leading to the outside and to the rest of the building, were unlocked at 4:20 when I brought in the basket of goods from the shop that is my contribution and the book that's Uncle Arthur's. I left almost immediately and didn't go back there until Jayne and I went in search of Kathy at 5:37. You can ask Leslie if she remembers if she locked the door when she finished. I should point out that all ninety-one auction items remain in situ."

"How do you know that?" Estrada asked.

"Because I saw them, and I compared the items in the room to the auction list. No noticeable gaps are in the inventory. The small, portable, expensive items—the diamond necklace being offered at fifteen thousand, the rare book at twelve thousand—are still there, as is the Wendy Lomax painting at seven thousand."

"You told us you only popped into the storage room. You expect me to believe you memorized the value of ninety items and could tell in a matter of minutes if anything was missing?"

I hate having to explain my thought process to the police. "I expect you to believe it, Detective Estrada, because that is what happened."

"I saw Gemma reading the auction booklet while we were having our tea," Jayne said. "She's good at remembering details."

I smiled at the detectives. "All of which is irrelevant. If nothing was taken, then theft cannot have been the motive. It's possible our culprit lifted one of the envelopes containing gift cards; I didn't check them all. What reason anyone might want to do so would be highly significant, wouldn't you agree?"

"We'll have everything compared to the lists," Ryan said, "but theft can't be dismissed outright as a motive. It's possible the door was left unlocked, and Kathy surprised the thief, and he, or she, lashed out."

"True," I said.

"Tea, Detectives?" Jayne said.

"No thank you," Ryan said.

"Can I take the tray out?" she asked.

"Go ahead," Estrada said.

"Everyone's going to ask me what's going on."

"To which you will not reply, will you, Ms. Wilson?" Estrada said.

"No." Jayne left with her laden tray. A wave of voices hit us as the doors swung open.

"Mrs. Lamb appears to have been strangled," Ryan said. "Marks are clear on her throat, and a length of pink rope was on the floor beside her. There are a lot of miniature, decorated teacups on the floor. Some are broken."

"I cut the rope away," I said. "In case she was still alive. She wasn't. The little teacups were strung together on the rope to make a decoration. We hung two of them in the hallway earlier, next to the other things we have for sale."

"Only one rope's there now," Ryan said. "I noticed them when we came in."

I nodded.

"Okay, Gemma, thanks. I—we have your number if we need anything more." He looked at Estrada. "Check with the forensics people, and see if they can tell us anything yet. Then we'll need to get the name and number of everyone out there. Ask if they saw anything significant. If they did, ask them to stay. If not, tell them we'll be in touch later for statements, and then they can go. I'll be out in a minute to make an announcement."

"Right." She gave me her standard look of disapproval and left the kitchen. It was no secret that Louise Estrada didn't like me, and she didn't trust me. Mistrust, I'm used to. I can't help it if people don't always understand my thought process. But open dislike? Irene Talbot, who as a reporter for the *West London Star* knows more about what goes on at the West London Police Station than the chief does, tells me it's personal. Louise wanted the job of lead detective, but Ryan Ashburton came back to West London and got it. She thinks he came back to be with me, which he didn't.

That Ryan and I are, once again, an item, no matter how tenuous and hesitant of an item we might be, no doubt reinforces Louise's feelings about me.

I try to remind myself that she's a good police officer. She might not like me, but she knows when I'm right and acts accordingly.

Ryan studied my face. I gave him a smile.

"I wish this hadn't happened to you again," he said.

"It didn't happen to me, or to Jayne," I said. "It happened to Kathy Lamb."

We walked out of the kitchen together.

"Ladies and gentlemen," he said in a good loud voice, "Can I have your attention, please?" Everyone stopped talking mid-sentence and turned to face him. Ryan never beat about the bush. "I'm sorry, but Kathy Lamb has died."

People gasped. A couple of women sat down quickly. One slumped in her chair. A man said, "Surely you're kidding."

Ryan didn't dignify that comment with a reply.

"That can't be right." Mr. Lamb pushed himself forward. "You're wrong. She has a bad heart. Get her to the hospital."

"Sit down, Dan," Elizabeth, his wife, called.

"Can I have your name, please?" Ryan asked.

"I'm Daniel Lamb. I'm Kathy's husband."

"Ex-husband," Elizabeth yelled.

Ryan's right eyebrow rose. "Do you know anything about what happened, sir?"

"Why aren't the medics rushing her out of here? Why won't you let me be with her? Will someone tell me what's going on?" Daniel Lamb glanced around the room. Sympathetic faces looked back. He let out a moan, and his shoulders slumped.

"I'm sorry," Ryan said again, "but we were too late."

Mr. Lamb shook his head. Leslie Wilson took his arm and gently guided him back to his chair. He'd aged about ten years in the last minute. Grief does that to a person. Notably, his new wife, Elizabeth, sat stiffly in her own seat and made no move to comfort him.

"Are you and Kathy Lamb divorced?" Ryan asked.

"Of course, they're divorced," Elizabeth said. "Dan's not a bigamist."

"What's your name?" Ryan said.

"Elizabeth Dumont. I chose not to change my name when Dan and I married. That happened only six months ago."

"What brings you and Ms. Dumont here today, Mr. Lamb?"

"We—" Elizabeth began.

Ryan cut her off. "Allow Mr. Lamb to answer the question, please."

"Kathy and I are divorced, as Elizabeth said. We came for the auction. I . . . we . . . Elizabeth and I want to support the museum. The museum means . . . meant a lot to Kathy. Was it her heart? She gave up smoking ten years ago, but before that she smoked a pack a day since she was a kid. It takes its toll, isn't that what they say?"

Elizabeth stared at him in something approaching fury, whether because he was talking so sadly of his ex-wife or at the comment about smokers, I didn't know. The overpowering odor of tobacco hung over her like a cloud.

"This was almost certainly murder," Ryan said.

The word ran through the room. I stood behind Ryan and slightly to his right. I watched everyone. Eyes opened wide, mouths gasped, legs wobbled.

Jock O'Callaghan got to his feet. "Murder, you say, Detective. What a coincidence that we have the Black Widow herself here with us today."

I didn't know what that meant, but I didn't have any trouble figuring it out. Elizabeth Dumont's face tightened even further. "You repeat that slander again, Jock, and I'll see you in court."

"I don't believe I mentioned any names, Elizabeth. What might make you think I was talking about you?"

She bristled but didn't answer.

"Is my presence necessary here, Detective?" Jock said. "I have an important . . . I mean"—he gestured to the elderly woman with him—"my mother needs to rest."

"I'm perfectly fine," she said, her voice calm and in control. "Continue, Detective."

Estrada came silently down the hall. She stood beside me, arms crossed over her chest.

"I'll need to speak to you in turn, sir," Ryan said. "If anyone saw someone in the back room with Kathy Lamb after the tea began, or if you have anything else you think significant, anything at all, please let me or Detective Estrada here know. Otherwise, Officer Johnson will take your names and phone numbers, and we will be in touch for your statements later."

People immediately fell into three groups. Some rushed for the detectives, shouting information and demanding answers. Some bolted for the door, wanting to get the heck out of here. A few remained in their seats, calmly sipping the last of the tea and waiting for the rush to be over. Ryan and Estrada would have their work cut out for them, trying to determine what was significant as opposed to what people wanted to seem significant because it might contribute to their own sense of self-importance.

The mayor, who'd been standing close to Stella Johnson, no doubt awaiting her chance to bolt, handed the officer her card. Johnson nodded and held the door open. Jock O'Callaghan was delayed in his escape by having to fish his mother's cane out from under the chair where it had fallen. She didn't appear to be in any rush to leave.

Maureen Macgregor shoved people out of her way. "Let me through. Let me through. I've left my store unsupervised long enough for this travesty. Get out of the way. You'll have your turn soon enough."

"Travesty!" A voice spoke loud enough to be heard over the din. People stopped and heads turned. Barb, the museum volunteer I'd nicknamed Helmet-hair, walked slowly through the crowd. "Why are you in such a rush, anyway? Hoping to get out of town before the cops figure out what happened here?"

Maureen sniffed. "That's ridiculous. Everyone here knows me."

"So they do. You made sure of it when you arrived with your finger-painting and argued with Kathy," Barb said.

Maureen sucked in a breath. Her face turned red.

Barb turned toward the police. She was a tall woman, almost as tall as Louise Estrada. The two women locked eyes over the heads of the crowd.

"You'll want to talk to this lady, Officers. The last thing any of us heard Kathy say was that she'd open the bidding at a dollar fifty for Maureen's ugly painting."

A low murmur spread through the room.

"Barb's right."

"I heard that too."

"Maureen was furious."

"Heck of an insult."

"You're crazy!" Maureen shouted. "Every last one of you."

Barb swung around. She extended her right arm. A long red claw pointed at Maureen. The action was somewhat overly dramatic, I thought, as though she were reenacting the Ghost of Christmas Yet to Come confronting Ebenezer Scrooge. "What did you do then, Maureen? Get your revenge? Make her suffer for your humiliation? Officers, I demand you arrest this woman for the murder of Kathy Lamb."

Chapter Six

Maureen was not arrested, but she was hustled mighty fast, protesting vociferously, into the kitchen of Mrs. Hudson's, where Ryan and Estrada could interview her in private. An officer was assigned to stand at the kitchen door to keep the curious out of earshot.

Unfortunately, I was lumped among the curious.

"Why don't you run along, Gemma," Estrada said. "We know where to find you."

I gritted my teeth and said nothing.

"You can go home, Jayne," Ryan said. "I'll call you when we're finished here."

She shook her head. "I'll be in the Emporium with Gemma. You won't . . . uh . . . touch any of my food, will you?"

"That shouldn't be necessary," he said. "We don't have to do much in the dining room area or in the kitchen. By all accounts, everything happened in the storage room. I see no need to open any of your supplies if the containers are sealed."

We left by the street door, nodding politely to Officer Johnson, busy taking down names and phone numbers.

Dan Lamb had insisted on staying until the body was taken away. He sat alone at a table for eight, body slumped, head in his hands. His angry wife had left as part of the first rush.

"What on earth is happening in there?" Ashleigh cried as Jayne and I came into the Emporium. "People are saying someone died."

"Sadly, yes." I spoke to the woman standing beside her. "Good afternoon, Irene. Need I ask what brings you here?"

"You needn't," Irene Talbot, crack (and only) reporter for the *West London Star*, said. "My sources tell me Kathy Lamb died in suspicious circumstances while officiating at the museum auction. Would you like to comment on that?"

"Is Sherlock Holmes a Russian spy? Of course, I'm not going to comment. Except to say that none of this has anything to do with me. With me or with Jayne. You'd be better off sticking your nose in—I mean doing your job elsewhere."

"The alley's crammed with police vehicles, and cruisers are parked all over the sidewalk out front. The cops, including forensics people, are walking in and out of Mrs. Hudson's. Where else would I be?"

"On the sidewalk? Maybe you can lurk about in the alley and get a statement from Ryan Ashburton." I opened the door for her.

"As if. He's even more closemouthed than you are. Jayne, do you have a comment for the press?"

Jayne pressed her lips tightly together.

"If you learn anything, Gemma, you'll give me an exclusive, right?" Irene said.

"I have no intention of learning anything that I don't read in your paper, Irene. Good night." Irene and I were friends, but when she was in snoopy-reporter mode and I was in not-wanting-to-be-involved mode, our friendship flew out the window.

"By the way," she said. "I decided not to take that job in Missouri. These days West London seems to be *the* place for criminal activity."

She left.

The shop was full of customers, every one of whom had stopped whatever they were doing to watch us. Moriarty crouched in his favorite place on top of the Gaslight shelf, ears up, whiskers twitching, tail moving slowly. Moriarty loved local gossip.

Ashleigh leaned close to me and whispered, "Nothing like being next door to a crime scene to get people dropping in."

"So I have discovered," I said. "Jayne, why don't you go upstairs if you need to rest?"

"I'm fine," she said. "I'll give you a hand here. I'm sorry Kathy Lamb died, but I didn't know her, and it didn't have anything to do with me."

"Except for happening in your place," I said.

She gave me a tight smile. "Except for that."

"Fortunately, we don't know many of those people, so we can keep ourselves well out of it for once." I raised my voice. "Anyone need any help here?"

Some people quickly bent their heads to examine the goods while others went back to browsing. A mother and daughter sorted through books on the Young Adult shelf, and an elderly lady curled up in the chair in the reading nook, flipping through *About Being a Sherlockian*, edited by Christopher Redmond. Moriarty jumped off the shelf and went to join her. He leapt into her lap, and she laughed and stroked his thick fur.

"You have been busy," I said to Ashleigh. "Quite a few books appear to have been sold. Also a rush on the mugs, I see. I'll have to order more. Where did Benedict Cumberbatch go?"

"Someone bought him. She didn't want him in his packaging, just carried him out, all six feet of him. I hope he fit into her car."

"That might be a problem," I said, "being made of cardboard, he doesn't bend at the knees."

"Has he ever been to Cape Cod?" an eavesdropping customer asked.

"Benedict Cumberbatch? Not that I'm aware of," I said.

"It would be fabulous if you could get him into the store," she said dreamily. "He could sign all the things with his picture on them." She added a calendar of the BBC series *Sherlock* to her stack of Cumberbatch-related items. Not a Holmes fan, I guessed, but a Benedict one.

At the Emporium, we cater to many tastes.

"The spot on the shelf that was occupied by *A Perilous Undertaking* is empty," I said.

"Sold out," Ashleigh said.

"Excellent. More came in this morning's delivery from the distributor, but I haven't unpacked them yet."

"I'll get them," Jayne said. "Are they upstairs?"

"Thanks. Back wall. Third box from the right. Bring some of *A Curious Beginning* too, please."

"Excuse me," the young mother said. "I'm looking for something with a strong female protagonist for my daughter. She's thirteen. Is there anything you can recommend?"

"I'm sure I can find something." I walked over to the Young Adult and Children's rack. "One of my favorites is . . ."

The shop continued to be busy. Even with Jayne's help, Ashleigh and I were on the hop for the next hour. I kept glancing through the still-closed sliding door into the tearoom but could see nothing of interest happening. The auction guests said what they had to say and left. Patrol cars moved off the street. The forensic vans had parked in the alley behind the tearoom. I peeked out the back door occasionally and saw men and women walking in and out of Mrs. Hudson's, carrying bags of equipment. I hoped Great-Uncle Arthur's copy of *The Valley of Fear* wasn't in one of them. The book was in excellent condition. Even the slightest damage would reduce the value considerably. And, more important, would break Uncle Arthur's Holmes-loving heart.

At one point, I glanced out the front window to see Ryan and Estrada waiting for a break in the traffic to cross Baker Street. They went into Beach Fine Arts, and a minute later the sign on the door was flipped to "Closed." We had a sudden rush of customers, and I didn't see the detectives come out again. When I next looked, the "Open" sign was back.

The shop's open until nine on Saturdays in summer. Ashleigh said good night at seven and left. "Big date tonight," she told me with a hearty laugh.

"Do you think she dresses according to her mood when she's on a date?" I asked Jayne after the old floorboards at the back door creaked and the door shut behind Ashleigh.

Jayne shook her head. "I hate to think what that might consist of. If she decides things are starting to get serious, and she shows up in a wedding dress, she'll scare the poor guy right out of Massachusetts."

"Maybe widow's weeds if she's had a bad day."

"Even worse," Jayne said.

At eight thirty, Ryan knocked on the sliding door. I was behind the sales counter, ringing up purchases, and Jayne hurried to let him in.

I handed the paper bag containing three books and two DVDs to the customer. She took it but made no move to leave. She pretended to leaf through the bookmarks and local tourist postcards stacked on the counter. She couldn't fool me. She was watching Ryan. Whether because she was hoping for some police activity or because he looked so darn good in his jeans, blue checked shirt, and black leather jacket, I didn't know. The stubble on his jaw was coming in thick, and his sharp cheekbones were highlighted in the shadows cast by the lights behind him. His blue eyes swept the shop, settled on me for a fraction of a second, and moved on.

"You should be able to open the tearoom at the regular time tomorrow," he said. "Mrs. Lamb is being moved now, and our people have most of what they need."

"Thank you," Jayne said.

"I hate to sound mercenary," I said, "but Uncle Arthur donated a rare and valuable book to the auction. Can I have it back?"

"All the items have been taken away for the time being," Ryan said. "Sorry, Gemma. I promise you, we'll look after it and get it back to you as soon as we can. Everyone else's property too."

Moriarty left the reading nook and ran over to join us. He arched his back and spat at Ryan. "Nice to see you too, Buddy," Ryan said. His opinion of the forces of law and order expressed, Moriarty flicked his tail, lifted his little chin, and sauntered away with a swing to his hips that reminded me of Maureen dismissing Kathy Lamb.

I wanted to ask Ryan if they'd learned anything of interest, but the hovering shoppers put a stop to that.

"Can you give me a moment in private, Jayne?" he said.

"Sure." She went into the tearoom, and he shut the door behind her. But not before I slipped through after her. He rolled his eyes but didn't ask me to leave.

"What can you tell me about that decoration? The teacups on the string? One's hanging on the wall and one is . . . uh, in the storage room. Do you have any others?"

"No," Jayne said. "They're handmade by a craftsperson in Brewster. I bought two as a trial to see how they did. If they proved to be popular, I was planning to place a larger order." She swallowed. "I don't think I want to stock them anymore."

"Understandable. We're keeping the detail of the murder weapon from the public for now. Please don't tell anyone that rope was used to kill Kathy."

"We won't," I said.

"If you want to go home, Jayne," he said, "I'll lock up when we're finished here and drop the keys off at your place."

"Thanks, but I'll stay awhile longer. I'll help Gemma."

"Okay." He slid the door open, and Jayne and I returned to the shop. Ryan closed it behind us and flicked the latch, and then he walked through the empty tearoom.

"I need to get all those borrowed tables and chairs out of there before opening tomorrow," Jayne said. "They clutter up the space."

"Why don't you stay closed," I said. "You need a rest."

"Closed! On a Sunday in July?"

"Sure," I said, warming to the idea. "Sleep in, then come around to my place. We can go to the beach, have a swim, and lie in the sun. It's supposed to be a hot day. You haven't been to the beach yet this year. I'll take the day off too. Ashleigh's working out okay." On Sundays, the shops on Baker Street were only open from noon until five. Ashleigh could manage.

"You mean play hooky?"

"I don't know what that is, but I like the sound of it." I grinned at her. She grinned back. I'd been thinking Jayne was looking tired. She worked hard in the summer. I worked hard too, but I didn't keep the killer hours she did. She got up at four, seven days a week, to get the bread and pastries started, opened the tearoom at seven for breakfast and takeout coffee, and worked until it closed at four in the afternoon. Then she usually helped with the cleanup and did accounts or worked on staff records. If they had a special function planned, such as today's auction tea, she stayed late to do prep for that.

It was now almost nine o'clock, and she was here, in the Emporium, helping me and worrying about opening tomorrow.

"Okay, I'm in. Let's do it!" she said. "I'll call Jocelyn and Fiona and tell them not to come to work." Her pretty face fell at the thought of her staff. "No, that's no good. What about Jocelyn and Fiona? I can't do them out of a day's pay."

"I'm sure they'll enjoy the day off too." Neither of them, I knew, had much in the way of extra income. "Tell them the cops said we can't open, but we'll pay them for the day anyway. You can tell the Business Improvement Association that too, if they complain about you being closed."

"Are you sure?"

"Sure, I'm sure. Haven't you exceeded last year's profits by seventeen percent? The shop's up by fifteen."

"Yes, but last year I was just getting started and—"

"It's settled then." I was already looking forward to an entire day off. In the summer too. I normally went to the beach on Sunday morning for a swim, but I never had time to linger. We'd do that tomorrow. Then we'd have lunch someplace charming and quiet and expensive. I'd heard good things about a new restaurant in Chatham. Maybe a drive up the coast in the afternoon. The roof of the Miata down, the salty wind in our hair. I'd like to get a new summer dress, and then we could stop at the Harbor Inn on the way back for drinks on the veranda. Unlikely that Ryan would be free to join Jayne and me at the Blue Water Café for dinner, but it was possible this case would be cleared up quickly and easily.

"I feel giddy at the very idea," Jayne said.

"Good. Why don't you go home? I can finish up here by myself. It's almost nine."

She glanced toward the sliding door. "I'll stay a bit longer. I hate leaving the place when people are in it."

The store began to empty out. "Do you have any ideas, Gemma?" Jayne asked when the last customer had left. Who, I am pleased to report, staggered under the weight of her purchases.

"Ideas about what?"

"About who killed Kathy?"

I shook my head. "I can't say I haven't been thinking about it, but nothing stands out in my mind. Although the relationship between her and her ex-husband is interesting."

"In what way?"

"I think he regrets leaving her. I think his new wife knows it, and she's angry about it. But I didn't observe either of them doing anything untoward."

I counted the day's receipts and began to tidy up. Jayne was sweeping the floor, with Moriarty scattering every patch of dust she gathered together, when the bell over the door chimed and Maureen came into the shop. She did not smile in greeting. She said nothing. She stood in the doorway and stared at, of all things, her own feet.

It was one minute before nine.

Jayne stopped sweeping. Moriarty leapt onto a shelf.

"Good evening," I said. "We're about to close, Maureen. Can I help you with anything?" I glanced past her out the window. The streetlights had come on, and cars moved through the deepening dusk. Beach Fine Arts was wrapped in darkness.

She took a deep breath. She lifted her head and looked at Jayne. She looked at Moriarty, watching her with his penetrating amber eyes. She looked around my shop, at the books, the toys, the games, the DVDs, the knickknacks. She looked at everything except me.

I did not have a good feeling about this.

"No," I said. "Absolutely not."

"I haven't asked you anything." She studied the reproduction of the cover of *Beeton's Christmas Annual* hanging on the wall behind me.

"You don't have to," I said. "The answer is still no."

"Ask what?" Jayne asked.

Maureen cleared her throat. She shifted her feet. She paid enough attention to everything in my shop to be able to pass a test later. She still didn't look at me.

Apparently, it would be up to me to start this conversation. "I couldn't help you if I wanted to, Maureen. I didn't know Kathy Lamb, any of the people who work at the museum, or other people in her life. I know no more about what went on today than anyone else who was there."

"Oh," Jayne said. "You want Gemma to find out who killed Kathy."

"The police think it was me," Maureen said. "I didn't do it, Gemma. I promise."

"I know you didn't," I said.

"Why would I—you do?" She looked directly at me for the first time.

"Kathy was much angrier at you than you were at her," I said. "If you'd been murdered, Kathy would have been the police's best suspect. I'll admit, if I must, that you were insulted by what she had to say about your painting, but that's not enough to kill someone over." I decided to be circumspect here and hold some of my observations—and opinions—back. No one on Baker Street liked Maureen, and Maureen seemed to, if anything, take pleasure out of that. Sometimes I thought she deliberately goaded her fellow shop owners, including me. Before I arrived in West London, Maureen had been the president of the Business Improvement Association. She'd held the post for one week. The way I heard it, the members of that organization threatened to burn her shop to the ground if she didn't step down.

I doubt they would have gone that far. But Maureen quit the post, and she's mocked and ridiculed the BIA and everyone in it ever since.

The point being, Maureen collected enemies the way some people collected Sherlock Holmes mugs or everything that had Benedict Cumberbatch's face on it. With pride.

When Maureen and Kathy had argued over the painting, I'd been the person closest to them. Maureen had been enjoying the spat. I thought it entirely possible she found the worst painting she could to donate to the auction, hoping to get a rise out of Kathy. Squabble over, aim achieved, happy with her afternoon's work, she'd retired in triumph to push her way into the mayor's circle.

No, Maureen Macgregor hadn't killed Kathy Lamb.

But others who'd overheard what went on between them might not have seen the satisfaction on Maureen's face or known how much she enjoyed her reputation as the Curmudgeon of Baker Street and did everything she could to encourage it.

What onlookers had seen, and what they told the police, was that Kathy and Maureen had argued loudly and publicly. Kathy had not wanted Maureen's contribution in the auction and had insulted the painting and humiliated its creator by offering a dollar fifty for it.

Even if anyone was inclined to suggest that normal people didn't kill over an inexpensive painting, Maureen had made enough enemies over the years that no one would leap to her defense. No one in West London considered her in any way normal.

"You want Gemma to prove your innocence," Jayne said.

Maureen nodded. I studied her face. She shifted from one foot to another. I waited. Finally, she forced the words over her tongue. "Yes, I do. P-p-please, Gemma. Can you help me?"

Moriarty leapt off the shelf. He walked over to Maureen and twisted himself between her legs. Happy to have a reason to break off eye contact, she bent over and gave him a hearty pat. He rubbed against her leg and purred loudly. She looked up and gave me a weak smile.

Little did Maureen know that if Moriarty wanted me to help her, that was an excellent reason for me not to. Moriarty and I didn't exactly get along. He was a great shop cat. He loved everyone and everyone loved him. But for unknown reasons, he was always trying to maul the hand that feeds him. I tried not to take it personally. Other animals like me. My dog, Violet, likes me. Stray dogs have been known to fall into step beside me. Even other cats like me, as I've found when I've visited friends who have cats.

Come to think of it, the only other person Moriarty doesn't like is Ryan Ashburton. I filed that thought away to ponder another time.

"I can't help with this, Maureen," I said. "I'm not involved, and I'm not planning on getting involved."

"All I'm asking is for you to do what you did those other times. You helped Donald Morris when he was accused of killing that woman writer and Leslie Wilson when . . ."

I refrained from saying that I'd helped Donald and Leslie because I liked them. Instead I simply said, "No."

She straightened, lifted her chin, and stared directly at me. "I knew this was going to be a waste of time, but I thought it'd be worth a try. It's not true, is it, what they say about you?"

"What do they say about Gemma?" Jayne asked.

"That she's smarter than the cops. I knew that was just talk. Simple minds assume that because you know all about Sherlock Holmes, you're some sort of consulting detective. As usual, no one listens to me. You won't help me because you can't. Admit it, Gemma Doyle."

The oldest trick in the book.

"It's after nine," I said. "Time to lock up."

"The police told me I'm not to leave West London. They've been talking to people who know me. Asking if I have a temper. If I've been known to lash out in anger. They're searching police records for dirt on me."

"Are they going to find anything?" I asked.

"They might. They might not. I'm a respectable businesswoman, Gemma. Like you and Jayne here. I have been for a long time, but maybe I have things in my past that don't look so good. Don't we all?"

"I don't," Jayne said.

Maureen gave her a withering glare. And then she remembered she was trying to be friendly, so the glare died. "The cops want to pin this on me. I know they do. All they're interested in is solving the case as fast as they can and getting their promotions."

"That's not how the West London police work," Jayne said.

Maureen's laugh had a history behind it. I might want to find out what that history is one day. "It's how they all work." She looked straight into my eyes. "They'll find a way to blame me, and the guilty person will go free. Maybe that person will kill again. But don't worry about it, Gemma. It won't be your fault. Like I said, I know you're not up to it."

"I'll ask a few questions," I said. "No guarantees."

The oldest trick in the book. And I stepped right into it.

Chapter Seven

Jayne arrived in time for breakfast on Sunday morning. I'm not much of a cook, but I pride myself on doing an excellent traditional full English breakfast.

I put a plate of grilled turkey sausages, scrambled eggs, sliced fresh tomatoes, sautéed mushrooms, and lightly buttered whole-wheat toast in front of her, and another at my place.

The Full English, adapted for modern times.

Jayne picked up her fork and dug in. "Did you change your mind overnight? About helping Maureen, I mean."

"Sadly, no." I sliced my sausage. Violet recovered from a bout of excessive enthusiasm at the arrival of Jayne and lay under the table, hoping for scraps to fall like manna from heaven. "I trust the West London police. I certainly trust Ryan. But it has been known for the cops to become fixated on a suspect and spend their time building a case against that person rather than searching for further suspects. Time and budgets are limited, and our chief likes a high solve rate."

"Ryan's not going to be happy."

"I'm not going to get involved, as in 'involved.' I'll chat to a few people in a light conversational manner and report what I learn to the officials."

"Right. You'll use a light conversational manner when you ask, 'So, did you kill Kathy Lamb?'"

"I have been known to be subtle, Jayne."

She popped a mushroom into her mouth and wisely refrained from answering.

I've found, in the few police cases I'd unwillingly been swept up in, that I'd been able to find out things the police could not. Jayne might roll her eyes at talk of a "light, conversational manner," but people tended to guard their words carefully when being questioned by the police. Conversation among peers and acquaintances was far more likely to be unguarded. And thus more revealing.

"I phoned your mother this morning," I said. "I asked her about the unlocked back door."

"I know. She called me as soon as she hung up and told me not to get involved with your wild schemes."

"Excellent advice. My mother would offer the same. She told me she honestly can't remember if she locked the back door when she left the room to take her seat in the dining room. I'll take that to mean she did not. In unusual surroundings, meaning not their home or place of business, a person remembers what they did more than what they did not do."

"I've lost count of the number of times I've forgotten if I locked the tearoom and had to go back and check."

"Exactly. Because you do it without thought, as a matter of routine. Locking up the tearoom is not part of your mother's routine, so she would remember if she had."

"She feels really bad about it," Jayne said. "She thinks it's her fault Kathy was killed."

"It's the fault of the killer and only the killer," I said. "The unlocked back door, I will admit, gives me cause for concern. If Kathy was killed by someone who walked into the storage room while the rest of us were having tea, then the list of suspects grows substantially. In that case, it might have been an attempted robbery gone wrong. A summary of the sort of items being offered at the auction was publicized widely, although not the prices."

"Can you check into the West London underworld and see if there was talk?" Jayne said.

I raised one eyebrow. "The West London underworld? I don't even know if there is such a thing. I suspect not."

"Oh."

"It's possible someone might have specifically been after *The Valley of Fear*. I'll ask Uncle Arthur to ask his contacts in the illicit rare book world."

"Arthur Doyle has contacts who deal in stolen books?"

"Arthur Doyle," I said, "has contacts everywhere."

"Oh. I wish I didn't know that."

"What is learned cannot be unlearned." I gave her a smile. "But you needn't worry. He once helped a man who was accused of stealing from a notoriously unstable collector. They've been friends ever since."

"Arthur proved his innocence?"

"Oh no. The man wasn't innocent at all. I think he still has the book. Arthur was able to shift suspicion to an even more notorious and unstable collector. He completely destroyed an infamous crime family while he was at it. You might have read about that in the papers."

Jayne gaped at me.

"More toast?"

"What? Oh, toast. No thanks. This is good. You're a better cook than you take credit for." She scooped mushrooms onto her eggs and took a mouthful.

"Every Englishwoman can make a proper English breakfast. Even my mother didn't burn the sausages. Occasionally."

"I guess our visit to the beach is off."

"Afraid so. Eat up and we can go. Good thing we planned to take the day off. Detecting, I've found, interferes with running a business." I carried my plate to the sink. "If you want to come with me, that is. Don't feel that you have to. I suggested a day off because you need a break. I don't want you to waste it running around West London on what might be a goose chase."

She popped a tiny heirloom cherry tomato into her mouth. "Gemma, I don't dare leave you alone. I hate to think what trouble you might get into without me. Need I remind you, there's a killer out there?"

"That," I said, "I am unlikely to forget."

"Where are we going to start?"

"I sensed a great deal of tension in that room yesterday, aside from the presence of Maureen."

Jayne nodded. "Conflict in the ranks, I'd say."

"As well as among the museum volunteers, there was dissent between Dan Lamb and his new wife, which implies dissent between them and Kathy. Jock O'Callaghan and Elizabeth Dumont clearly have a history, but that's likely not to have anything to do with Kathy's death. I'm going to start with the museum. Kathy wasn't popular with everyone there. She only assumed control of the board recently, and I overheard talk yesterday of volunteers who quit when Kathy took over."

"We're going to assume this wasn't a random theft gone wrong, then?" Jayne said.

"You told Ryan you had two of those hanging teapot decorations—is that right?"

"Yes."

"It would be beyond coincidence for the thief to wander in the back door and just happen to have a similar item in his or her pocket. One was taken off the wall, and one remained. The thief must have grabbed it as he, or she, went past. Whether they intended to use it as they did isn't for us to say, but that eliminates, at least for now, the idea that someone came in the back door, intending to steal whatever they could grab."

"Why are we helping Maureen, anyway? It seems entirely possible that she killed Kathy. I saw her in the hallway only minutes before we went into the storage room."

"Lots of people were in the hallway, using the loo or checking out the items for sale. That's part of the problem. Everyone in the room, with the possible exception of Jock O'Callaghan's elderly mother, was milling about while we waited for the auction to start. I don't like Maureen more than anyone else in town does, but I believe she's innocent. In this at least," I explained my reasoning to Jayne.

"Makes sense," she said, mopping up the last of the eggs with her toast.

* * *

Although Scarlet House is only a short walk from my house, we took the Miata, leaving a sad-faced Violet peering out the window after us. In case the museum visit led to other calls, I didn't want to have to come back for the car.

It was shortly after ten o'clock, and the tourists were out in force. Traffic moved slowly as they headed for the beach or Sunday brunch, and the boardwalk was crowded with people shopping for fresh fish, eating ice cream, or watching seals play in the cool waters under the pier.

I pulled into the parking lot off Harbor Road. Signs informed me that the main museum house was closed, but the barn and grounds were open. It was Sunday, so no one was working on the house, but the repairs and restoration had begun. Scaffolding covered the front and one side wall.

"It's too bad what happened," Jayne said. "They can restore the house, but it won't be the same if it's not original. Has anyone wondered if the fire was connected to Kathy's murder? They said it was an accident, but maybe it wasn't."

"I did think about that," I said. "I'll have to ask Ryan. The arson investigator might want to look at it again in light of Kathy's death. If she had enemies at the museum, perhaps they set the fire, hoping it would look as though it was her fault. When that didn't work . . ." I let the sentence trail off, and we got out of the car.

A man came out of the barn, a lamb and a pack of excited toddlers chasing after him. "Mornin'," he said, touching the edge of his floppy-brimmed hat. He wore the clothes of a Colonial-era farmer: dusty white shirt with sleeves rolled up, a brown leather vest, dark baggy trousers that ended at the knees, black stockings, and shoes with buckles. "This little guy," he said to the children, "is a late lamb. She arrived long after most of the other lambs, which were born in the spring." He carried a baby's bottle. "Would you like to feed her?" He handed the bottle to a young girl. She took it, held it out, and the lamb latched on immediately. The girl giggled so hard her pigtails bounced.

I felt myself smiling. One of the kids carried a round flat rock. He put it in his mouth and took a bite. A piece broke off, and he chewed. Not a rock then, but an attempt at baking by someone without Jayne's skill. "Yuk," he said. He spat it out and dropped the remainder to the ground. We heard voices from inside the barn, and Jayne and I slipped in. The barn was dark and cool and smelled of clean straw and well-cared-for animals.

"Welcome." A group of adults stood around a woman dressed in a long brown dress under a white apron, with a white bonnet on her head. "Why it's my friends Goody Doyle and Goody Wilson," she said. "Ladies, please join us."

The modern-clothed group nodded politely. The costumed woman was Sharon Musgrave, Chipmunk-woman who'd sat at our table yesterday.

"Are we being particularly good today?" I whispered to Jayne.

"Goody means 'goodwife.' The Puritan version of *Mrs.*"

"Don't think I care much for that form of address," I said. "Sounds like something I'm expected to live up to."

"I was explaining to these out-of-time visitors," Sharon said, "that because the house is temporarily uninhabitable, we're living in the barn. I do miss my lovely, soft four-poster bed, the one my husband and sons made with their own hands, and my big fireplace, but we know how to make do in 1648." She smiled at us. Gone was Chipmunk-woman, nervous, awkward. In her place was Goodwife Musgrave. Strong, confident, proud—a woman who knew how to make do.

"Oh, my gosh, Madison! I'd better check on the kids." A man ran out of the barn.

The women thanked Sharon and followed him.

"This looks interesting," I said.

Sharon beamed. "Every cloud has a silver lining, doesn't it? Terrible what happened to the house, but I love the opportunity to be as industrious as our ancestors had to be." She spread her arms to take in the barn. "We can make this perfectly habitable while the repairs are being done."

The small enclosures for the animals took up half the barn. Two goats gave me suspicious looks across their gate. A huge pig nursed eight tiny, squealing, pink bundles. The rest of the barn was used to store equipment and sacks of feed. The floor had been thoroughly swept, pallets with straw mattresses placed against the wall, and a rough-hewn table with four equally rough stools placed in the center of the space. Stones were piled to make a hearth, and a big iron pot rested on a rack placed above the fire. I smelled cooking vegetables and a rich broth. "Chicken stew for dinner," Sharon said. "With biscuits freshly made over an open fire. Not as convenient as an oven, but they'll be just as tasty." She smiled at us. Her bonnet was starched to within an inch of its life, and her apron as white as new-fallen snow. Her dress fell to about a half an inch off the ground, but the hem was clean, as were her shoes. A discreet red badge with the Scarlet House logo was pinned to her apron, the only touch of color on her. "I sometimes think we've missed so much in the rush to industrialization."

Goody Musgrave, I thought, was living in a fantasy world as complete as Disneyland.

The straw in the pens was fresh, the floor clean, the goats and pigs glistening as though they'd had a bath this morning. I doubted that the flour for her biscuits had maggots or grit mixed in with it or that she'd chased, killed, and plucked the chicken to throw in the pot. If the vegetables weren't ready for harvest, she'd go to the supermarket, and if their pigs died, there was always the butcher shop on Baker Street.

"You're so right." I said. "You do good work here. It's important to remind people of our history. Those children will always remember being able to feed the tiny lamb."

"I baked cookies first thing this morning, following a traditional recipe, made in the traditional way. Would you like to try one?" She gestured to the table, on which lay a cracked wooden platter containing six flat, round, lumpy beige items that had all the culinary appeal of a rock.

"No thank you," I said. "We had a late breakfast."

"Terrible what happened yesterday," Jayne said.

Sharon shook her head. "Just awful. I can't believe it. All that work and nothing came of it."

"Work?" I asked.

"The auction. We hoped to raise as much as a hundred thousand dollars. We had some marvelous things donated. The people of West London are so kind, aren't they?"

Jayne and I exchanged a glance. I gave her a slight nod.

"I meant the death of Kathy Lamb," Jayne said

Sharon tittered in embarrassment. "Oh, that too. Most unfortunate." She lifted the lid of her pot and stirred the contents with a giant wooden spoon. I wandered away to study the authentic farming tools hanging from hooks on the walls.

"Kathy was the chair of the board of your museum," Jayne said. "Are you going to be able to carry on without her?"

Sharon snorted. "Carry on? Heavens, I don't like to speak ill of the dead . . ."

Sure you do, I thought as I examined a wicked piece of curled metal that looked like something the Grim Reaper might carry. As the Grim Reaper wasn't real, the purpose of it I couldn't even guess.

". . . but Kathy wasn't the right person to run the museum. She had some ideas she thought were new and original, but we'd discussed them in the past and rejected them for practical reasons. She wouldn't see sense and refused to listen. No one on the board liked her. She wouldn't have lasted much longer."

"I suppose," Jayne said, "you'll need a new chair."

"I for one am hoping Robyn will agree to come back. Now, she was an excellent chair. She truly had the interests of the museum at heart. She wasn't trying to find something to make her seem important because her husband dumped her for an *older* woman." Sharon laughed.

"Uh . . ." Jayne said.

Sometimes a witness doesn't want to tell you what they know, so you have to trick them into revealing it.

Sometimes you have to gently prod information out of them; thus I had asked Jayne to open the questioning.

And sometimes, best of all, all you have to do is stand back and let them at it.

"A nasty divorce?" I asked.

"The worst." Sharon settled happily into gossip mode. "It dragged on and on, must have been dreadfully expensive, and Kathy got more and more bitter. The whole thing was only settled a couple of months ago. Everyone took sides, his or hers, and lifelong friendships ended. Things got so bad, Dan had to quit the West London Yacht Club, where he'd been a member forever, because the people there took Kathy's side."

"Several people from that club were at the auction," I said.

"Because she begged and wheedled them into coming. Still, Dan did okay, didn't he? What did he care that the divorce lawyers were draining him dry? Elizabeth paid for it. Easy enough to make new friends too. The day he was kicked out of the WLYC, he joined hers."

"Which one's that?"

"The Cape Cod Yacht Club. The place just up the street." She waved her hand in what she thought was the direction of Harbor Road. "It's not nearly as swanky, or so I've been told, as West London is." She sniffed. "I wouldn't know. They'd be unlikely to let the likes of me through their doors. Not that I'd ever want to."

"Kathy used her work at the museum to help her get over the pain of her divorce," Jayne said. "I'm sure you all provided a marvelous support system for her."

Sharon snorted. "We would have if she wasn't so darned bossy about it. She needed something to salvage the shards of her self-respect. She lost her house and ended up living in a cheap apartment." Sharon couldn't hide the slight smile that touched the edges of her mouth. "That put her in her place fast enough. At first, people felt sorry for her, and she used that to her advantage, to wiggle her way onto the board and then get herself voted chair. It was all sneaky and underhanded. Robyn, who always played fair, didn't know what was happening before it was too late and she was out."

"I didn't see Robyn at the tea," I said. I'd never met Robyn, and I didn't know what she looked like, but I'd overheard someone say she wasn't there. The best way to get information out of people, I have found, is to let them assume you know more than you do.

Sharon put the lid back on the pot and wiped her hands on her apron. "As if. She wouldn't go anywhere near any event Kathy was in charge of. It absolutely broke poor Robyn's heart when Kathy formed that cabal against her and drove her out."

A family came into the barn. The "farmer" wasn't with them. The kids turned immediately for the animal pens, and their mother said sharply, "Stay away from them. Those animals might be dangerous."

"Will you look at that scythe," the father said. "It's a real original. My granddad had one like that when he still had the farm. It wasn't used any more, but it had been his grandfather's. Before the days of automation, they cut the wheat and hay by hand."

"I wanna see the pigs," the little boy declared, not the least bit interested in how great-great-granddad had worked the farm.

"Jayne," I said. "Why don't you tell the visitors all about animal husbandry in the old days."

"What?"

"The animals are quite safe," I said, "as long as you don't try to get into the pens or pick them up. Introduce the children to the baby pigs, Jayne." I gave her a jerk of my head.

"Oh, right. The pigs." She headed across the barn. "The baby pigs are called piglets and they're about . . . uh . . . four weeks old. Their names are Miss Piggy and Kermit and—"

"Cookie Monster," one of the kids shouted as he ran after Jayne.

"I guess it will be okay," the mother said, as though she had any choice but to follow. The father continued to examine the farm implements. So that was what that thing was. A scythe. Used for felling hay and other crops. Not for the first time, I was glad I lived in the twenty-first century and owned a bookshop.

"Poor Robyn," I said, nudging Sharon back onto the topic at hand.

"She won't be sorry to hear that Kathy died," Sharon said, cheerfully tying a noose around Robyn's neck. "I suppose the museum should do the decent thing and send flowers. I'll call Robyn when I go on my break, and suggest she take care of that."

"Why don't you do it before you forget?"

"My phone's in my purse, which is locked in my car. I can't have the dratted thing ringing in here, can I? It would ruin the mood totally."

"Guess what we've found," the father bellowed into his phone. "An old barn like the one Granddad had. Really takes me back to those summers on the farm."

"Baby pigs remain with their mother until they're . . . uh, one year old," said Jayne, who knew as much about farming as I did. For all I knew baby pigs stayed with their mothers until they graduated from high school.

"I'll watch the stew for you while you run and get it," I said.

Sharon hesitated. "I shouldn't leave the barn unattended."

I dug in my pocket. "Why don't you use mine?" I unlocked the phone. "If you don't know her number, we can look it up on four-one-one. What's Robyn's last name?"

"Kirkpatrick."

"Kirkpatrick. Does she live in West London?"

"No, she's in Chatham, but she loves Scarlet House. Her husband's name is Eric. The phone's probably under his name."

"Here it is. Eric Kirkpatrick. Chatham." I pressed the appropriate key and handed the phone to Sharon.

She accepted it. She didn't want to. She didn't want to use a cell phone in the middle of her seventeenth-century fantasy, but she was too polite to say no. I thanked the god of amateur detectives for well-mannered people.

She waited a few seconds and then her voice took on the robotic tone that meant she was talking to a machine. "Hi, Robyn. It's Sharon here at the museum. I was thinking we should send flowers or something to Kathy at the funeral home. Or wherever they . . . uh . . . took her.

You've probably thought of it yourself—I know you're always on the ball about that sort of thing, but just in case, I wanted to make the suggestion. Thanks. Call me. Let's do lunch soon. We have so much to talk about now that we—I mean you—can get control of the museum back. Don't call on this phone. I borrowed it. Bye." She hung up and handed the phone back to me.

"Now baby goats, on the other hand, don't need their mothers as much as piglets do." Jayne struggled to make up tidbits of animal husbandry. I didn't have much more time.

A burst of laughter announced that another group had come into the barn. Sharon blinked and slipped back to her seventeenth-century world. "Welcome," she said. "I'm Goody Musgrave. You look as though you have had a long, hard journey. Come sit by the fire, and I'll tell you my tale."

I called to Jayne, and we left Sharon to her fantasies.

"Learn anything?" Jayne asked as we walked to the car.

"Quite a lot," I said. "Give Ryan a call. Ask him if the police will be releasing Kathy's body soon, and if so, ask if he knows the funeral arrangements. Don't tell him you're with me. Just say that, as she died in your place, you'd like to pay your respects."

Chapter Eight

Ryan didn't answer, so Jayne left the message. As we drove toward Chatham, I told her what I'd learned.

"You think someone would kill over a place on the volunteer board of a small-town history museum? That seems like a heck of a stretch to me, Gemma."

"I've discovered there's no accounting for what some people will consider serious enough to kill over," I said. "The smaller the stakes, often the bigger the desperation. This Robyn Kirkpatrick was spotted outside the tearoom while the fund-raising tea was getting underway. That implies a degree of obsession to me. But I'm not—not yet anyway—as interested in Robyn as I am in Sharon."

"Sharon? Why? She seemed harmless to me."

"*Seemed*, isn't good enough to prove innocence, Jayne." We came to a red light, and I pulled my phone out of my pocket and pressed my thumb into the button to unlock it. "Take this. Look up the last number dialed on four-one-one-dot-com, and find me the address."

She did so and read it out.

"Thank heavens," I said, "some people still have land lines. When Sharon called Robyn, she got voicemail. Either Robyn isn't at home, or she didn't want to pick up for a number she didn't recognize, which is common enough these days. If she's not home, this might be a wasted trip. But it is Sunday morning, and chances are good Robyn and her husband are either at church or brunch. We'll check their house, and then I'll decide. I want to pay a call on Mr. Lamb as well. That might be more difficult to arrange, as I don't want to talk to him in the presence of his wife."

"As long as you don't send me to talk about pigs endlessly," Jayne said. "There's only so much a woman can pretend to know about pigs, Gemma."

"I fear you've ruined those children for life with all that incorrect knowledge," I said. "By the time pigs are a year old, they're on the dinner plate, not living happy piglet lives in Farmer's Brown's family compound."

"You could have done better?"

"I didn't even know a baby pig's called a piglet until today."

The Kirkpatricks lived on a well-maintained street of well-maintained houses not far from the ocean in the beautiful town of Chatham. We drove slowly down the street. A few people worked in their immaculate gardens, making them even more immaculate. An elderly couple sat on the swing on their front porch, watching the world go by. A woman walked a Pomeranian. She passed a man with a Great Dane, and they exchanged words of greeting while the dogs sniffed at each other. The Pomeranian couldn't reach his twitching nose past the Great Dane's ankles.

This was not the sort of neighborhood in which I could park on the side of the road and observe the inhabitants without being noticed. At the Kirkpatrick's house, no cars were in the driveway, and the double garage doors were closed. I parked on the street, and Jayne and I walked up the pathway between rows of perfectly trimmed bushes overflowing with fragrant pink roses.

I rang the bell, and the sound echoed throughout the house.

"Please tell me we're not going to break in like we did at the Kent place when no one answered," Jayne said.

"As I have no reason to suspect the maid is not telling her we're here, the answer is no." The house was nice, built on a quarter acre of tree-lined property in the seventies or eighties. The windows had recently been upgraded, and the house given a new roof. Nice, but not the sort of home in which the residents had a maid.

I pressed the bell again.

No answer.

"Let's go," I said. "We'll try again later. If they're still not home, I'll have to call ahead, although I always hate giving people time to prepare for my visit."

We headed back to the car. "I dribbled salad dressing down the front of my favorite green dress the other day," I said to Jayne as I pulled the Miata out of the driveway.

"Did you just think of an important detail, Gemma? You remembered something about salad dressing or green dresses, and now you know who killed Kathy Lamb?"

"I remembered that I can't get the stain out, and so I'd like to get a new dress. There are some nice shops in Chatham. It's almost noon, and they'll be open soon. We can come back here later and see if anyone's home."

My shopping expedition was a success, and I bought a sleeveless blue and green cotton dress with a full, knee-length skirt, and a matching blue cardigan in case of evening chill.

"Feel like lunch?" I said to Jayne as we left the store.

"After that huge breakfast you made me?"

"Let's check out the Kirkpatricks again then," I said.

This time, an almost-new Lexus was parked in their driveway. I pulled in behind it, and the door was opened almost immediately in answer to the bell.

"Can I help you?" The woman was in her mid-fifties, short at about five foot one, lean, and toned in a way that told me she worked out regularly. Blond hair with caramel highlights fell to her chin. Dark eyes and an olive complexion hinted at her southern European ancestry, but her accent was pure middle-class New England. I'd never seen her before.

"Mrs. Kirkpatrick?"

"Yes."

"My name is Gemma Doyle, and this is Jayne Wilson."

"From the Sherlock Holmes store and the tearoom."

"Oh. Yes, that's right." I wasn't often caught off-guard. Usually I was far quicker to recognize people than they were to remember me. "I'm sorry, but have we met?"

She shook her head. "No, but my husband loves your store. He has a terrible weakness for historical mysteries. He pointed you out to me once when you were walking down the street."

"You come into the tearoom quite often," Jayne said.

Robyn smiled. "Whenever I have out-of-town guests, I like to take them for afternoon tea. It's always such a treat. What can I do for you two? Would you like to come in?"

We did so, and Robyn showed us to the living room. We took seats on comfortable chintz chairs.

"Can I offer you some tea?" Robyn asked.

"No thank you," I said. "We don't want to take up much of your time. I'll get straight to the point. Did you hear what happened yesterday at Mrs. Hudson's?"

"My phone hasn't stopped ringing since yesterday afternoon. Everyone pretends they're breaking bad news, but I can tell they think I'll be delighted, although I'm not. How can I be happy that a woman died?"

"*Delighted* is a strong word," I said.

"Kathy Lamb and I had a strong relationship," she said. "Strongly negative. To put it bluntly—and I'll assume that's why you're here—we hated each other."

I was wrong-footed again. Most people danced around their feelings for the recently departed with phrases like "I won't speak ill of the dead" or "We had our differences, but."

"She kicked you off the museum board." If bluntness was the order of the day, I could also be blunt.

"She did. She engineered a coup and managed to persuade enough members to vote against me. I was angry at the time, but I soon got over it. Unlike some people, I don't allow my position on the board of a historical museum to define my self-worth."

"You didn't come to the auction tea?"

"No, I didn't. As I said, I got over it. The museum is no longer any of my concern."

"But you stood outside, watching people arrive."

Her right eye twitched. Not as calm as she wanted me to think. "Why are you here, Ms. Doyle?"

"Someone killed Kathy Lamb in my place of business. I don't like that."

"I'm sure you don't." She picked a piece of invisible lint off her immaculate white trousers. "I find your question insulting, but I assume you'll go running to the police if I throw you out of my house."

"I never run to the police," I said, "unless I have something to tell them."

"I was in West London yesterday to do some shopping. I like the fishmonger on Harbor Road better than the one in Chatham. After I bought our night's dinner, I thought I'd drop into your store and get a gift for Eric. His birthday's coming up, and I read a review of *Gaslight* by Stephen Price in the *New York Times*. I know Eric hasn't read it yet. It was only after I'd parked my car that I remembered someone telling me about this auction. I saw my former colleagues going into Mrs. Hudson's Tearoom. I didn't want a potentially unpleasant encounter with Kathy, so I went home without buying the book. I'll return for it another time. Now, if there's nothing else."

"Tell me about Sharon Musgrave."

Robyn let out a bark of laughter. "Sharon. I'm surprised she hasn't moved into the museum, she spends so much time there. "Get a life," is the phrase that comes to mind when I think of Sharon."

"You mean she cares too much about it?" Jayne asked.

"I mean that place is her life. I didn't mind if she spent all day every day there. Saved me having to find other volunteers or balance people's schedules. Others didn't agree. They thought Sharon was too fixated on the place. She wouldn't agree to any improvements or changes in the way we did things. She must be out of her tiny mind now that half the house has burned down."

"Not really," I said. "She's enjoying making do in the barn."

Robyn laughed again. Underneath the groomed appearance and New England manners, she had a mean streak as wide as any Sherlock Holmes would have come across in the back alleys of London. "I'm sure she is. She's not only a volunteer at the museum, playing dress-up in the kitchen, but she also keeps our books. Sharon and I never got on particularly well; I thought her obsession over the museum was potentially harmful, but I was pre-pared to keep her on because I didn't want to rock the boat. Kathy didn't see it that way, and they clashed imme-diately. Poor Sharon was about to be shown through the original seventeenth-century doors, but Kathy died before she could get rid of Sharon. I wonder what's going to hap-pen now." Her eyes glittered with malice.

"Get rid of her? Why would Kathy do that if Sharon was such a good volunteer?"

Robyn looked at me. Something stirred in her eyes, and the corners of her mouth moved. She'd once again caught me out and was pleased to have done so. "Oh, you didn't know? Sharon burned the museum house down."

Jayne sucked in a breath. "What?"

She stood up. "If you'll excuse me, we're expecting guests this evening, and I have things to do."

I also stood. Robyn was a good deal shorter than I am, but we seemed almost to be eye to eye. I was aware of Jayne scrambling to her feet.

"The arson investigator and the police aren't saying who was working that night," Jayne said.

"Not publicly, but everyone at the museum knows. Why Kathy didn't fire Sharon on the spot, I don't know. She probably enjoyed dangling the threat in front of her for a while. Sharon must have had a couple of highly unsettling weeks, waiting for the ax to fall."

With that, she showed us to the door.

*   *   *

"If Sharon caused the fire in the museum," Jayne said, "and Kathy was considering firing her because of it, Sharon would have reason to want to see Kathy dead."

"Agreed," I said. "If that's what happened and if Sharon was at fault rather than it being an accident."

"We now have a viable suspect. Good work, Gemma."

"We do," I said. "But it's not Sharon."

"What? You think Robyn might be the guilty one? She's put the museum behind her."

"So she wants us to think. Robyn's an interesting woman. Everything about her, from her mannerisms to her clothes and makeup, to her house and car, tells me she's disciplined and organized. A woman in control. People who like to be in control don't take it well when control is taken from them."

"I like to be in control," Jayne said. "At work, anyway."

I gave her a quick smile. The tearoom kitchen could be used to illustrate the dictionary definition of chaos. Jayne ran Mrs. Hudson's with efficiency without being demanding. Her staff knew what they had to do, and they did it without her peering over their shoulders and criticizing. She had her way of doing things, but she was always open to new ideas. Jayne was anything but a control freak.

"Robyn," I said, "is almost as good a liar as I am, but I hope I don't make such sloppy mistakes."

"You think she lied about why she was outside the tearoom? West London's a busy town in the summer, Gemma, and Baker Street's at the heart of it. Seemed natural enough to me that she'd be in town to do some shopping and be curious to see who was coming to the museum auction."

"No one who's a frequent shopper at the West London Fish Market would go there at four o'clock on a Saturday afternoon. All they have left is fishy rejects and melting ice, and not much of that. She's never before been inside the Emporium, despite her husband being a regular. But on the one day we were hosting the museum, she decides she needs to buy him a gift. The book she mentioned came out in 2016. She would not recently have seen a review in the *New York Times*. Robyn Kirkpatrick was standing outside Mrs. Hudson's because she was furious that they were having a major event and she had not been invited. Not only not invited, but I'd be willing to bet she offered to help—on her conditions, of course—and was rebuffed."

Jayne let out a long sigh. Traffic between Chatham and West London was heavy, and we were stuck behind a van packed to the rafters with a gang of college-age kids, their brightly colored paddleboards stacked on the roof. "Suspicion is one thing, Gemma, but proof is entirely another. I don't see how you're going to force Robyn to confess."

"I'm not planning to do anything of the sort. I'm gathering data to present to the police. As for Robyn, she's merely on my suspect list."

"We have a suspect list?"

"We do now. I haven't forgotten Sharon. My working hypothesis is that someone who was in Mrs. Hudson's for the auction went to the storage room during the break, removing the teacup chain decoration from the wall as they passed. If Robyn did come in the back way, she did not have the opportunity to grab the chain."

"What are we going to do next?" Her bag began to ring.

"I don't know. I need to talk to Dan Lamb before I go much further, but that needs to be handled with some delicacy. Why are you looking at me like that?"

"The word *delicacy* rarely applies to you, Gemma."

"Answer your phone," I said.

She pulled it out of her purse. "Hi, Ryan. Did you get my message?" She listened for a short while and then said, "Great, thanks," and hung up. "The police see no reason to hold Kathy Lamb's body if the autopsy turns up nothing unexpected."

"When's the autopsy?"

"Later this afternoon."

"That's fast. It must be a slow day at the hospital. And on a Sunday too."

"He said something about the pathologist being on hand because he starts his vacation tomorrow."

"Did he say what funeral home's handling the arrangements?"

"Glenbow in West London," Jayne said.

"How involved is your mother with the museum?"

"Not too involved. She's still devoting a lot of her time and effort this summer to the theater festival."

"How's the festival doing?"

"A sold-out season. The dramatic departure of the headlined actor and what happened after that proved a boon for ticket sales."

"Glad to hear it. Speaking of the festival, you haven't seen Eddie lately, have you?" I said, referring to a stage actor who Jayne had begun dating when the play first came to town.

"No, I haven't, Gemma. It was nothing but a brief infatuation that passed almost immediately. Not that my relationship, or lack thereof, with Eddie or anyone else is any of your business."

"Just checking," I said.

She harrumphed. "Are you wanting to talk to Mom about the people involved in the museum?"

"I'd like to get her take on what we've learned."

"Do you want me to call and ask her if we can drop by?"

"Yes, please."

Jayne did so, and when we arrived, Mrs. Wilson came out of the house to meet us, accompanied by her dog, Rufus. If Rufus was disappointed not to see Violet leap out of the Miata, he hid it under his explosion of excitement at the arrival of Jayne. While they romped, I greeted Leslie with a hug. She was looking well, and I was glad to see it. Earlier events at her beloved West London Theater Festival had been hard on her. She called to Rufus, and we went into the comfortable, although outdated, kitchen. Then again, maybe it was comfortable because it was so outdated. There wasn't a steel appliance or metal stool to be seen, just aging linoleum, laminate countertops, and backsplash tiles featuring tulips and Dutch windmills.

Jayne and I took seats at the scarred pine table. "I assume you two are here to ask me what I know about Kathy Lamb and who might have wanted to kill her," Leslie said as, without asking, she put the kettle on (for me) and took a pitcher of iced tea (for Jayne) out of the fridge.

"Why do you assume that?" Jayne asked. "Can't I drop in for tea with my mother?"

"You can drop in for tea with your mother anytime, dear, and you know that. It just seems that where murder happens, you two are sure to follow."

"That's not right," Jayne said. "Gemma follows the clues, and I follow Gemma. Half the time I don't even know where I'm following her to. Or why."

"Just take care," Leslie said. "Someone wanted Kathy Lamb dead, and that someone isn't going to want to be found."

Jayne shivered and wrapped her arms around herself.

"I always take care," I said to Leslie. "Of Jayne and myself."

"I know that," she said. "How can I help you?"

"I'm not planning to get involved," I said, "but sometimes I can find out things before the police do. If

I learn anything, I'll hand it over immediately." I didn't need to add *this time*. "No secrets."

"Good," Leslie said.

"Tell me about the people at the museum. Kathy Lamb was the chair of the board, but she hadn't been in that position for long."

Leslie fussed with the tea things. She put a tray on the table along with a plate of freshly made oatmeal cookies. "The previous chair was a woman by the name of Robyn Kirkpatrick. Robyn had been there for a long time, and some of the other board members thought she was too stuck in her ways. I'm not on the board myself, Gemma, but we volunteers hear things."

"Gossip is the stuff of life," I said.

"Did Sherlock Holmes say that?"

"No, but Gemma Doyle did. How did Robyn react to being ousted?"

"She wasn't pleased, but she took it in stride. She was asked to remain on the board, but she said she didn't want to overshadow the new chair, and handed in her resignation. That was the right thing for her to do. With Kathy as chair and Robyn still involved, the board would have turned into a battleground."

"They couldn't work together?" I asked.

"Kathy and Robyn have never gotten on. Robyn was a traditionalist. She wanted Scarlet House to be like every other historical re-creation museum. Kathy used words like *avant garde* and *innovative*. Personally, I was on Robyn's side. I like our little museum as it is. I think it's a marvelous way of introducing visitors, children in particular, to the history of the Cape."

"Do you know Sharon Musgrave?"

Leslie rolled her eyes. "Oh yes. We all know Sharon. Everyone calls her Poor Sharon, although not to her face."

"Why?"

"The museum is her life. Her life is the museum. We want people to love the museum and to value it, but there's such a thing as too much love. Sharon was angry when Kathy took over and announced she was looking for"—Leslie made quotation marks in the air with her fingers—"'bold and innovative ideas to recreate Scarlet House as befits the twenty-first century.' I thought she sounded like she should be working at NASA, not our local museum."

"Do you know what started the fire?" Jayne asked. "The fire department report said it was an accident caused when a volunteer left a candle burning."

Leslie let out a long breath. "I don't *know*, dear. Not for sure. Sharon was the volunteer in charge that evening, so it was her responsibility to lock up for the night, and rumor has it she gets a mite freehanded with her homemade rose hip wine, if you get my meaning."

"You mean Sharon's a drunk?" I said.

"I wouldn't quite put it that way, but she does like to play at being a pioneer housewife. She actually eats all that stuff she makes as part of her kitchen demonstrations because she can't admit that modern civilization does have its advantages." Leslie's face curled up at the memory of Sharon's authentic historic cooking. "Like ready access to salt. Homemade wine can be mighty potent, or so I have heard."

"Interesting," I said.

"Don't read too much into this, Gemma," Leslie said. "I'm telling you what I've heard, but it's all just gossip and innuendo."

"On its own, information such as this is not all that helpful," I said. "People have their own agendas, and they often misinterpret things. Put it all together, and if a pattern emerges, then the drops of information may become significant. I've been told Sharon's also the museum's bookkeeper."

"She is, and that's why I suspect Kathy didn't fire her after the fire—or used that as her excuse not to do so. It's not so easy to get a qualified bookkeeper for a nonprofit."

I finished my tea and stood up. "Thank you."

"Any time," she said. "Some people are saying Maureen Macgregor did it. You don't think so?"

"I've come to no conclusions yet," I said.

Once we were heading back to town, I said to Jayne, "Considering that we're playing hooky, as you call it, how about an afternoon at the beach after all?"

"Perfect," she said.

Chapter Nine

And it was. We stopped at Jayne's flat for her swimming costume, and then at my house for mine. I promised Violet a long walk later and threw beach chairs, umbrella, towels, and books into the car.

The public beach was crowded, but we found a perfect patch of sand to lay ourselves out on. Jayne paddled in the warm water of Nantucket Sound while I swam up and down the shoreline for thirty minutes. I didn't think about the Lamb murder. I simply didn't have enough data to put anything together yet.

Swim over, I toweled off and dropped onto my beach chair. "Good swim?" Jayne murmured sleepily. She was stretched out on a towel in the full shade of a beach umbrella.

"It was." I opened my book. I'd brought *The Women of Baker Street* by Michelle Birkby home from the shop. I read for several hours while Jayne dozed, enjoying Birkby's interpretation: Mrs. Hudson and Mrs. Watson as the sleuths. Every once in a while, I adjusted the umbrella to keep Jayne's pale bikini-clad body in the shade. Close to us, an enormous family had set up what might serve as a base camp on the way to Mount Everest. Shade tent, umbrellas, blankets, tables, beach chairs and loungers, a portable grill, three coolers stuffed with drinks on ice, and containers of ready-made salads and meat for the grill. Children and dads played ball or splashed in the shallows while teenage daughters giggled in the surf and eyed the pack of teenage boys who'd appeared as if in a puff of smoke. Eagle-eyed matronly mothers settled into their seats. Two elderly ladies in baggy, form-covering bathing suits kicked off their sensible shoes and chased each other into the water, squealing with delight.

I read for a long time, alternating this with quick refreshing dips into the water, simply enjoying being at the beach and having time to myself. Eventually, the scent of roasted meat dragged me out of my book. The family was settling down to dinner. I nudged Jayne with my toe.

She groaned, rolled over, and blinked sleep out of her eyes.

"Time we were off home," I said.

"What's the time?"

"Half five."

She sat up with a louder groan. "Half past five! I can't believe I missed our whole day at the beach."

"You needed the sleep and slept like a baby. It did you a world of good." I began packing up our things. The time off had also done me a world of good.

I dropped Jayne at her place and headed home. The streets were busy with tourists leaving the beach and going out for dinner. My phone rang as I pulled into the driveway. It was Ryan, and for a moment, I thought he might be calling to suggest dinner because the case had been solved.

No such luck.

"I'm coming out of the autopsy now," he said. "It was as pleasant as ever. I never get used to these things, Gemma."

"That's a good thing," I said. "You don't want to ever regard death by murder as normal."

"True. There were no surprises, and we learned nothing we didn't already know. I need a break. What are you up to?"

"I had a pleasant day with Jayne. We played hockey."

"You played hockey? Today?"

"Isn't that what Jayne called it? We skipped off work."

"Hooky. You played *hooky*."

"Oh, right. That was it. I was surprised you Americans used the same word for an illicit day off as a game played with long sticks."

Ryan laughed, deep and hearty. "You cheer me up no end, Gemma Doyle." I smiled to myself. I knew full well the difference between hooky and hockey. (At least, I had since this morning.) I could tell by the heaviness in Ryan's voice that he needed a good chuckle.

"Want to come over for dinner?" I asked. "I can order in Chinese or pizza." I unlocked the door and went into the mudroom. Violet barked a greeting. "Violet says please come."

"I wouldn't want to disappoint Violet. I'll drop by, but I won't be able to stay for long. I have a meeting with the chief to discuss the autopsy in an hour."

"I need to take Violet for a walk. Why don't you join us?"

"I'd like that," he said. "Get the hospital smell off me. Be there in ten."

I used the ten minutes to leap into the shower and wash the sand off and then quickly dressed in shorts and a T-shirt. Violet and I were ready and waiting when Ryan drove up.

He came into the kitchen and gave Violet a hearty pat and me a deep kiss. In that order. Then he threw a plastic bag onto the table. I opened it to see a first-edition copy of *The Valley of Fear.* "We're done with most of the items donated to the auction and are returning them to their owners."

"You found nothing?"

"Either our killer wasn't interested in the items, or they were interrupted before they could lay their hands on what they were after. Everything on the list was present and accounted for, and Leslie Wilson says nothing appears to have been disturbed. We didn't bother to fingerprint the auction items—there would have been far too much to go through. Some of them must have been handled many times by many different people. Ready for a walk?"

He spoke to me, but Violet barked her agreement.

Ryan took my free hand as we walked down the street. He didn't say anything, and I let the companionable silence stretch as long as he wanted. When we reached a small local park, I let Violet off the leash. Ryan and I sat on a picnic bench under a huge old maple and watched her rush about, sniffing at the base of every tree. This wasn't a leash-free park, but she was good enough to return to me at a call, and no one else was around at dinnertime on a Sunday. I kept one eye on her in case she left a deposit that needed to be gathered up.

Ryan put his arm around my shoulders, and I leaned into him. "Tell me what you learned today," he said.

"Learned?" I asked innocently. "About what?"

"The Kathy Lamb case—what else?"

"Why do you think I learned anything?"

"Because you're Gemma Doyle. And before you go any further, I should tell you Maureen spilled the beans."

"What beans?"

"Louise and I paid a call on her earlier. We had further questions about what happened yesterday between her and Mrs. Lamb. A lot of people overheard them arguing at the auction and were quick to tell us about it. Other than that, we have nothing that points to Maureen. No one saw her taking down the string of teacups, for example, or going into or out of the storage room. But when someone fights with someone only minutes before they die in suspicious circumstances, we take that seriously."

"As you should."

"Maureen, being her normal cheerful self, told us we might as well go back to the donut shop and stop wasting everyone's time, as you were on the case."

I groaned. "I'm sure that went down well with Louise."

"After I peeled Louise off the ceiling, I told Maureen not to get too cocky. She said she didn't much care whether Kathy lived or died. I think that's Maureen's way of proclaiming her innocence."

"It is. It's also true." I told Ryan why I believed Maureen hadn't killed Kathy Lamb.

"Be an unusual defense in court," he said. "Your honor, the accused didn't kill the victim because making people hate her was nothing but her hobby."

"I'd be interested to find out what made Maureen so nasty," I said. "There has to be something very dark in her past."

"Some people are plain born mean. But that's irrelevant right now. I can tell you Maureen has come to police attention previously, before she moved to West London, but that was a long time ago. Don't bother asking me for the details, because I won't tell you, and it has nothing to do with this case or her present situation."

"I suspected as much," I said. "She has a distrust of the police that usually comes from bad experiences."

"It also comes from having a guilty conscience. Never mind Maureen; you still haven't told me what you learned today."

I told him about our visit to the museum and to the homes of Robyn Kirkpatrick and Leslie Wilson. "In short, I learned nothing conclusive, but a pattern's starting to take place."

"A pattern of Kathy having enemies?"

"Yes. Speaking of enemies, what did Louise have to say about Maureen's revelation?"

He took my chin in his hands and lifted my face to his. "Louise is not your enemy. Unless you make her so."

"Sorry," I said. "Trying to make a joke."

"Don't do it again. Naturally enough, Louise wasn't pleased to hear you're getting yourself involved, but she wasn't as angry as she would have been earlier, and she isn't threatening to go to the chief to have me removed. Believe it or not, she's starting to have some faith in your instincts."

"Really?"

"Really. But all it'll take is one snarky remark from you, and she'll be on your case again."

"Me, make a snarky remark?"

He looked to the heavens.

"I've told you what I learned," I said. "Little though that is. Do you have anything to share?"

"I need to get back. You know I can't reveal details of private conversations, Gemma." I knew, but it was difficult for me to investigate when information went in one direction only.

"What's the story of Dan Lamb's second wife?" I asked.

The edges of his mouth turned up in a grin. "I was wondering if you knew about that. Elizabeth Dumont. I'm not breaking confidences to tell you she's come to the attention of the WLPD before. In this case, Elizabeth claims to be to be shocked and dismayed at the sudden death of Kathy. Between Dan and Elizabeth, I thought his distress the more believable."

"What do you mean she's come to police attention before?"

"Time I was going." He hopped off the table. "It's a matter of public record. You should be able to find the details easily enough. The case got a lot of press in the area a couple of years ago."

I called to Violet, and she trotted over. I pulled a twig out of her tail and fastened the leash to her collar. "What do you know about the fire at the museum? Do they still think it was an accident?"

"The fire department investigator is confident the blaze was caused by a candle that was left unattended and burned down. Some papers, info brochures about the museum, were on the table next to it, and the window was open. It's likely, but can't be proved, that a gust of wind caught the sputtering candle and pushed the dying flame too close to the papers. The museum closed at eight, and the docent claims she locked up and left at that time. Louise spoke to her, and she was pretty shook up about it. No one else was seen on the property until the fire trucks arrived. You didn't see anyone, did you?"

I shook my head. "The docent was Sharon Musgrave."

His eyes flickered, meaning yes. "That information isn't being made public."

"No matter. Except that everyone knows. Sharon's very much involved in the museum. Involved to the point of obsession, they say."

We turned into Blue Water Place, my street. The soft evening light caressed the gardens, and white flowers glowed. Seeing home come into sight, Violet quickened her pace.

Ryan stopped by his car. "I have to go. The chief doesn't like to be kept waiting." He kissed me on the top of the head. "I can't tell you not to investigate, Gemma. I learned that the hard way. But I can tell you to take care."

"Don't I always?"

He shook his head and flicked the fob on his keys. His car beeped in response.

Violet and I watched him drive away, and then we went inside. The book on the kitchen counter reminded me of something I had to do, and I pulled out my phone to send a quick text to Uncle Arthur.

*Auction didn't happen. I have yr book. Can you
check with yr rare book world contacts & ask if
anyone placed order for theft of same?*

It was night in Spain, but Arthur would get the
message when he woke.

Chapter Ten

Shortly before ten on Monday morning, I joined the lineup at Mrs. Hudson's for my morning tea and muffin. The main room had been returned to normal. The extra tables and chairs were gone, and no sign of recent police activity remained.

"Everything okay this morning?" I asked Fiona when it was my turn to be served.

She lowered her voice. "Thanks for paying us for the day off, Gemma. That was nice of you."

"You're welcome," I said.

"The police must have finished up, as they were all gone when I got here. The museum people came in first thing and took away their chairs and those card tables."

"I see the teacups on a rope decoration isn't on the wall anymore. Did someone buy the last one?"

She glanced down the hall. "Oh. They're gone. I hadn't noticed." She shrugged. "I didn't ring anything up."

"I'll pop in and say hi to Jayne."

I passed Jocelyn coming out of the kitchen, laden with breakfast sandwiches and coffee cups. "Thanks for the day off, Gemma. I took the kids to the beach, and we had a great time."

Jayne was rolling out pastry when I came in. She greeted me with a smile. "Good morning."

"Morning to you. Quick question. What happened to the last teacup chain?"

"I took it down as soon as I came in this morning, and threw it into a desk drawer. I don't think I want to sell those anymore. Not the fault of the woman who makes them, but if I have them around, they'll remind me of what happened every time I see them."

"Fair enough," I said. "Fiona didn't know anything about them, so the police must be keeping the murder weapon to themselves, as Ryan said they would. Be sure you don't mention to the maker why you're not getting more."

"I won't."

"Have a good day."

"You too." She waved sticky fingers at me.

I unlocked the sliding door and went into the Emporium. Moriarty greeted me with his customary hiss of disapproval. I'd learned the hard way not to put my breakfast down and turn my back, so I carried the paper bag and takeout cup to the front door. I swallowed a yelp of surprise as I saw Maureen's face pressed up to the glass, her hands forming a frame around her head.

I unlocked the door and opened it. "Good morning, Maureen."

She marched in. "Did you figure it out yet?"

"If you mean did I solve the murder of Kathy Lamb in one day, the answer is no. I did make some inquiries however."

"What did you find?"

"Nothing I'm going to tell you." I said. "When—*if* I learn anything, I'll take it to the police."

"I hired you. You have to report to me."

"Maureen, I'm not a consulting detective, and even if I was, I don't recall money changing hands or contracts being signed."

She sucked on a lemon for a minute, and then she swallowed her bitterness and said, "That's true, but I thought you'd help me out of . . . friendship."

I flicked the sign on the door to "Open" and crossed the floor to the sales counter. I sipped my tea and took the muffin out of its paper bag. "Did you think of anything that might be significant? Anything you might have overlooked on Saturday in the excitement?"

"No," Maureen said. "Nothing. I spent a lot of time chatting to the mayor. She invited me to sit at her table so she could get my opinion on the improvements to Baker Street the town is planning for next year."

"They're planning to improve Baker Street next year? That never goes well. It's always twice over budget and three times over expected duration."

"You should keep up with the business news, Gemma."

I refrained from pointing out that I'd have more time to keep up with the business news if I wasn't investigating a murder on her behalf.

"The mayor asked me to join the planning committee as a representative of the BIA, but I said my store has been so busy this year, I simply don't have the time."

Maureen lied comfortably and easily. But more than that, she lied when she didn't need to. I knew she wasn't popular with the BIA, so they'd never let her represent them, and I'd seen the hapless mayor trying to avoid Maureen's company.

"I was far too engaged chatting with Her Honor and her table to be watching everyone coming and going," she said.

The door opened, and the first shoppers of the day came in. Two women who'd spent far too long at the beach yesterday, judging by the state of their noses. Sisters, with identical smiles and cheerful blue eyes. Pale faces and arms, now bright pink, and ash-blond hair indicated their Swedish ancestry. Not a people accustomed to long days in the hot sun.

"Let me know if you need any help," I called.

"We will," they said. They headed straight for the Gaslight shelf.

"Time to get to work," I said to Maureen.

She glanced at the women and took a hesitant step toward me. She lowered her voice. "The police paid another call on me yesterday."

"Did they?" I said.

"They had nothing but the same questions. Why did I fight with Kathy? What did we argue about? Did Kathy and I know each other before Saturday?"

"What did you say to that?"

Her eyes slid to one side. "I told them I never met her before she came into my store begging me to donate something for their silly auction."

"Was that true?"

She turned and looked me full in the face, making direct eye contact. "Of course, it was true."

Maureen wasn't a good liar after all. She could spin stories that made her look good without effort, but she couldn't tell an out-and-out falsehood without flashing lights going off all over her face. I filed that information away. That Kathy and Maureen had encountered each other before might mean something, and it might not. West London was a small town, particularly when all the tourists went home.

"Chin up, Maureen," I said. "At least you're not in jail. Yet."

The customers put their selection of books on the counter. I turned to them with a smile, and Maureen slunk off back to her lair. "We spent all day yesterday at the beach," one of the women said in a broad Minnesota accent. "We finished the books we'd brought for the holiday already and need to stock up. Was I ever thrilled when the clerk at the hotel told us about this store." Her pick was *Murphy's Law*, the first Molly Murphy mystery by Rhys Bowen. Her sister had grittier taste, and she'd chosen *A Hunt in Winter* by Conor Brady.

I was kept constantly on the go in the shop until Ashleigh came in at one. "It's been a busy morning," I said. "I'm going upstairs to do some work in the office, but if you need me, just ring."

"Sure," she said, giving Moriarty a scratch under his chin.

I did have work to do, but I didn't do it. Instead, once I was settled behind my desk, I made a phone call to Glenbow Funeral Home. I asked about visitation for Mrs. Lamb and was told the hours today would be four until six, and five until seven thirty tomorrow. I opened the computer and, rather than checking my accounts receivable and payable, accessed Google.

The police will tell you that in a murder case not involving a bar fight, gangs, or criminal activity, the first suspect, and often the guilty party, is the husband or wife. Even more likely, the ex-husband or ex-wife, if the parting had been acrimonious. I'd been aware yesterday, when I headed off to the museum, that I should be starting my investigation with Dan Lamb. There are definitely some disadvantages to being a consulting detective—not that I am one—rather than the police. For one thing, I couldn't make people talk to me or even let me into the room. I didn't know Dan or Elizabeth. I hadn't spoken to them at the auction. I couldn't think of a pretext to go around to their house and start interrogating them.

A visitation, however, was open to the public, and other members of the family were likely to be there.

In preparation, I needed background on Kathy and her life. I started with the Scarlet House website. It featured plenty of pictures of Kathy, showing off the house, posing in front of the huge open fireplace, presiding over meetings. In none of them was she in costume or doing any of the pretend work that demonstrated how our ancestors managed. That, I assumed, was left to the docents like Sharon. I next searched Google for items of interest about her and her family. I found very little, and none of it interesting. Kathy had been born in Boston. She and Dan had married when she was twenty-three and he twenty-seven. Dan's family had lived on Cape Cod for several generations, and the newly married couple settled in West London. Dan had been married previously; his first wife had died of an unspecified illness when their son, Bradley, was only one year old.

Dan and Kathy had one child together, Crystal. Kathy had worked as a secretary for an insurance company until she retired at age fifty-five. The Lambs divorced shortly after that, and Kathy assumed the position of board chair of Scarlet House.

All terribly dull. There wasn't a single thing in Kathy's online life that would indicate she was the sort of person someone would want to get rid of.

Elizabeth Dumont, however, was another story. As Ryan had told me, Elizabeth made the press seven years ago, before I came to America, when her husband—her extremely wealthy and much older husband—died in a boating accident. The Dumonts were, at the time, members of the highly prestigious West London Yacht Club.

Edward Dumont had been an excellent sailor, so the old police reports said, and on the day he died, the weather had been good and the seas calm. He'd been sailing alone, which was a normal thing for him to do. When he did not return to port by nightfall, the Coast Guard had been notified. The following day, his boat, the *Lizzie*, had been located, washing in on the tide, with no one on board and no sign of anything unusual having occurred. Edward Dumont had been caught some weeks later, among a load of flounder, by a fishing trawler.

I reached for the phone.

"Good morning," said Ryan Ashburton.

"Do you have time to talk?"

"I'm well, thank you. How are you, Gemma?"

"I'm fine," I said. "Sorry."

He chuckled. "Don't worry about it. Your enthusiasm gets the better of you sometimes. Can I assume you're calling about the Lamb case?"

"You can. I've been reading up on the parties involved. What can you tell me about the death of Edward Dumont? Have you read the files?"

Ryan was in the office. I could hear the buzz of conversation in the background and the chug-chug of a cheap desktop printer struggling to spit something out. A man shouted, "Hey, watch out."

"I have, and I can tell you pretty much everything I know, which isn't a whole lot. The case is still open, but not being actively investigated. Edward Dumont was a good sailor. An excellent sailor by all accounts. He was in his seventies, but healthy and in good physical shape. As his body had been in the water for some weeks, the autopsy was inconclusive, but it did rule out a heart attack or aneurism."

"Neither of which would have explained why he'd fallen off his boat in any event."

"Exactly. The police were interested in Elizabeth Dumont's activities that day, but she'd been seen around town. Shopping, at the hair dresser, having lunch with friends, and then meeting other friends for drinks in the late afternoon."

"Could have been setting up an alibi."

"Or having a pleasant day while her husband was enjoying his hobby. Yes, she was in the frame for a while, but nothing came of it. Friends reported that the marriage was going through a difficult patch, and some people at the yacht club told the investigating detective that Edward had been heard to threaten to divorce her."

"Difficult in what way?"

"Elizabeth told her friends Edward accused her of having an affair. She denied it. She claimed he had a jealous streak and was always suspecting her of being up to something. It was of interest to us that Mr. Dumont had taken out a pretty strong prenup, meaning she got almost nothing if they divorced, but his will left everything to her. They had no children."

"The police had no case against her?"

"Nothing but yacht club gossip. He was a wealthy man, and wealthy men often have enemies. Some shady real estate deals, some business acquaintances suspected of having ties to organized crime. Suspicion soon turned from Elizabeth Dumont and a hired killer to the mob. But nothing came up there either. The original detective has since retired and moved to Florida, but the case remains open."

"Thanks, Ryan."

"What are your plans for the rest of the day?" he asked.

"I'm going to try and get some of my sorely neglected business accounts done. I might pop into the visitation for Kathy Lamb later and express my condolences."

"I've got the warrant," Louise Estrada called.

"Be right with you," Ryan said to her.

"Warrant for what?" I said.

"Gotta run," he said.

Chapter Eleven

At twenty-two minutes to four, I opened my mouth. "Partners' meeting. Back in twenty minutes. Got it," Ashleigh said.

I closed my mouth. Then I opened it again. "Am I that predictable?"

"Gemma, I could set my watch by you."

"Not today. I'm going out. I might be quite awhile. I'll call if I don't plan to be back before your dinner break."

"Guess I'd better find another way to set my watch."

I went into the tearoom and then into the kitchen. Jocelyn was taking dishes out of the dishwater, and Jayne was taking off her apron. "Be with you in a minute, Gemma," she said.

"I can't make the partners' meeting," I said. "I have to go out. Want to come?"

"Come where?"

"The visitation for Kathy Lamb."

"Is that today?" Jocelyn said. "I thought I might go. Pay my respects. I might have been the last person who saw her alive. Other than her killer," she added quickly.

This was news to me. "What do you mean?"

"I was coming out of the kitchen, ready to start serving, and almost bumped into her. She was carrying that awful painting by Maureen."

"Did you see anyone with her?"

"Nope."

"Anyone go down the corridor after her?"

"Nope. Not when I was there, anyway. The police sent someone around to my house to interview me. I told them that."

"If you want to go to the visitation, it's today from four to six and tomorrow from five to seven thirty at Glenbow Funeral Home."

"I'll go tomorrow after work," Jocelyn said. "I can get Mom to pick the kids up from summer camp." She began putting the dishes away.

"I'll come with you now, Gemma," Jayne said. "Jocelyn, can you and Fiona lock up?"

"Sure."

I didn't usually bring my car to work, but hoping to get to the visitation, I had today. I'd never been inside Glenbow Funeral Home, but every time I drove past, I thought it an unsuitable location unless the owners were heavily into nineteenth-century gothic. The building had begun life in the mid-1800s as an orphanage, and in my rare fanciful moments, I imagined that an aura of despair still hung over the place. It was all sharp angles, rough stonework, narrow-windowed turrets, and cracking gingerbread trim. They could have filmed a Dracula movie in there. All that would be needed was cracks of lightning above and villagers with torches and pitchforks below.

"I love this old building," Jayne said as I parked the car.

"Really?"

"Look at the detail in the gingerbread trim and the way the sun turns the stone gold."

I looked. All I saw was the Bride of Dracula peering out a downstairs window.

We climbed the wide stone steps. The door opened noiselessly, and the Bride of Dracula stepped back to admit us. On second glance, she wasn't a vampire bride, just an attractive young woman with long, straight black hair and too much red lipstick, dressed in the severe black suit of her profession. "Good evening," she said in deep, serious tones.

"Mrs. Lamb?" I asked.

She gestured toward the hallway. "Second door on the right."

The room was well appointed with solid wooden furniture, a thick red carpet, comfortable sofas and armchairs, dark wallpaper, and paintings of pastoral rural life in previous centuries. Heavy red drapes were pulled back to let the slanting afternoon sun stream in. People milled about, some laughing and chatting as though they were at a cocktail party, others shifting awkwardly from one foot to another. The casket was against a far wall, almost buried under mounds of flowers, whose too-sweet scent overpowered the room. An enlarged head-and-shoulders photo of Kathy Lamb, stern and unsmiling, was propped onto a stand next to the visitors' book.

"We should have gone home to change," Jayne whispered to me. Most of the mourners had come in suit and tie or dresses with stockings and pumps. Jayne was in jeans and a T-shirt, and I wore a cheerful sleeveless dress patterned with giant yellow sunflowers.

"Can't be helped now," I whispered back.

A young woman broke away from the crowd and approached us. She might have stepped out of the board-room at a bank, dressed in a well-tailored dark gray skirt-suit, white shirt, pearl necklace and matching ear-rings, and black shoes with one-inch heels. The pearls appeared to be genuine; the shoes were Ferragamo; and the suit, I estimated, cost about two thousand bucks. Her brown hair with golden highlights fell in a perfect shiny bob to her chin, and her makeup was subdued and tasteful.

I held out my hand, and she took it in hers. Her grip was light and her palm cool. Her eyes were red, but her makeup showed no sign of tears streaking through it. "I'm sorry for your loss, Crystal," I said.

Her smile wavered, and she sorted through her memory banks, searching for my name. "I'm sorry, but I don't remember where we've met."

We hadn't. I hadn't seen a picture of Crystal Lamb in my internet searches, but I recognized the thin line of her mouth and the slight tilt to her eyes as those of her mother, Kathy. "Gemma Doyle," I said. "This is Jayne Wilson. We knew your mother."

"Thank you for coming," Crystal said. She looked past us, and a genuine smile crossed her face. "Gerald, how lovely of you to come." She almost pushed me aside in a rush to greet the newcomer.

Jayne and I wandered into the room. I recognized quite a few people I'd last seen at the auction on Satur-day, both museum volunteers and guests.

"Hi," Sharon Musgrave said. She was suitably dressed for the occasion in a black dress with black buttons down the front and starched white collar and cuffs. "Isn't this a nice turnout? Kathy would be pleased. She always loved being the center of attention."

I thought that a rather unseemly dig to make at the woman's funeral, but I took the opportunity to dive straight into the subject I was interested in. "It looks like a good number of people from the museum came."

"Oh yes. Her death came as such a shock to us all. I hope Robyn will put in an appearance." Sharon lowered her voice. "If she wants back onto the board, she should. She needs to show that she's put her differences with Kathy behind her, don't you agree?"

"Totally," I said. "Who will be in charge of the board in the meantime?"

"Ben Alderson's the vice chair. He's over there. Tall guy with gray hair."

I recognized him from the tea. He was a good-looking man in his seventies, with excellent bone structure; a tall, lean build; and a still-thick mop of curly gray hair. I headed toward him. Behind me, Jayne said, "Nice talking to you, Sharon."

I broke into the circle around Ben. "Good afternoon. Nice to see you again, Mr. Alderson."

"Although the circumstances aren't nice," Jayne added quickly.

"Ms. Wilson," Ben said. "I'm sorry I didn't get a chance to thank you and Ms. Doyle for the tea on behalf of the museum."

"Yes, well . . ." Jayne said.

"With the auction cancelled, the museum must be scrambling to find the funds to pay for repairs that have already begun," I said.

Ben turned to me. His smile was forced. "I don't think this is the right time."

"I'm thinking of helping out," I said. "Making a donation, I mean. The museum's important to the town."

"In that case, why don't we set up a lunch meeting?" He pulled his phone out. "I'm free next—"

"What about overhead? Do you have many paid employees?"

"We pay a bookkeeper," the woman next to Ben said. "We're lucky to get her at an excellent rate because she's one of our dedicated volunteers. You were talking to her just now. Sharon Musgrave."

"So I was," I said. "Didn't realize. Nice meeting you all."

I walked away. Jayne ran after me. "Geez, Gemma, you could try to be subtle. This is a visitation."

"I thought I was being subtle," I said. "I pretended to be interested in donating to their museum. Although that might have been a mistake. Ben seems nice enough, but I don't want to get roped into having lunch with him."

Jayne shook her head.

"If I'd been subtle, as you call it, I might not have learned that important piece of information."

Jayne let out a long sigh. "Okay, I'll bite. What important piece of information did you learn?"

"That Sharon is paid to be their bookkeeper."

"We knew that already."

"We knew she kept the books—your mother told us that—but she didn't mention that Sharon's paid to do so. I assumed it was another part of her volunteer role."

Mentally, I kicked myself. "Never assume. In the words of the Great Detective, 'There is nothing more deceptive than an obvious fact.'"

"What's that from?"

"*The Boscombe Valley Mystery*. That makes Sharon's role at the museum even more important to her than just a chance to play dress-up. Her financial situation is uncomfortable, if not desperate, so . . ."

"How do you know that? I thought you'd never met her before Saturday." Jayne glanced over at the woman in question. "That dress she's wearing looks expensive."

"And it was. Many years ago. That she can't afford to buy anything new for something as important as a visitation for someone significant in her life indicates she's short of funds but trying to keep up appearances."

"Maybe she didn't have time to go shopping."

"Maybe," I admitted. But it was more than that. Sharon hadn't put on weight since the outfit was new but what weight she carried had shifted over the years, so the dress hung badly on her frame, clinging in some places and baggy in others. The rim of the collar showed the remains of stains that no longer came out in the wash. A button had been lost and replaced with one that didn't quite match the others, and a half-inch dip in the hem behind her right knee indicated that she'd sewn it up herself.

"Don't gape, Jayne," I said.

"I'm trying to see what you see," she said.

"What I see at the moment is Dan Lamb sitting alone. Let's have a word." I plunged through the crowd. Since we'd entered, more people had been arriving, and the room was rapidly filling up. Coffee, tea, water, and a platter of cheese and crackers had been laid out on the long table.

Dan Lamb sat in a comfortable armchair under a window overlooking a well-maintained, orderly garden.

"I'm sorry for your loss," Mr. Lamb," I said.

He blinked up at me. "Gemma from the bookshop, right?"

"The very one."

He smiled at Jayne. "And Mrs. Hudson herself."

My friend smiled in return.

He glanced around the room. "You know, I think you're the first one today to call it my loss. It's a difficult situation I find myself in, ex-husband of the deceased."

Notably, Elizabeth Dumont was not present. I decided to take Jayne's advice and be subtle, and not ask him outright why his wife hadn't come. Elizabeth might not have liked Kathy, and no doubt the feeling was mutual, but you'd expect Elizabeth to be with Dan to provide a show of support, if not support itself.

"You were married for a long time," Jayne said. "Naturally you're mourning."

Another smile. "Thank you for saying that. Some might disagree."

What do you know? Subtlety sometimes works. When he'd said "some," Dan's smile faded, and he twisted his wedding ring. A clear tell that he was thinking about his second wife, Elizabeth.

Was Elizabeth jealous of Kathy? Even after death?

Although Elizabeth was technically his third wife. His first, according to what I'd learned, had died a long time ago, leaving him with a small child.

"You doing okay here, Dad?"

"I'm fine, thanks. Ladies, this is my son, Bradley. Brad, Gemma and Jayne own the tearoom in West London."

"The infamous tearoom," Brad Lamb said.

"I wouldn't put it like that," I said.

"I would," he replied. "My stepmother died there, didn't she?" He stared into my face, almost begging me to rise to the bait. I didn't. Jayne said nothing.

"Do you still live in West London?" I asked him.

Brad shrugged. "I don't live anywhere these days. Nowhere and everywhere."

An artist of some sort. Musician, most likely. Guitar player, probably, judging by the calluses on the tips of his fingers. Long past his glory days, if ever he'd had any. Brad wore a well-worn gray T-shirt featuring AC/DC, an Australian hard-rock band. His brown hair was heavily streaked with premature gray and badly needed a wash. It was pulled back from his face in a straggly ponytail with a rubber band. The tips of his fingers were yellow from nicotine, and his teeth were stained. He smelled strongly of tobacco, both stale and fresh, but I didn't detect traces of anything illegal. He didn't look much like either his father or his sister, who, I remembered, was his half-sister. Except for the eyes, he must take after his biological mother.

"Do you sail, Gemma?" Dan asked me, obviously trying to change the subject from his son's living arrangements and employment opportunities.

"I've done some over the years. My uncle Arthur has taken me out a few times."

"Good man, Arthur. How's he doing?"

"Well, thank you. He's in the Mediterranean now."

I wasn't surprised that Dan knew my uncle. Arthur Doyle was well known in the Cape Cod boating community.

"I haven't been into the store for a while," Dan said. "Life seems to have gotten busy since I . . . lately that is."

"She keeps you running to her beck and call, you mean," Brad said.

Dan gave his son a glare.

"Kathy had many friends," Jayne said, trying to cover up the awkward silence. "Lots of people have come today."

"If you look around this room," Dan said, "you'll see two totally separate groups. Over to our right, sticking close to the refreshments table, is the commodore of the Cape Cod Yacht Club and some of the members. They're pretending not to notice the group pretending not to notice them. Those are the representatives of the West London Yacht Club. The Cape Cod group has come supposedly to support me, as Elizabeth and I are not only members there, but Elizabeth is heavily involved in just about every special event they put on. Mainly they're here for the gossip and in the hope of free food. The richer people are, the more they want something for free, I've learned. Today, I fear they're to be sadly disappointed. In the food, if not the gossip. Kathy belonged to the West London Yacht Club for many years, and that group is here to pay their respects to her. They'll have nothing to do with me."

"I met Jock O'Callaghan at the tea," I said.

"He was friends with Kathy. Despite the fact that my father was a member of the club before Jock so much as plopped his diaper-clad bottom into a boat, after our divorce and my engagement to Elizabeth, I was informed I was no longer welcome in those august halls." He shrugged, pretending the eviction hadn't stung him to the core. "I joined the Cape Cod club, where Elizabeth was already a member."

"That's right," Brad said. "Elizabeth was thrown out of the WLYC after she murdered her first husband."

Jayne sucked in a breath.

"Brad." Dan's voice was low.

"Or so people said." Brad looked at me. "If you want to know what I think, I wouldn't put it past her." He made a show of searching the crowded room. "Where is my dear second stepmother anyway? Too busy at home counting her money to come?"

"That's enough, Brad," Dan said.

"Enough for now." Brad wandered away, heading for the refreshments table.

"I'm sorry about that," Dan said. "My children didn't take Kathy and my divorce well."

"Common enough," I said.

"Brad's mother died when he was a baby, and Kathy was the only mother he knew. I wanted an amicable divorce, but . . . well, it didn't go that way, and the children were forced to take sides. Elizabeth and her first husband never had any children. She had . . . difficulty warming to mine. Divorces can get expensive. Brad needed money to keep his band together, and I had to turn him down."

"You don't have to explain to us," Jayne said.

As I was attempting to be subtle, I refrained from adding, "But please do."

Two elderly women joined our small group. "Dan," they said stiffly. "It's been awhile."

"So it has," he replied without smiling.

Jayne and I walked away. "Can we go now?" Jayne whispered to me. "This is all incredibly awkward."

"I see one person I want to talk to. Why don't you have a chat with Crystal? She's helping herself to a coffee at the moment and not talking to anyone."

"What am I going to chat to her about?"

"Noticeably, she hasn't so much as glanced at her father in the time we've been here. Find out if she's as angry with him over the divorce as her brother is."

"Easy for some people," Jayne muttered.

I made my way through the crowd to the West London Yacht Club circle. One of Ashleigh's favorite outfits is people-who-lunch-at-the-yacht club. This bunch took that up a notch. Dyed, sun-kissed hair, dark tans, heavy gold jewelry, blue and white jackets with epaulets, white or striped trousers, deck shoes worn without socks. That was the men. The women's shoes were either espadrilles or designer heels.

"Gemma. Nice to see you." Jock O'Callaghan welcomed me to the circle with a hearty hug and a kiss on both cheeks. I was somewhat taken aback, not only by the power of his aftershave, but because I hadn't thought we were at the hugging stage yet. "Some of you must know Gemma Doyle, from the Sherlock Holmes Book-shop." He introduced them, and I caught a blur of names.

Everyone nodded politely. Most of these people had been at the tea. They were an older group, all of them old-money New England.

"Was Kathy a member of your club?" I asked.

"For many, many years." Jock shook his head sadly. "She'll be sorely missed."

"She enjoyed sailing then?" I said.

He laughed. "Kathy? No, she never went out on a boat if she could help it, but she loved the sailing community and was a vital part of our group."

"And we at the club loved her in return," an elderly man with a blue cravat tied at his neck said. "You could always count on Kathy to pitch in when she was needed."

"Everyone was so dreadfully sorry that we were going to lose her at the end of the year," a woman said. "Couldn't be helped."

"I don't think we need to talk about that anymore," the older man said. "And certainly not here."

"It was Kathy's husband who sailed." Jock's eyes moved to where Dan sat all by himself. The women who'd greeted him with no enthusiasm had moved on.

"I'm surprised Dan had the nerve to show up here," another one of the women said. "After the way he treated her over *that woman*."

"She, at least, had the good sense not to come," someone else said. Everyone nodded.

"Who are you talking about?" I asked. I had no need, I decided, to try to be subtle. This bunch were eager to dish the dirt.

"Dan's new wife," said a woman with a Boston Brahmin accent and a face that might have been born with a disapproving frown. "Elizabeth Dumont."

"The Black Widow herself," her friend said.

I gave them questioning looks.

"Edward Dumont, Elizabeth's first husband, was a close friend of mine," Jock said. "A good man and a great sailor." Everyone nodded. "He died seven years ago."

"He was murdered seven years ago," the man with the cravat said. "By her. Elizabeth."

"Blimey," I said. An English expression I rarely use, but it would serve to remind them that I'm an outsider and might not know the details.

"You're not from around here, dear," the sour-faced woman said. "So you might not have heard about it."

"What happened?" I asked. "Why isn't she in jail?"

"Because it couldn't be proved. Elizabeth had an alibi for the time, but we all know she put a hit out on him." She went on to give me a detailed, and highly sensationalized, version of what Ryan had told me.

"She denied it all." Jock shook his head. "Bad business."

"She didn't even offer her resignation from the club. Can you believe the nerve!" the woman said, and her friends shook their heads.

"I was forced to have to tell her to leave," Jock said. "It was all extremely unpleasant."

"We kicked her to the curb. She went to the Cape Cod Club," the man said. "I wasn't surprised. They'll take anyone."

"Anyone with money," Jock sniffed. As though his fees weren't more than Fiona or Jocelyn's annual income.

"You can imagine our shock when we heard that Dan had left Kathy to take up with her, of all people," the first woman said.

Dan's a fool. Always was, always will be. He didn't even have the sense to know he wasn't welcome at the

WLYC any longer. He showed up, all smiles and all ready to go sailing, the day after his engagement to Elizabeth was announced."

"Which was the day after he told Kathy he wanted a divorce," one of the women said.

"Like Elizabeth before him, he had to be ordered to leave," Jock continued. "It wasn't pleasant, I can tell you."

"You managed it perfectly, Jock," the woman said. "Anyone else would have lost their cool and embarrassed us all."

Thank you," Jock said. "Now, I, for one, am ready to toast Kathy with something stronger than tea. Anyone interested?"

The group chorused their agreement, and I slipped away. I found Jayne chatting to Tina Norman, an Emporium regular. "The newest Victoria Thompson book's come in," I told her.

She grinned at me. "Can't beat that for customer service. You know what I like better than I do."

"What brings you here today? Did you know Kathy Lamb?"

"Not really. I went to school with Crystal and Brad. I dated Brad for a short time until I realized that before he and his band had even reached the big time, they were already gathering groupies."

"I'll take a guess the big time never arrived."

"Nope. I haven't heard from him since school, but I read about his mom's death in the paper, so thought I'd pay my respects." She blew out a puff of air. "I shouldn't have bothered. He wasn't interested in talking over the old times."

"I'm surprised you were in school with him. I'd have put him at a great deal older than you."

"He's thirty-seven. Same as me."

Brad was leaning up against a wall, not talking to anyone, just looking around the room and scowling. Life on the road as a musician can be hard. So can a life of bitterness.

"Ready to go, Jayne?" I asked.

"Yes."

"I'll pop into the store tomorrow for the book," Tina said.

People were beginning to leave, and we followed the West London Yacht Club out.

"What did Crystal have to say?" I asked once Jayne and I were settled into the Miata and heading back to town.

"I assumed you wanted to know what sort of relationship she had with her mother, and you sent me to talk to her, thinking that she'd get on better with me than with you."

I gave her a grin. "I'm impressed. You read my mind."

"Your influence must be rubbing off. I don't know if that's a good thing or not. I'd say Crystal had a good relationship with her mother and is taking her death hard. She might have been putting on an act, but I don't think so. I asked her where she worked, and she's a vice president at a bank in Boston."

"Which bank?"

"She didn't say. I guess I should have asked."

"Unlikely that matters. Her clothes are expensive, but that position should pay well. She's unmarried."

"You know that because she wasn't wearing a wedding ring, right?"

"A simple observation."

"What she did say that I found interesting is that she hates her stepmother."

"Do tell."

"Crystal and Brad are really angry about their parents' divorce. Crystal hasn't spoken to her father since he left Kathy."

"Did she give you any idea why they're so angry?"

"According to her, Elizabeth's a home wrecker and Dan too weak and spineless to stand up to her."

"Always the woman's fault," I said.

"Yeah. Anyway, one other thing you might find interesting."

"Go ahead."

"The divorce was very bitter and got drawn out for a long time. That means expensive. Kathy spent almost everything she had on lawyers. It was only finalized about six months ago. She ended up getting a fair settlement, but Dan didn't have all that much left to share with her. She got the house, but she couldn't pay the taxes and upkeep on it and had to sell it. She moved into an apartment that she hated. Crystal thinks Elizabeth was paying Dan's legal fees, egging him on to keep fighting Kathy."

"That would cause a lot of bitterness, all right."

"So, are we getting anywhere?"

"If Elizabeth was the murder victim, I'd say we were. Crystal and Brad to start with, Dan if he regretted marrying Elizabeth, not to mention that she's not too popular with her late husband's friends from the yacht club. We've found all those people with motives, and we're not even looking into Elizabeth. Elizabeth wasn't murdered—Kathy was, and I don't know that I've learned much that will help."

"What about Elizabeth? Maybe she did it. She was at the tea."

"Ah, yes. Elizabeth. The yacht club people call her the Black Widow."

"What does that mean?"

I told Jayne what I'd learned about the death of her first husband before saying, "I'm going back to the shop. Do you want me to drop you at your place?"

"Please."

I made a detour to take Jayne home. As I drove through town, I thought about the afternoon. Not only did I not have any good suspects for the murder of Kathy, I had a plethora of groups to sort out. Kathy's family, including Dan, her former husband. Dan's new family, meaning Elizabeth. The West London and Cape Cod Yacht Clubs. The museum. Not to mention the ubiquitous person or persons unknown.

Chapter Twelve

I made it back to the Emporium in time to relieve Ashleigh for her dinner break. As I helped customers, rang up purchases, gave recommendations and directions to local restaurants, tidied the shelves, and rearranged stock, I thought about what I'd learned about the death of Kathy Lamb.

Nothing I could take to the police. I hadn't forgotten Robyn Kirkpatrick, thrown off the board of the museum in a power play by Kathy, or Sharon Musgrave, who not only needed to keep working at the museum because she loved it, but because she needed the small income she got from doing their books. Did Sharon know Kathy wanted to fire her because her carelessness had caused the fire?

Not for the first time, I regretted having no authority to make people let me into their houses and talk to me. I'd love to go with Ryan when he called on the suspects, and observe their reactions to his questions, but that, I knew without even asking, wouldn't happen. Any help Ryan wanted from me had to be kept strictly unofficial.

I'd spoken to Dan Lamb, his children, the people from the West London Yacht Club, and Robyn and Sharon from the museum. The one person I hadn't yet talked to was Elizabeth Dumont.

Before going any further, I'd have to do that. All I knew of Elizabeth was what I'd observed at the auction tea and what others had told me, but that was enough to indicate that she wasn't the sort of woman who'd simply open up and tell me all I needed to know.

I waited impatiently until the shop was empty of customers, and then I accessed the computer behind the sales counter. I called up the activities page of the Cape Cod Yacht Club. As it was July, they were busy. Tomorrow the club was holding a regatta for the under-twelves: no use to me. Classes every day for teens ages thirteen to sixteen: again, no use to me. Cocktail party and initial meeting on the veranda for members interested in planning next year's anniversary celebrations: bingo! Should be right up Elizabeth's alley. Dan had mentioned that she was an active organizer at the club.

My phone pinged with an incoming text from Uncle Arthur.

Nothing.

Arthur was a man of few words, and that one word was enough. On the off chance someone had commissioned a theft of a Conan Doyle first edition, I'd asked him to see if there was any talk in the shadier parts of the collecting world. He had done so, and had come up empty.

Which didn't mean there was nothing to find, but Uncle Arthur would have done what he could, and I was satisfied.

* * *

Tuesday morning I brought a few extra things into work with me, so I drove rather than walked. I opened the shop at the regular time, and Ashleigh arrived promptly at one.

"I'm sorry to do this to you again," I said to her, "but I need to go out for a few hours this afternoon."

"Not a problem," she said. Moriarty jumped onto the counter to greet her.

"If you need any help, I can try to hurry back."

"I've got this, Gemma. We've got this, don't we, big boy?" She scratched behind Moriarty's ears. He purred.

"There are people I can call on to help in a pinch."

"Not necessary."

"It can get busy in July in the afternoon."

"Busy is good, isn't it, Moriarty?"

He meowed his agreement.

"Well, yes, but—"

"Don't spare me a second thought," Ashleigh said.

Today she looked as though she were about to head off to ballet class, with her hair scraped back so tightly the edges of her eyes lifted. She wore a black tank top and black tights under a lacy pink skirt accented by thick wool socks and flat shoes.

"Maybe I won't go out after all," I said.

"If I need help, I have your phone number," she reminded me. "You can help me here, can't you, buddy?" The cat's body shivered in delight.

I sighed. "Okay. I guess that'll be all right."

Moriarty looked at me for the first time. He smirked.

* * *

At three o'clock, I climbed the seventeen steps to my office. I did not plan on going to the Cape Cod Yacht Club as myself. Using the things I'd brought from home, I went to a great deal of trouble to prepare for the visit. When I came back down, the bottom step creaked under my weight, as it always does, and Ashleigh looked up.

"You can't go up there," she said to me. "The second floor's private."

Moriarty arched his back and hissed. Ashleigh put her hand on his back. "Sorry. He's usually quite friendly. Can I help you find anything?"

"Do you have *From Holmes to Sherlock* by Mattias Boström?" I asked.

"Yes, we do." She came out from behind the counter. "It's over here." She crossed the floor to the nonfiction section, and I followed, trying not to trip on the unaccustomed high heels. Moriarty jumped off the counter and bolted for his bed beneath the center table.

Ashleigh put her hand on the volume in question and began to draw it out. "Are you looking for a book for yourself or for a gift? We have a good selection of—"

"Don't bother," I said in my normal voice.

She whirled around. "Gemma?"

"The one and only."

"What the heck?"

"I'm off to the yacht club. I'd prefer not to be recognized. Pop into the tearoom and tell Jayne I won't make our regular meeting, please. Carry on!" I went out the back door to the parking spot in the alley where I'd left the Miata, feeling rather pleased with myself.

As I'd told Ashleigh, I didn't want to be recognized. It's not as hard, I have found, as some might think to dramatically change one's appearance. People expect to see what they expect to see. A gray-blond wig, a pair of giant sunglasses, a bit of makeup to add lines to the edges of my mouth and nose, a silk scarf around the throat to hide the lack of loosening skin, the sort of clothes I'd normally never be caught dead in, shoes with higher heels than I ever wear, to add height, and a bit of padding to my chest and hips. All that, plus an upper-crust New York accent, and we have a wealthy, widowed lady in her well-preserved fifties recently moved to West London from Manhattan and hoping to join a yacht club for the social life.

My disguise might make me look a bit plumper than is fashionable among wealthy East Coast women, but I can't make myself look thinner than I am, nor can I become shorter, so I had to add weight and height.

I drove past the harbor to the Cape Cod Yacht Club. It was another beautiful day, and the sun sparkled on the Atlantic Ocean. Plenty of boats were out, their brightly colored sails and hulls brilliant against the dark water. The CCYC is newer than its rival, the West London club, so it doesn't have quite as much prestige, but otherwise it's on par in the quality of the sailing and sailors (excellent) and cost of membership (eye-watering). According to Uncle Arthur, it's not quite as snooty.

I parked in a lot crowded with expensive vehicles, plucked my Louis Vuitton clutch bag off the front seat, and walked to the front doors of the main building. My steps were slightly hesitant; I was not quite sure where I was going or whom I hoped to meet. I opened the door and almost collided with Detective Louise Estrada on her way out. My stomach turned over.

"Pardon me," my archnemesis said.

"Quite all right," I replied.

Louise continued on her way.

I stood in the entrance, looking around the building, getting my bearings. A substantial number of people bustled about, most of them dressed in some version of sailing clothes. Ages ranged from primary school to almost a century. The opposite wall was all glass, giving a fabulous view over the harbor, row upon row of straight tall masts pointing into the blue sky, to the ocean dotted with boats of all types and sizes. I am not a sailor. My parents didn't sail—they didn't so much as row. I didn't even have toy boats to play with in the bathtub. When I was growing up, my father's uncle Arthur was mostly away at sea, and on the rare occasion he visited us, he would take my sister and me to the British Museum or the National Gallery, not to the seaside. Since we've been living together in West London, I've been out with him several times on his boat, *The Irregular*, but after a few attempts to teach me to steer the craft or raise a sail, he decided I'm better suited in the galley making rum punches or on the computer planning our land excursions.

I walked up to the reception desk. The handsome young man, all freckles and blond hair, gave me a smile so brilliant I was glad I hadn't removed my sunglasses. "Good afternoon. May I help you?"

"I hope so. I . . . I'm new to town, and I'm thinking of joining a sailing club." I smiled shyly at him. "My late husband was a marvelous sailor, and I'd like to take it up again."

Out came a stack of brochures. I tucked them into my bag.

"Our membership director is Mrs. Burnside. She's in her office at the moment, and she'd be delighted to answer any questions you might have."

"That would be nice."

"Let me show you to her office."

"I'd rather have a look around first, if you don't mind. I was at the West London club yesterday, and they were so friendly. Gave me free run of the place. Oh, it looks like you're having a party on the deck. How lovely." I wandered off. He picked up his phone and punched buttons.

A sign at the entrance informed me that the outdoor bar and restaurant was closed this afternoon for a club meeting. I went outside. White pillars, dark wood floor, blue and white wicker furniture, giant iron tubs of red geraniums and trailing vines. A glass railing marked the edge of the veranda, and beyond was a patch of perfect grass, some flower beds, and a dock that appeared to be the valet dock for motor boats. Young men and women in the club's colors helped passengers disembark, and then took the boats to a slip.

All terribly posh.

On the veranda itself, about twenty-five people mingled and sipped drinks. White-and-black-clad waiters carried silver trays with flutes of sparkling wine. A long table had been set up at the front, with seats for three and pads of paper and pens and water glasses laid out. Rows of chairs had been arranged to face the table, ready for the meeting to begin.

Quite a few people smiled politely, although vacantly, at me. I recognized some Emporium shoppers and some who regularly frequented Mrs. Hudson's. A few of these people had been at the visitation for Kathy Lamb yesterday, but none had been at the museum auction.

Except for one. I spotted my quarry helping herself to a glass of wine off a young waiter's tray. Elizabeth Dumont. There was no sign of her husband, Dan Lamb.

Once she had her drink in hand, Elizabeth went to stand at the railing, looking out to sea. I joined her.

"What a marvelous view," I said.

She didn't look at me. "It is."

I held out my hand. "I'm Gail McIntosh. I'm new to the Cape and thinking of joining this club."

She glanced at my hand through her thick glasses and took it a fraction of a second before enough time passed to be rude. Her grip was firm. I thought of three-day-old fish and let my own fingers flop.

"Are you a member here?" I asked.

"Yes."

"Do you like it?"

"It's fine."

In this fashionable, well-heeled crowd, Elizabeth stood out for her lack of style. Her gray hair was cropped short, her eyebrows were bushy, and she wore no makeup. She dressed as though she didn't much care what anyone thought, in well-worn Bermuda shorts and a pink T-shirt with a flower pattern. Her shoes were Birkenstocks, and her only jewelry consisted of small gold studs in her ears and a thin wedding band on her left hand. Instead of Chanel Number Five or Elizabeth Taylor's Diamonds, she smelled of stale tobacco. She stared over my shoulder. I laughed lightly. "Have you been a member long?"

"A few years."

Two women began fussing at the long table, placing a binder and a water glass at each place. The meeting was about to begin. I was getting nowhere, and getting there fast.

A woman dressed in a summer business suit crossed the veranda rapidly, heels tapping on the wooden decking, heading my way.

"There you are!" she said to me. "I'm sorry to have left you on your own. I'm Theresa, the membership director here."

We shook hands. A waiter passed and I pointedly stared at him.

Theresa got the hint. "Would you care for a glass of wine?"

"That would be lovely, thank you."

"If you'll excuse me," Elizabeth said. "Our meeting's about to begin."

"Meeting?" I blinked in embarrassment. "Oh dear. I'm so sorry, I didn't mean to interrupt. What's your meeting about?"

"Club business."

"I'm sorry, I didn't get your name."

"I'm Elizabeth Dumont."

"Elizabeth is one of our die-hard members." Theresa handed me a glass full of dancing bubbles. I touched my lips to the rim, but didn't drink. "I don't know what we'd do without her."

"An exaggeration." Elizabeth attempted to sound modest, but her chin lifted at the praise. "You'd manage perfectly fine."

"Elizabeth has recently married," Theresa said. "Isn't that nice? Her husband is new at our club, and we're absolutely delighted. Perhaps you'd enjoy talking to Mr. Lamb and some of our other new members to find out all about joining our little yachting family."

"Ladies and gentlemen, if you can take your seats please," a woman said in a voice designed to carry.

"Why don't I show you around the club, Mrs. . . . ?" Theresa put her hand lightly on my arm.

"McIntosh."

"We have full banqueting facilities and a justifiably famous restaurant as well as . . ." Her voice droned on, outlining the excellence and exclusivity of the Cape Cod Yacht Club.

Short of tearing my arm away, dropping into a seat, crossing my arms over my chest, and not budging, I couldn't refuse to go with her. Disguise or not, I didn't see a way to demand of Elizabeth, "Did you kill your husband's previous wife?"

This had been a wasted trip. Elizabeth herself seemed calm and in control, a woman comfortable in her environment and confident of her place in it. Then again, if she'd had the nerve to murder her rival a few feet away from a room full of people, she wasn't the nervous sort.

She hadn't mingled much with her fellow club members, but I got the feeling that was her choice, not theirs. She wasn't ostracized here. People had greeted her, and Theresa had praised her.

Maybe that was the most I would learn today.

"Nice meeting you, Elizabeth," I said.

"I'm sure you'll like it here if you decide to join." She turned to walk away.

I slapped my forehead. "Lamb. I heard that name just this morning. One of my friends was telling me about it. That woman who died on the weekend—terrible tragedy. The papers say the police are treating it as a suspicious death." I pretended not to hear Theresa's sharp intake of breath. "Lamb isn't a common name, is it? Was she your sister-in-law maybe?"

The look of bored politeness on Elizabeth's face changed in an instant. Pure rage flared in the depths of her eyes, and a vein pulsed in her neck. "How dare you!"

I lifted my hand to my throat and took a step backward. "Oh dear, did I say something out of turn? My husband always said my mouth was my worst enemy. I'm only trying to make conversation."

"What sort of a boat do you own, Mrs. McIntosh?" Theresa said.

"Were you related to the dead woman?" I asked Elizabeth.

"We have mooring for any size of boat or yacht." Theresa's voice rose in panic.

"I knew her," Elizabeth said.

"You must be in mourning then. I'm sorry to disturb you."

"Plus winter storage for those who don't go south for the season."

Elizabeth stared at me. "Kathy Lamb was a thoroughly nasty, jealous, bitter woman. No loss to anyone. Least of all to me."

I laughed in embarrassment.

"And a wide range of social activities for all ages," said an increasingly desperate Theresa.

"Her death worked out to your advantage then," I said.

Elizabeth's eyes narrowed. "Who are you, anyway?"

"Do you have grandchildren, Mrs. McIntosh?" Theresa grasped desperately at conversation of last resort.

"Why yes, I do," I said. "I have seven. Four boys and three girls. Will you look at the time? I have an appointment soon. Why don't I take your card and come back another day." I allowed Theresa to lead me away. Other than forcing her to break down and confess, which wasn't going to happen, I'd learn nothing more from Elizabeth today.

Behind me, Elizabeth's phone rang. She pulled it out and snapped, "Dan, where the heck are you?"

I stopped walking abruptly and leaned against the railing. I looked out to sea and took a deep admiring breath. The air was full of the scent of the ocean mingled with flowers, freshly cut grass, good perfume, and a slight trace of bacon grease wafting from the kitchen. "This view is magnificent," I said to Theresa. "Much better than the one at the West London club."

I had no idea if it was or not, as I've never been to the West London Yacht Club, but my words had the desired effect. Teresa stopped trying to hurry me away. "We're very proud of it."

"Not again!" I overheard Elizabeth say. "You went yesterday. I told you not to go, but you insisted. Wasn't once enough?"

Fortunately, Theresa had the common sense to realize that I wanted to admire the view in peace. She stopped talking and let me enjoy the beauty of my surroundings.

"This meeting is important to me," Elizabeth yelled into the phone. "I told you that."

I was only party to half of this conversation, but that was enough. I couldn't hear his words, but the whiny, pleading tone of Dan's voice came across. Elizabeth was getting angrier and angrier. "I want—no, I *expect* your support. You don't have to make an appearance again. You weren't married to the horrid woman any more. Let her children handle the visitation."

She paused. Dan said something I didn't catch.

"Don't give me that. I'm surprised anyone even bothered to show up. Morbidly curious, no doubt."

There was a long pause. Elizabeth breathed. "I expect you to be at the club in fifteen minutes, Daniel. No excuses." In the old days, she would have slammed the receiver down so hard it bounced; today she shoved the phone into her jacket pocket with an angry grunt. She marched across the veranda. "Let's get this meeting started. Now!"

I headed for the doors. "Your grandchildren will enjoy our extensive range of children's programming," Theresa said. "Both on the water and on land."

"How nice," I said. "Thank you so much for your time. I'll be in touch."

She whipped out her phone. "Why don't I take your contact information, Mrs. McIntosh? I can send you further information electronically."

I waved my hand in the air. The large stone in the ring on my left hand wasn't a real diamond, but it was a good imitation. "I'll call you. Oh, I see someone I know. Thank you for your time."

I left Theresa with her mouth open, clutching her phone. I hadn't been lying this time: I had seen someone I knew. About the last person I would have expected to find here.

A man and a woman stood by the club's notice board chatting. He was dressed in Ralph Lauren, his hair wind-blown, his cheeks pink, looking as though he'd just come back from a sail. Her long blond hair was tied into a casual ponytail, and she wore jeans with a plain T-shirt and trainers, as though she'd just finished work,

Which she had.

"Good afternoon," I said.

They both smiled politely, although vacantly at me. "Good afternoon."

"This is a lovely club," I said. "I'm new to town and thinking of joining."

The man's smile broadened. He was in his early thirties and handsome in that clean-cut American way: short dark hair, strong jaw, good teeth. "You'd be most welcome. We're a great bunch." He held out his hand. "I'm Jack Templeton and this is my friend, Jayne Wilson."

I accepted his handshake and nodded at Jayne. She narrowed her eyes and studied me closely.

"If you're new here, you must try Jayne's place," Jack said. "It's called Mrs. Hudson's Tearoom. It does a fabulous traditional afternoon tea."

"Perhaps I will," I said.

"It's on Baker Street," he said, "next door to a pretentious bookstore called Sherlock Holmes."

"Pretentious, is it?"

"Totally. Run by some nutty English woman."

Jayne leapt to my defense. Sort of. "Gemma might seem different from most people sometimes, but she's anything but nutty. She's the smartest person I've ever met. Don't tell her I said that."

"My lips are sealed." He turned the full wattage of his smile onto Jayne. "I have to be going. Great seeing you, Jayne. I'll call you later, and we can arrange that dinner."

"I'll look forward to it," she said.

He gave her a wink and me a polite smile, and went into the bar.

"I hope you're not thinking of going on a date with him," I said in my normal voice.

Jayne sucked in a breath. "Gemma?"

"Let's get out of here." I headed for the doors. Jayne followed at a rapid clip.

"What the heck are doing in that get-up?" she asked.

"'Pretentious,' indeed. Never mind 'nutty.' I'll accept your compliment, though. Did you come in your car?"

"I walked. I left Fiona and Jocelyn to lock up the tearoom. Are you going to tell me . . . ?"

"I have the Miata. I'll meet you at the corner of Harbor Road and Smith Street in five minutes."

"Can't I come with you now?"

"I don't want people to see us leaving together. I might need to come back at a later date. They've done a nice job with the gardens here, haven't they?" I wandered over to examine the roses.

Roses examined, along with the condition of the rest of the garden, I headed for my car. I was driving cautiously and sedately out of the Cape Cod Yacht Club when a black Lexus tore past me on the other side of the driveway, missing my side mirror by inches. I pulled to the verge, stopped the car, and watched in my rearview mirror as the Lexus squeezed into a spot close to the doors. The driver leapt out, and her door struck the car next to her. She paid it no mind, but grabbed her purse and ran up the steps into the club.

Robyn Kirkpatrick, former board chair of Scarlet House, in a heck of a hurry.

Perhaps because she was late for a meeting? If she was a member here, she'd be acquainted with Elizabeth Dumont.

Jayne was waiting for me as arranged. I stopped at the curb, and she hopped in. "Spill," she said. "I didn't recognize you at first. Where the heck did you get all that stuff?"

I pulled off the wig and gave my head a good rub. "That thing is hot."

"Gemma! Talk."

"A few items I've collected over the years," I said, "thinking they might come in handy someday."

"Is that diamond real?"

"No."

"Are you going to tell me why you thought it necessary to age yourself twenty years to visit the Cape Cod Yacht Club?"

"I wanted to check out Elizabeth Dumont in her own environment. I thought it better to do so in disguise."

Jayne fell against her seat with a sigh. "You never fail to amaze me."

"Thank you," I said. "What were you doing there?"

"I wanted to help you with the investigation. I dated Jack Templeton for a while in high school."

"Is that so?"

"He moved to Boston, made a lot of money in an internet start-up, and is now back in West London. I'd heard he belonged to the club, and thought I might be able to find something out about Dan Lamb and Elizabeth Dumont, so I gave Jack a call. I was planning to talk on the phone, but he said he was at the club and suggested I pop down and meet. It was nice seeing him again." She smiled to herself. "We've lost touch over the years."

I harrumphed. "You're not planning to have dinner with him, I hope."

"Why, yes, I am. Turns out he got divorced not long ago. He's been thinking about looking me up and was pleased when I called."

"You aren't afraid of being known as Jack and Jayne?"

"I, for one, am not so childish."

I harrumphed again. "I don't suppose you learned anything apart from the news that your childhood crush is once again single?"

I pulled into the alley behind the Emporium and the tearoom, and switched the engine off. I turned to face Jayne, and she grinned at me.

"I think I did. Learn something, I mean. Elizabeth and Dan aren't getting on too well. Rumor is he regrets marrying her, but she controls the purse strings, and he'll be cut off without a cent if he leaves her. Elizabeth was absolutely furious when Dan tried to maintain a friendship with Kathy, and now that Kathy's dead, she still doesn't seem to be able to get over it. She ordered Dan to have nothing to do with planning Kathy's funeral. Can you believe it? Kathy was the mother of one of his children and as good as the mother to the other. No one at the yacht club can stand Elizabeth, but she's one of their richest members and puts a lot of money into the club, plus she runs most of the committees, so everyone pretends they love her to bits. As for Dan himself, they all feel sorry for him."

I stared at her.

"What did you learn?" Jayne asked.

"Less than you did, it would seem," I admitted at last. "And I didn't even get a dinner date out of it."

"I don't like to say, Gemma," Jayne said, "but have you put on weight lately?"

Chapter Thirteen

I went upstairs to my office to lick my wounds. Not only had Jayne learned more than I had, but she hadn't needed to bother with the pretext of pretending to be something she wasn't. She'd simply asked.

I had to consider that maybe I was going about this detecting the wrong way. *Too clever by half*, Ryan Ashburton had once called me.

I washed the aging makeup off my face and struggled out of the clothes and extra padding (have I gained weight, indeed!). When Sherlock Holmes was facing a difficult case, he settled into his comfortable armchair by the fire, steepled his fingers, lit his pipe, and instructed Doctor Watson to leave him alone.

I, on the other hand, had a business to run.

I went downstairs and told Ashleigh she could take her dinner break. While customers browsed, I surveyed the shop, taking mental inventory of what had been bought while I'd been out and what I needed to reorder.

Unlike me, the Great Detective didn't live in the age of constant interruptions. I've found that I don't need quiet, solitude, and three pipes to think things over. I can do that while my mind is going through mechanical tasks.

Elizabeth Dumont was now firmly at the top of my suspect list. She clearly had motive—jealousy of her husband's previous wife; opportunity—she was at the tea; and means—along with everyone else at the auction, she could have grabbed the teacup chain on her way to the back room.

To top it off, Elizabeth had been a suspect in the death of her first husband.

I thought of her anger on the phone when Dan told her he wanted to go to the funeral home again today, rather than come to Elizabeth's meeting.

The Black Widow.

Might Dan be next?

"Excuse me," a woman said, "but I'm wondering if you can recommend a good book."

"Something suitable for your beach vacation?"

She laughed. "How'd you know I'm on vacation?"

I didn't have to be Sherlock Holmes to figure that one out. Pink shorts, flip-flops, sunburned nose, and a trace of chocolate ice cream on her pink T-shirt. "I hope you're having a good time in West London."

"Fabulous. I love it here. When I was a child, we came to Cape Cod every year, but I haven't been back since. I'm so glad we decided to come again. I was told this was a great place to look for historical mysteries. They're my favorite."

"Then you are indeed in the right place," I said. "Do you like the gritty stuff: dark alleys, tough men and desperate women, and dangerous killers? Or ladies in silk gowns and gentlemen hailing hansom cabs?"

"Dark and gritty," she said with a laugh. I walked with her to the pastiche shelf and pulled out *Dust and*

Shadows by Lyndsay Faye. "Sherlock Holmes and Dr. John Watson on the grim streets of Whitechapel in pursuit of Jack the Ripper."

She accepted the book with a shiver of delight. "When my husband and I were in London a few years ago, we went on a Jack the Ripper walking tour. It was so interesting."

"Do you have a DVD player?"

"There's one in the common room at our B and B."

"You might enjoy the BBC TV program *Ripper Street*. It's excellent and faithful to the times. Not for the faint of heart, though."

"Show me to it," she said with another laugh. I handed her the DVD package, and she exclaimed over the picture of the characters in their costumes.

"Matthew Macfadyen—be still my beating heart," I said.

Eventually, she left with a huge smile and a bag full of books and DVDs, leaving the shop momentarily empty of customers. Thinking of handsome men, I pulled out my phone and called Ryan. He answered on the first ring.

"Do you have fingerprint analysis on the teacup decoration back from the lab yet?" I asked.

"I'm well, thank you, Gemma," he said. "And yourself?"

"Oh, sorry. I forgot the pleasantries. How are you?"

"The better for knowing that you'll never change. The answer is yes, but nothing conclusive. Plenty of partial and smudged prints. Other than the deceased, yours was the only set we could identify positively."

I let that one go. "Kathy's prints were on it?"

"She would have struggled to get it away from her throat."

I paused for a moment, imagining the scene. I hadn't expected the fingerprints to be conclusive, as the decoration had been hanging in a room packed with people, never mind the chain of ownership, but it never hurt to ask. "Is your investigation focusing on anyone in particular?"

"The only reason I can answer that question, Gemma, is because the answer is no. Not everyone loved Kathy Lamb, but she didn't go around deliberately making enemies."

"I can think of one person who hated her."

"Go on."

"Elizabeth Dumont. Dan's new wife. People at the yacht club say Elizabeth was furious at Dan for wanting to maintain a cordial relationship with his ex-wife."

"How do you know that?"

"I . . . I mean Jayne, simply asked a friend of hers. It's not a secret."

"And it isn't a secret to us either, Gemma. Louise spoke to several of the club members, and they told her much the same."

Once again, I thought of all the time and trouble I'd spent trying to ferret out information that turned out to be freely available. I should have pulled a stool up to the yacht club bar and said to the person next to me, "Whatcha havin'?"

"Have you considered that Dan Lamb might be in some danger?" I asked.

"What does that mean?"

"Elizabeth's angry at Dan because he's mourning Kathy. How angry, I have to ask. We can't forget what happened to the first Mr. Elizabeth."

"I'm not forgetting, but I don't see it, Gemma. Kathy's funeral will be over in a few days. She'll be out of the picture for good. The only reason Elizabeth was ever suspected of killing her first husband was for his money. Her situation now is, to put it mildly, comfortable. Dan Lamb's, on the other hand—and this is highly confidential—is not. The man's completely broke. The divorce cleaned him out. Sorry, but I gotta run. Louise is making get-off-the-phone gestures. Are you going to be home tonight?"

"I am."

"I might drop in if nothing comes up. Would that be okay?"

"It would be more than okay," I said.

He hung up without words of affection, which meant Louise Estrada was standing next to him, glowering and tapping her foot.

I went to the front window and stood there, watching the activity on Baker Street. Traffic was heavy as cars drove through town and pedestrians browsed the shops. A group of women came out of Beach Fine Arts. Maureen appeared in the doorway, watching them turn into the accessories store next door. Judging by the look on her face, they had not bought anything in her shop. She caught me looking, and her face turned even darker. She tossed her head and went back inside.

Here I was, trying to help her, and all Maureen could give me was an ugly look. Oh well, I hadn't decided to get involved because I liked her or had any expectations that we'd soon become best of chums.

I hadn't learned anything this afternoon that wasn't common knowledge, but I had discovered one potentially important piece of information. Either Robyn Kirkpatrick was a member of the Cape Cod Yacht Club, or she had some business there. She'd been in a hurry, which indicted she was late for an appointment or for a meeting. The only meeting going on at the club this afternoon was the one I'd crashed.

She almost certainly knew Elizabeth Dumont. Were two separate strands of Kathy's life coming together: the museum, and Dan and Elizabeth?

And what of Elizabeth? I'd heard the anger in her voice when Dan told her he wanted, once again, to be with Kathy. I'd seen the rage on her face. I'd heard her give him an order.

Had Dan decided to keep peace in his marriage and go to the yacht club instead?

Easy enough to find out. I waited impatiently until Ashleigh got back from dinner.

"I'm going out again," I said as she put her purse under the counter.

"Take all the time you need," she said. I studied her, searching for a hint of sarcasm. She gave me a sweet smile.

The parking lot at the funeral home was almost empty. It was after seven o'clock, and the visitation would soon be over. I hurried in, saying to the young man who opened the door for me, "I hope I'm not too late. I just got off work. Mrs. Lamb?"

"Not at all, madam," he said somberly. "The family will be receiving visitors for a few more minutes."

I went down the hall and into the room. A handful of people milled about while an attendant cleared plates and glasses off the refreshment table. Kathy's daughter, Crystal, today wearing a different designer suit, greeted me as I entered, and I expressed my condolences. Brad, Dan's son, stood next to a window, his phone out, his thumbs moving. Dan Lamb had taken a chair close to the casket, and there he sat, shoulders hunched, head bowed, alone.

"Is your father okay?" I asked Crystal. "I don't want to bother him."

She slowly turned her head to look at him. Her dark eyes were like chips of coal. "Bother him? He should be bothered." She switched her somber but welcoming smile back on for an elderly couple on their way out. "Thank you so much for coming, Mr. and Mrs. Frankenheimer. Please give Joanne my best when you're next talking to her."

The last of the visitors were leaving now, but no one approached Dan Lamb to say goodbye. He sat by himself, a picture of lonely misery.

All of a sudden, out of nowhere, I felt bad. This wasn't any of my business, to intrude on this family in their time of grief. Let the police handle it, and let Maureen get herself out of trouble.

I turned to leave, but my way was blocked by Crystal's well-draped back. She wasn't attempting to prevent me from leaving, but someone from entering.

Elizabeth Dumont.

"I don't think you're wanted here," Crystal said.

"I don't much care what you think," Elizabeth replied. "I need to speak to my husband."

"Not in the presence of my mother, you aren't." Crystal raised her voice. "Father, your fancy lady is here. You can talk to her in the alley next to the trash cans."

Dan didn't move. I doubt he even heard her. Brad looked over. He put away his phone, and a smile crossed his lips. The smile was not at all friendly. I stepped away and positioned myself behind a chair, with my back to the wall, the better to see and hear without being observed.

"Get out of my way, Crystal," Elizabeth said.

"Or what?" Crystal put her hands on her hips.

"Or I'll walk right through you."

Crystal braced herself. I prepared to intervene should they come to blows. Then Crystal's shoulders deflated ever so slightly, and she moved a fraction of an inch to one side.

Elizabeth pushed past her. She marched across the room, with firm determined steps, to stand in front of Dan Lamb. Every muscle of her body emanated fury. He looked up and blinked. "Elizabeth. Thanks for coming, honey. I'll be ready to go in a few minutes."

"Too late, Dan," she said.

"I'm sorry I missed your meeting, honey. I'll make it up to you."

"No, you will not," she said. "You've humiliated me for the last time."

"Sorry," he said again. He pushed himself to his feet.

"In case you've forgotten, we were due to have drinks at the club with John and Ellen Ireland." Elizabeth made no attempt to lower her voice. The few remaining visitors openly stared. I openly stared. "That meeting was important to me. My reputation at the club depends on getting the Irelands to sponsor the proposed children's regatta weekend. I tried telling them you'd taken ill, but that blathering idiot Ellen said she'd heard you were despondent—she used that very word—over the death of Kathy and you refused to leave her side. People are gossiping about me, Dan. Laughing at me behind my back. I don't like that."

"Sorry," Dan said again. "I'm ready to leave now."

She lifted one hand and slapped him hard across the face. His eyes opened wide, but he didn't move. Brad sucked in a breath, and Crystal might have actually laughed. An attendant stepped hesitantly forward.

"Don't bother coming home tonight," Elizabeth said. "Or any other night. We're finished."

She turned and headed for the door. "Nice of you to drop by," Brad called. Crystal gave Elizabeth a grin. "Good one," she said.

"Now, that was entertaining," Crystal said to the room once Elizabeth had left. "I'm outta here. Coming, Brad?"

"I'll help Dad," Brad said.

"Suit yourself. Sounds like he needs to find himself a hotel room."

"How about I bring him around to Kathy's for the night?"

"You do that, brother dear, and I'll have to shoot him. And then you for being such an idiot." Crystal picked up her Prada bag, tucked it under her arm, and walked out.

"It's time for us to lock up, sir," the attendant said to Dan.

I edged away from the wall and around the chair. Brad noticed me for the first time. He glared at me. "You hanging around for any particular reason?"

"I'm here to express my condolences."

"Noted," he said. "Now get out."

I did so.

Chapter Fourteen

After leaving the funeral home, I went back to work, locked up at closing time, and headed home. Ryan hadn't said if he'd want dinner when he came over, but I wanted to have something ready in case he did. Great-Uncle Arthur's a great cook and he ensures that our freezer is always packed full of homemade frozen meals. I took out two servings of lasagna to thaw and was washing lettuce in the sink when headlights filled our driveway.

Violet and I met Ryan at the door. He looked tired, I thought, as he gave me a deep kiss and Violet a hearty pat. He then helped me make the salad, and we sat down to eat at the kitchen table.

"Elizabeth Dumont has threatened to divorce Dan," I said around a mouthful of lasagna.

Ryan shook his head. "Gemma, do you know everything that goes on in West London?"

"Only the important things," I said modestly. I filled him in on the scene I'd witnessed earlier, without saying anything about Crystal or Brad. Their open hostility to Elizabeth would have had nothing to do with the death of Kathy.

"The woman has a temper that is terrible to behold," I said.

"Which, I'll admit, is interesting," he said. "But I have nothing at all to tie Elizabeth to the killing of Kathy. Speculation, even on your part, doesn't do me any good. Not with no physical evidence to back it up. If Elizabeth has a temper, as you say, and she doesn't worry about acting out in public, it doesn't seem as though she'd have killed her rival in such a quiet, private way."

I took a bite of salad. "I'll agree that she'd have been more likely to bash Kathy over the head with a serving tray."

"My mom's asking me when I'm going to bring you around to their place for dinner."

I almost choked on a lettuce leaf. "Your mother wants to feed me? When she saw me at the theater the other week, she spat on the floor. Figuratively speaking, of course."

"She's my mom," Ryan said simply. "She wants me to be happy. You make me happy."

I smiled at him.

"I have to get going soon," he said when his plate was scraped clean. "Early start tomorrow." The population of West London grew exponentially in the summer, but the resources of the police department did not. They had other cases on the go as well as the Lamb murder. "How about a short walk first?"

"I'd like that," I said. Violet barked her agreement, and we both laughed.

"Maybe get an ice cream down at the harbor." Ryan stood up. "Just this once, can we pretend we're on a date? Like a real date. No talk of 'murder most foul.'"

"I can do that," I said.

I put Violet on her leash and a light sweater on me, and we left the house. Ryan took my free hand, and we walked down the hill together. It was a beautiful clear night. A big moon shone overhead, and the lights of the boardwalk and the harbor sparkled in the distance. A couple of doors down, my neighbors sat on their front porch, and they called out greetings as we passed.

Not many people were around at this time of night. A group of teenagers jostled in the line at the ice cream stand, and Ryan and I waited our turn before placing our orders. Ryan asked for a triple-scoop triple-chocolate surprise, and I had a small French vanilla. The clerk passed me a dog treat for Violet.

Licking our cones and simply enjoying each other's company, we walked toward the West London Lighthouse, throwing its guiding light out to sea. When our treats were finished, we turned and headed back to Blue Water Place.

We chatted about nothing in particular, and I filled him in on Uncle Arthur's news.

"Sounds like he's having a great time," Ryan said. "I've only been to Europe once. The summer before I joined the police, I went with some buddies to Paris. I loved it. The museums, the history. The cafés and restaurants."

"You'd love London," I said, "and I'd love to show it to you."

"Maybe we can go there together someday. I'd like that." Then, out of the blue, he said, "Do you know that I love you?"

"Do you?" I asked.

"Totally and completely. But you're not an easy woman to love, Gemma Doyle."

I stopped walking. I stared out to sea as a lump formed in my throat. "I don't try to be difficult, Ryan."

"You can't stop getting yourself wrapped up in police cases."

"It's never what I want," I said in a low voice. "Stuff just happens around me."

"I know that. It's who you are. If I love you, I have to love who you are."

"If it helps," I said, "I love you too."

I turned and looked up at him. The streetlight overhead shone on his warm blue eyes and his wide smile. He bent to kiss me, and I lifted my chin to accept the kiss and return it.

I was almost jerked off my feet as Violet, at the other end of the leash, decided she'd had enough of this talking and kissing stuff, and headed off after a squirrel.

* * *

The following morning, brilliant sunlight streamed through the kitchen window, and Violet chased dust mites around the kitchen. I nibbled toast while, through the wonders of the World Wide Web, I searched for information on Bradley and Crystal Lamb.

Last night, when I'd arrived at Kathy Lamb's visitation, I'd decided to abandon my inquiries into her murder. I'd soon changed my mind. That scene between Dan and Elizabeth had been both interesting and informative. As had the reactions of Kathy's child and stepchild to their father and his new wife.

I hoped never to be invited to Christmas lunch at the Lamb house.

I had no reason to consider Brad or Crystal as suspects in the death of Kathy. Obviously, they—Crystal, in particular—were on their mother's side in their parents' divorce, but my interest was piqued. As it often is when I witness a display of such unguarded emotion.

I learned that Brad was the guitar player and backup vocalist for a band called Out to Lunch. Whether because of a poor choice of name, because they weren't any good, or due to bad luck, Out to Lunch played nothing but third-rate clubs and seedy bars throughout New England. And not much of those lately. Their website showed no upcoming gigs, and I wondered if the band was still together. I found Crystal's bio on the page for a tennis club in Boston, where she was a member. She'd graduated from West London High School, then gone on to the University of Massachusetts in Amherst, where she got a business degree. She was now a vice president at a New England bank. No husband or children were mentioned.

Sherlock Holmes had the Baker Street Irregulars to keep him informed. I have the internet.

* * *

"Do you know what they wanted?" Ashleigh said to me when I came downstairs. I'd spent some time in the office, reading through publishers' catalogs and placing orders for books that would be suitable for stocking in the shop for Christmas. I'd found several I was excited about, including the fourth (and the last) in the Hudson and Holmes series by Renalta Van Markoff. That one had been pushed into publication mighty fast following the celebrated author's death a short while ago.

"What who wanted?" I asked. The shop was busy with customers browsing, but no one needed our attention at the moment.

"The police, of course," Ashleigh said. "Weren't you looking out the window with a magnifying glass or something?"

"Unlikely I, or anyone else, would use a magnifying glass to look out the window," I said. "I get your point; however, I have absolutely no idea what you're talking about."

She tried to hide an "I know something you don't know" look. She failed.

I hadn't paid much attention to Ashleigh's outfit today because for once it was quite normal, whatever that means. She looked nice in white capris, blue-and-white-striped T-shirt, blue trainers with white laces, and small gold hoop earrings. Now, I looked closer. She'd done something with her hair. Normally straight and either tied into a ponytail or falling to her shoulders, she'd styled and sprayed it into a halo of wild curls held back by a clip. Those earrings looked a lot like the ones I normally wore to work. Mine were real gold, a birthday gift from my parents. Ashleigh's had been bought at Walmart.

She was, I realized with a shock, dressed in imitation of me!

I gaped. Moriarty smirked. I decided not to say anything; better to pretend I hadn't noticed. "I like your hair that way."

"Thanks. The police, you didn't see them?" she said.

"No."

"Your boyfriend and that tall woman cop. They went into Beach Fine Arts a couple of minutes ago. Parked right out front, in the loading zone, which means they were on police business, right?" She walked over to the window and peered out. "They're still in there."

I joined her at the window. Some of the customers had caught our conversation, and they followed us. We all stood there, staring onto the street. As we watched, the door of Beach Fine Arts opened, and Ryan and Louise Estrada came out. His face was unreadable, but the look on hers was one of satisfaction. She said something to him; he shook his head. They got into their car and drove away.

Maureen ran out of her store. She barely made it across the street without causing a four-car pileup. We all turned away from the window and bustled about, pretending not to have been watching.

"Gemma!" Maureen screeched as the front door of my shop bounced off the wall. "You're not working fast enough."

I pointed to the line of "I am SHERlocked" mugs I was arranging on the shelf. "I'm working as hard as I can, Maureen."

"Never mind that rubbish. I mean on my case."

"What happened?" Ashleigh asked.

I was about to suggest Maureen and I go upstairs, or at least to a quiet table in the tearoom, but she shouted so everyone could hear. "They've dug up some ridiculous triviality in my past and are using it to frame me for the killing of Kathy Lamb."

My customers, along with Ashleigh and Moriarty, gave up all pretext of minding their own business.

"No one's going to frame you, Maureen," I said. "Why don't you calm down and—"

"Calm down! I don't need to calm down! I need you to do what I hired you for."

"I wouldn't say *hired* is the right word."

"Okay, so Kathy and I had an argument that time in Hyannis. She should have been watching where she was walking, that's all. She wasn't hurt. Not badly anyway. No charges were laid. I said sorry, although I didn't mean it. It was her fault. I had nothing to be sorry about. Okay, I didn't mention it after Kathy died—why should I? I didn't want to waste police time on such a minor triviality. This is what happens when I try to do the right thing. No wonder I never bother." She turned on her heel and stormed out.

A customer looked at the DVD in her hand: *Sherlock Holmes and the Case of the Silk Stocking*. She put it back on the shelf. "No need to get this," she said. It's going to seem mighty tame after all that."

*   *   *

"Feel like an outing?" I asked Jayne.

She eyed me suspiciously. "An outing where?"

"Why are you looking at me like that?"

"I don't trust your outings. Are we going to climb trees, crash through fences, or wear disguises? I'm not dressing all in black."

"That will not be necessary. We're going to pay a call on Elizabeth Dumont."

"You mean a call as in walking up to the door and ringing the bell?"

"That's exactly what I mean."

"Like normal people do?"

"Jayne! Do you want to come or not?"

She sighed. "Someone has to keep you out of trouble."

"Good. We'll leave after the store closes at nine. I'll pick you up at your place."

"Isn't that late for a social call?"

"Better chance of finding her at home."

"Meaning you're not going to call ahead."

"Of course not. If she's not in, we'll try again another time."

"Are you going to accuse her of killing Kathy?"

"Pretty much. Although I will attempt to be slightly more subtle than you're suggesting."

Jocelyn had taken a pot of tea and four place settings into the dining room. Two three-tiered trays were set out on the kitchen counter, waiting to be ferried to tearoom guests. I helped myself to a cucumber-and-cream cheese tea sandwich, my favorite.

"Gemma! Those are for our customers."

"I didn't get any lunch." I took a bite. "Can't you make another?"

"Yes, I can make another, but I don't want to."

"Sorry," I said, not meaning it.

Jocelyn came in. She reached for the trays and stopped. "One looks short."

"So it is," Jayne said, taking a loaf of bread out of the bin. "We've had a raid."

"I'll be at your house around ten after nine." I tossed the last of the sandwich into my mouth, hopped off my stool, and hurried out of Jayne's domain before she could order me to make the replacement sandwich.

*   *   *

It might not be significant that the police had dug up a previous altercation between Maureen and Kathy. After all, West London is a small town, and Maureen isn't known for her friendliness. Still, the visit by Ryan and

Estrada to Beach Fine Arts reminded me that I was getting nowhere in this investigation. Apparently, Ryan and Estrada were also getting nowhere.

Time, I thought, *to beard the lioness in her den.*

I had no expectations that Elizabeth would break down and tearfully confess in front of me. Even if she did, I had been reminded recently, in a case that ended on the stage of a theater, that a confession isn't worth much in a court of law, not in absence of physical evidence.

No, about all I wanted was to assess the woman face-to-face in her own home. I believed Elizabeth had killed Kathy because of jealousy. I might not think Dan Lamb, short, flabby, aging badly, to be worth killing over, but there's no accounting for taste.

Ryan dismissed Elizabeth as the potential killer because she acted out her anger in public. At first, I'd agreed, but now I wondered if that was a mistake. Different circumstances require different methods. Ryan was letting me be more involved in this case than he had in the past, but I was still reluctant to tell him I thought he was wrong.

Not without more to go on than my gut instinct.

Thinking of Ryan made me remember last night. Our walk for ice cream. That he told me he loved me, and I replied in return. Love—isn't that what's supposed to make the world go 'round?

Too bad life has to get in the way. I didn't tell Ryan I was planning on paying Elizabeth a visit. That would put him in the position of having to tell me not to, and put me in the position of either arguing with him or lying to him.

And then I'd go anyway.

I picked up Jayne shortly after nine. I felt a twinge of guilt because I know how early she needs to get to bed, but when bearding lionesses, I like to have some backup.

"I just got off the phone with Jack," she said as she fastened her seatbelt.

"Leaving town, is he? Dinner date's off, is it? Too bad."

"He called to set up something for tomorrow night and to tell me he's looking forward to catching up. Wasn't that nice?"

"I suppose so," I grudgingly admitted.

"I've been meaning to say, Gemma, that you've been happy lately."

"I have?"

"Yes, you have. It's very noticeable. When you're not worrying about who killed Kathy Lamb, you have a genuine glow about you. Things are going well with Ryan, I can tell."

"Well enough," I said.

"I don't like to say, 'I told you so,' but I told you so."

"You did not."

"Yes, I did. I told you he was the man for you. You wouldn't listen to me at first, but then you did, and now you're both blissfully happy." She sighed. "The only thing better than being in love is having your best friend taking your advice and falling in love with the right man."

"I hope this conversation has nothing to do with Jack Templeton."

"Why should it?" she said sweetly.

I grumbled. Fortunately, at that moment we arrived at our destination.

Elizabeth Dumont's house occupied a prime piece of oceanfront land on Harbor Road past Scarlet House and the Cape Cod Yacht Club. The property was fenced, but the gates stood open. I glanced at them as we drove past. Judging by the pattern of weeds in the cracks in the pavement and the lack of tracks made by the wheels of the gates, they were not normally kept closed. Lush green lawns spread out on either side of the driveway, but there were no trees and no flower beds. The house was ultra-modern, all gray concrete and dark glass, straight lines and sharp angles.

"Cold," Jayne said with a shiver.

"Maybe it's nicer at the front overlooking the water," I said.

The driveway ended at a set of dark gray double doors that weren't brightened by so much as a pot of annuals. The garage doors were closed, and no vehicles were outside. I parked and we got out of the Miata.

All was quiet except for the soft pounding of the surf against the shoreline. The sun had set, but it wasn't yet fully dark, and deepening dusk hung over the house and grounds. The motion light above the door had come on as we drove up.

I pressed the bell, and we waited.

Nothing. I rang again.

When the sound of the chimes had died down, I held my hands to my face and peered through the small window set into the door. Inside, all was dark.

"Doesn't look like anyone's home," Jayne said.

"It's a big house. If lamps are on at the front, it's unlikely we can see them from here."

I rang the bell again, but again got no response.

"Let's go," I said. "I'll have to call and arrange a time to visit, although I'd rather not do that." I turned to leave, and my elbow hit the door. It swung open a few inches.

I looked at Jayne. "What have we here?"

"We can't just walk in," she said.

"No." I pushed the door open at the same time as I knocked loudly and called out, "Ms. Dumont, are you at home?"

The sound of glass breaking.

"Elizabeth? Are you all right?"

Sea air ruffled my curls; the sound of the waves was louder. "Call nine-one-one," I shouted to Jayne. I pushed the door aside and ran into the house, followed by Jayne's "What's going on?"

I pulled my phone out of my pocket and switched on the flashlight app. I was in the entrance hall. Black and white ceramic tiles, closed door leading to a coat closet, a bench for removing shoes, a container holding two umbrellas. An ashtray on the side table held the crushed end of a single cigarette. The lights at the back of the house were off, but a soft glow came down the hallway. I ran toward it, yelling, "The police have been called." Past the darkened kitchen and dining room, through the TV room, and into the living room. The far wall was almost all glass, and I got a glimpse of moonlight shining on the ocean. French doors led to a swimming pool and patio. Two table lamps were on, casting a warm yellow light around the large space. The furniture was wicker; the cushions, blue and white; the paintings on the walls, of sailboats at sea. The side tables held photographs of smiling people crewing boats, as well as a plethora of ashtrays, some containing ash and cigarette ends. The floor was gleaming hardwood, wide planks quite possibly salvaged from an old barn. A thick white carpet trimmed in blue filled the center of the room. A woman lay face down on it. It was Elizabeth Dumont, and she was very still.

Chapter Fifteen

Jayne stood behind me, talking rapidly into her phone.

"Stay here," I yelled. A breeze blew in through the broken glass of the French doors and ruffled the edges of the white-and-blue-striped drapes. I grabbed a heavy ashtray off a side table and used it to sweep aside shards of broken glass, and then I stepped through. Pieces of shattered glass glimmered in the moonlight. Lounge chairs were laid out around the pool, and teak furniture formed an outdoor dining area.

"What are you doing?" Jayne called.

I lifted one hand. "Shush."

I listened. Surf pounded the shore; cars drove by on Harbor Road. The thud of feet hitting turf came from my right.

I ran after them, using the beam from my phone to light the way. A small cabin, probably used to store pool equipment, was at the edge of the patio. I ran past it and shone my flashlight onto the ground around me. The light caught traces of fresh indentations in the recently mowed grass. I followed the footprints to the corner of the house. As I rounded the building, I saw a figure crossing the front lawn, heading toward the open gates and the road beyond, moving fast. I took off in pursuit.

The figure was wrapped in dark, bulky clothes; of average height and weight, from what I could tell from afar; and able to run at a good clip, at least over a short distance. He or she didn't look back, but had to have been aware of me following. I didn't bother to yell at the person to stop.

The dark figure reached the end of the driveway. Through the gates and onto the sidewalk. Cars drove past. It was not yet ten o'clock, and traffic was heavy in both directions. I was far behind my quarry, and by the time I burst through the gates, the running figure had disappeared. No pedestrians were on the sidewalks to my left, but the street took a sharp bend to the right at this spot, so I headed that way. This was a wealthy residential area, the trees large and old, hedges thick and lush, many of the houses fenced and gated, and all set well back from the road. A few yards ahead, a side street headed inland. I slowed to a halt and looked around me.

My quarry could have gone anywhere: up the side street, into one of the yards, behind a hedge, crouched in the shadow of a car. If the person had a vehicle parked nearby, he or she might have simply driven away, blending anonymously into the steady stream of evening traffic. I hadn't noticed any cars parked at the side of the street when we arrived, but Jayne and I had come from town, to the left.

I heard sirens fast approaching and gave up the chase. I trotted back to the entrance to Elizabeth's property as a police car, blue and red lights flashing, tore up the driveway. I retraced my own steps, across the lawn, around the house, past the pool, through the broken glass of the French doors.

Jayne was talking to an officer, waving her hands in the air. Another knelt by Elizabeth Dumont's unmoving body.

"Good evening." I stepped through the shattered glass of the doors. The cop with Jayne practically jumped out of his skin. He reached for his gun, and Jayne yelped.

I lifted my hands into the air. "Only me, Officer Richter. We're the ones who discovered the body."

Officer Stella Johnson pushed herself to her feet. "The detectives have been called. Did you do this, Ms. Doyle, Ms. Wilson?" She asked the routine question, but her heart wasn't in it, and she clearly didn't expect a positive reply.

"We did not," I said. "We were paying a friendly house call, and it would appear we arrived only moments too late."

"You can both wait in the kitchen," she said. "The detectives will want to talk to you."

I turned and shone my flashlight app onto the French doors. The lock was not engaged, meaning the door was unlocked. I tucked my hand into the folds of my shirt to avoid leaving fingerprints and tugged at the door.

"Don't touch that!" Richter shouted.

It didn't move, and I studied the doorframe.

"What were you doing outside?" Officer Johnson asked me.

"Trying to apprehend the killer."

I pointed my flashlight outside, searching the shattered glass. "You'll want to check those glass fragments for cloth and threads. Ah yes, I see a few have been caught, looks like some sort of fleece. I had to knock some of the bigger pieces of glass aside to get out."

Unlike our alleged killer, I was wearing a sleeveless shirt and capris. My arms and legs would have been badly cut on the exposed glass.

"The kitchen," Johnson repeated. I knew Officer Stella Johnson well. Her grandmother was a good friend and regular card partner of Great-Uncle Arthur. The benefits of living in a small town: I usually met the same police officers at every scene.

"In a moment," I said. I crouched down beside Elizabeth, keeping my hands to myself. Either Jayne or one of the officers had turned the body over, no doubt to check for signs of life, and Elizabeth Dumont stared up at me, unseeing. She had, as far as I could tell, been felled by a blow to the side of her head. I had no need to search for the weapon. An iron statue, about two feet high, of a thin, graceful woman lay on the floor beside her head. A side table next to the French doors had been overturned. The table was about the size that would hold a small piece of sculpture.

"And did you?" Johnson asked.

"Did I what?"

"Apprehend a killer?"

"Obviously not."

"You're going to have to wait in the kitchen, Gemma. You too, Jayne. The detectives won't be happy to see you poking about the scene."

"As if I ever poke," I said. I tucked my hands behind my back to keep from touching anything and examined the carpet, searching for footprints. It hadn't rained for days, and no one, not even Jayne or I or the police, had tracked mud into the house. Elizabeth herself was barefoot and dressed in her nightwear. Cotton pajamas, gray and pink striped, with loose trousers and a baggy, V-necked gray shirt with a cartoon drawing of a sailboat on it. She smelled strongly of tobacco, and I assumed she'd finished a cigarette shortly before her caller arrived.

More sirens approached, and Johnson's radio crackled. "Around the front of the house, facing the sea," she said. "The glass in the door's broken. Uh, Detective Estrada, Gemma Doyle is here."

A screech sounded over the static.

"Perhaps we'll wait in the kitchen." I pushed myself to my feet. "Come on, Jayne. Let's get out of these people's way."

Elizabeth's kitchen was large and furnished with all the latest in high-tech gadgets. Dishes were piled in the sink, no doubt waiting for the maid to arrive in the morning. One plate, one set of cutlery, a small frying pan, and a pot with a few grains of rice clinging to the bottom. One wine glass next to an empty bottle of California chardonnay and an overflowing ashtray. All the cigarettes were the same brand.

"She ate dinner alone," Jayne said.

I gave her a grin. "You're learning."

"I'd rather not be."

Taking care once again to cover my fingers, I opened the fridge and studied the contents. Nothing out of the ordinary: some cheeses, cold meats, fruit and vegetables of varying freshness, cream for coffee, the usual assortment of condiments. A bottle of Veuve Clicquot, half full. I stuck my head into the walk-in pantry. One wall was being used as a wine rack. There must have been fifty bottles there, all of which, to my largely untrained eye, looked expensive.

"What do you think happened here, Gemma?" Jayne asked.

"Obviously, Elizabeth was not expecting visitors. She was in her nightwear—ordinary pajamas, not a negligee of some sort—therefore not ready for a romantic assignation. She knew her visitor and invited him or her into the house. She did not expect this person to stay for long, certainly not for the night, and so she left the back door unlocked. Not a totally casual visitor, pizza delivery person or someone similar, as they walked together through the house into the front room, likely to take a seat while they talked. Either the person came intending to kill Elizabeth, or something was said that made him or her do so. It's possible this person had been in the house before and knew there were small items of statuary that could be used as a weapon, but I can't dismiss the idea that they might have simply hoped there would be something at hand. Not bringing a weapon doesn't presume lack of planning."

Jayne wrapped her arms around herself. "We surprised him in the act."

"Him or her," I said. "Sadly, it would seem we were minutes too late. Our killer would have planned to simply walk out the way they came in, but hearing us at the back door meant they had to find another way out."

Jayne reached for a cupboard.

"Better not touch anything." I said.

She pulled her hand back as though it had been burned. "Will they fingerprint the kitchen?"

"They'll probably fingerprint the entire house. This could have been an attempted robbery gone wrong, but none of the signs point that way."

Jayne stuffed her hands into her jeans. "Why do you suppose this person didn't simply wait for us to go away? We would have if no one answered the bell. It was only when you heard them breaking the glass in the door that you came in, right?"

"Right. I was prepared to turn around and leave if no one answered, even in the face of the open door. They panicked, most likely. Which indicates this person is not a hired killer."

Not that I considered that to be a possibility.

"Did you see him?" Jayne asked.

"Only from a distance, and nothing was identifiable about him. About all I can say is that he was not obese and not handicapped, judging by the ease with which he ran across the lawn. He or she. Him or her. I wish we had a gender-neutral singular pronoun."

As we talked, more police were arriving. Flashlights moved outside the kitchen windows, and officers called to one another in loud voices. "I hope they're not trampling evidence," I said.

"I think we can manage not to do that." Ryan Ashburton came into the kitchen, rubbing at his chin. "We've got a K-9 unit trying to find the trail. What are you two doing here?"

"You paid a call on Maureen this afternoon," I said. "I realized you're still barking up that wrong tree, so I decided it was time to talk to Elizabeth Dumont myself. Face-to-face, as it were. Jayne came along to keep me company."

Jayne attempted a friendly smile.

A dark cloud settled over Ryan's face, and his mouth formed a tight line. I knew that look, and it never meant anything good was coming my way.

"Fancy meeting you two here." Louise Estrada said. "Officer Richter tells me Jayne Wilson was inside the house when they arrived. She made the nine-one-one call and met the responding officers at the back door, but you, Gemma, had gone outside. Did you kill the woman?"

I ignored the question. "We arrived to find the house in darkness. No cars were parked in the driveway."

"So you walked in?" she asked.

"As a matter of fact, that's exactly what we did. The door was unlocked, which was surprising. All was quiet, but someone was in the house. Someone who didn't want to meet us at the door."

"As much as I hate to ask, I will anyway," Estrada said. "Why didn't you assume the woman didn't want to talk to you? If you come poking around my house late at night, I'm not going to answer either."

"The unlocked door meant Elizabeth had a visitor she didn't expect to stay for long. The lack of a car in the driveway meant either the visitor walked or, more likely, hid his or her car on the street if they had one, not wanting it to be seen, which implies a not entirely aboveboard visit. The door was off the latch and swung open when I touched it. I called out loudly that we were here."

"That's right," Jayne said. "We didn't sneak in or break the lock."

"The abrupt increase in noise coming from the sea and the sensation of air rushing into the house clearly meant a door or window had suddenly opened. The sound of breaking glass meant someone had not simply opened the door and walked out to enjoy the evening."

"Right," Jayne said.

I had been speaking to Estrada, but I took a peek at Ryan out of the corner of my eyes. The darkness had not passed. "Naturally, we tried to help."

"How do I know you didn't smash the door yourself?" Estrada said. "To make it look like you had an excuse to come in uninvited."

"Because I told you what happened," I said. "And because I came here to speak to Elizabeth Dumont. I had no reason to break in."

"The French doors aren't locked," she said. "I noticed that myself. Unless you unlocked them—and I wouldn't put it past you—the breaking of the glass was all for show."

"Partial observation is no better than no observation, Detective Estrada. The lock on the door is not set, as you observed, but you failed to see the security bar in place on the bottom runner. Our killer had just murdered a woman when he heard people at the door. Rather than remain quiet and hope the visitors will simply go away, he—or she—panicked. He tried to get out the door, but it wouldn't open. Rather than take the time to figure out why it wouldn't open, he smashed the glass. Almost certainly you'll find a piece of statuary or something similar on the patio. You'll also find fragments of green fleece on the broken glass." I held out my bare arms. "You might notice that I am not wearing any sort of sweater."

Estrada glared at me. Ryan said nothing.

"I'll be happy to come down to the station in the morning and make a full statement. As for now, Jayne and I will leave you to it."

"Not so fast," Ryan growled. "Detective Estrada, will you leave us, please."

She looked between Ryan and me. Then she said, "I'll see what's happening with the dog," and walked out.

"I'll wait in the car." Jayne fled.

"Gemma," Ryan said, "this time you've gone too far."

"I haven't done anything. Surely you don't think I broke into this house and killed Elizabeth?"

"I value your observations and insights, and that's no secret. There's a difference between observing people and actively being involved. You can't keep popping up at crime scenes and getting in the way."

"We're hardly in the way. I can't make observations from my house. Even Sherlock Holmes had to venture out of 221B Baker Street to see for himself. I've pointed out valuable evidence to you. One of your less-experienced officers might have removed the security bar to get out the door and not thought about it. I chased the person in question off the property but lost him on the street."

"You attempted to apprehend a cold-blooded killer alone, at night, unarmed. This gets worse and worse. Gemma, I can't have you—" He stopped at a burst of sound from the hallway.

"In here," a man cried. A dog barked.

A uniformed officer ran into the kitchen, preceded by a large German shepherd wearing an orange vest with the words "Police" stamped on it. The dog lunged toward me, and I leapt back, crashing into the counter. The stone edge caught me in the hip and a shot of pain ran through me.

The dog snarled and showed me every one of his very impressive teeth. The handler cried, "Diablo, down!" as he tugged at the leash. The dog dropped to his haunches and sat there, eyeing me, while every muscle in his body quivered.

"Oh, for heaven's sake," Ryan Ashburton said.

Chapter Sixteen

The appropriately named Diablo might have identified me as the murderer, but even Louise Estrada didn't really think I'd killed Elizabeth Dumont. She escorted me to my car and the waiting Jayne. "Get lost, Gemma," she said. "And please, no more 'helping.'"

Ryan had walked out of the kitchen without another word, leaving Estrada to mumble about ruining evidence and interfering with crime scenes.

In real life, police dogs don't track individuals the way they do in the movies. No one waves a piece of cloth under their nose and says, "Find Billy." The dog simply follows the most obvious or most recently laid trail. Diablo had picked up two strong scents at the scene of Elizabeth's body, followed her killer and me to the street, and when the trails divided, he traced one line of scent back to the house to corner me in the kitchen.

"Are you in trouble?" Jayne asked me.

"No more than usual," I said.

"That bad, eh?"

"That bad." I didn't know if Ryan would be able to forgive me, yet again, for what he calls interfering. The path of true love never runs smoothly, but never less than between an ambitious and very good police detective and a well-meaning but highly perceptive member of the law-abiding public.

* * *

I was woken the following morning by a phone call.

"Good morning, Gemma," Irene Talbot said. "I hear you found the body of Elizabeth Dumont last night. The police are saying her death was suspicious. Do you have a statement for the press?"

"Is Sherlock Holmes a Mafia enforcer? No." I hung up.

I flopped onto my back and stared up at the ceiling. Sunlight peeked around the curtains and drew patterns on the walls. Violet leapt onto the bed and licked my face. "At least you still love me," I said to her.

Greetings over, she jumped down and trotted into the kitchen.

After we left Elizabeth's last night, I'd dropped Jayne off at her house and gone straight home. I sat up for a long time, reading and waiting for the police to call me.

No one had.

I didn't try to go back to sleep after Irene's call, but took Violet for a long walk. When we got home, I found a police car in front of my house and Detective Louise Estrada sitting on the steps. Ryan was not with her, and I feared that was not a good thing.

"Good morning," I said, keeping my tone light. "I hope you haven't been waiting for long."

Violet ran to greet our visitor. Estrada stood up slowly, stretching her long, lean body, ignoring the dog's attempts to make friends. "I need you to take me through the events of last night."

"Might as well do it inside rather than provide entertainment for the neighbors." Across the street Mr. Gibbons was watering his flowerpots, not noticing that he was soaking his feet instead, and next door, Mrs. Ramsbattan had decided that her mailbox needed a good scrubbing at eight o'clock in the morning.

I led the way into the kitchen and put the kettle on. "I'm having tea, but I can do coffee if you'd prefer."

Estrada sat at the table. "Nothing, thanks." The dark circles under her eyes indicated she had not been to bed last night. She needed coffee, but she didn't want to accept my hospitality. I took the French press off the shelf and beans out of the fridge. "I can do some scrambled eggs if you're hungry."

"This is not a social call," she snapped.

"I didn't think so," I replied, taking out the eggs and cream. "I find interrogation goes better with a meal."

"Talk to me," she said.

"I can talk and make coffee and scrambled eggs at the same time." And so I did. I told her not only everything that had happened last night, but also about my thought process leading me to decide to visit Elizabeth Dumont at her home. I served the detective a mug of coffee, which she finished in record time. I poured her another, made tea for myself, and then dished up scrambled eggs and whole-wheat toast for us both.

"You thought Elizabeth Dumont killed Kathy Lamb?" Estrada picked up her fork.

"I did," I said.

"Do you still think so?"

"No. It's possible two ruthless killers exist in Kathy, Elizabeth, and Dan's small world, but I consider that possibility to be highly remote."

"As do we," she admitted. She scraped her plate clean. "Thanks for this." She finished her coffee.

"You're welcome." *Was it possible that Detective Estrada and I might be able to be friends someday?*

"We're looking for one killer," she said. "I pointed out to the chief this morning that only two people are known to have been present at both deaths: Gemma Doyle and Jayne Wilson."

Maybe not friends exactly.

"Except, Detective, I was not present when either of those women died. I was simply unfortunate enough to come upon them after the deed was done."

"So you say." She stood up.

Violet had been lying on the floor by the mudroom, watching the breakfast preparations and listening to our conversation. She leapt to her feet, butt shaking, tail wagging, tongue lolling, clearly expecting a pat.

Estrada walked straight past her. She opened the back door and then turned to look at me. "Don't leave town." The door slammed shut.

"See if I make her eggs and coffee again," I said to Violet.

My phone hadn't vibrated as I talked to Estrada, but I checked it anyway. Nothing from Ryan. I hadn't asked Estrada why her partner hadn't taken part in the interview. I hadn't wanted to give her the satisfaction of telling me he was mad at me.

I cleared the dishes off the table, poured myself a fresh cup of tea, and settled down to check the Twitter feed of the WLPD. It told me the chief was due to give a press conference at ten this morning. I briefly considered going but decided not to. If my name was mentioned as a "person of interest," I didn't want to be anywhere near a pack of ravenous reporters.

Someone had killed Elizabeth Dumont. It was beyond possibility that her death was unconnected to that of Kathy Lamb. Who, I thought, might have wanted to kill both women?

Dan Lamb was the most obvious suspect. Certainly for the killing of Elizabeth, who had earlier that day told him she was divorcing him. Elizabeth was wealthy, very wealthy, and according to Ryan, Dan was not. Did he want to get rid of her before she could divorce him and write him out of her will?

Possible.

Elizabeth would have let him into her house and greeted him in her pajamas. He likely had his own key.

He would, however, have known about the security bar on the French doors.

For that reason alone, I moved Dan down my list of suspects until I could find out more about his where-abouts last night.

Dan, as far as I knew, had no reason to kill Kathy. They were divorced, and it had been expensive and acri-monious, but that was over. He would gain nothing monetary by her death. I'd seen for myself his grief at her death, but that proved nothing; many a killer had come to deeply regret what they'd done.

I thought back to my visit to the yacht club, to Jayne's friend Jack telling her Elizabeth was unpopular with most of the members. There's a mighty big difference between unpopular and hated enough to be killed.

Other than Dan, current husband and ex-husband, what did Elizabeth and Kathy have in common?

I'd thought nothing until I saw Robyn Kirkpatrick arriving at the Cape Cod Yacht Club in enough of a hurry to indicate she was late for a meeting. Prior to that, I'd not seen any connection between Scarlet House and Elizabeth. Elizabeth was clearly not a supporter of the museum: she'd come to the auction under some sort of duress, probably to keep an eye on Dan in the presence of his ex-wife. Might Robyn be the link between the two dead women?

Robyn was in her fifties, but she looked like a woman who visited the gym regularly. She could have easily run across Elizabeth's lawn to disappear into the night.

I reminded myself that Robyn had not been in Mrs. Hudson's for the auction, and thus would not have had the opportunity to grab the teacup chain off the wall.

On the other hand, Sharon Musgrave, also heavily involved with the museum, also no friend of Kathy's, had been at the auction tea. Sharon had not killed Elizabeth. She was shorter and stockier than the person I'd seen last night, and I doubted she'd have been able to run at that pace.

It was possible, I had to admit, that the person who'd run from me was not the same one who'd killed Elizabeth: he or she might have come into Elizabeth's home—as I had—and found her dead. Hearing me arrive, and not wanting to get involved, they'd left through the

French doors. If that was the case, it would severely complicate things, so until I learned more I'd act on the assumption that the person I'd chased last night was the one responsible for the death of Elizabeth.

Might Robyn and Sharon have been working together? Had one of the women killed Kathy and one killed Elizabeth? I knew of no reason Elizabeth would be a threat to their positions at the museum.

Which didn't mean there wasn't one. Only that I hadn't found it.

I opened the web page for Scarlet House. Repairs were progressing on the house, I was told, but in the meantime, summer programming would continue in the barn. I wondered where they were getting the money for the renovations. Surely they wouldn't try to have the auction again? Some would think that in extremely poor taste.

I needed to go back to the museum to find out what was going on. The web page told me the board of the museum was meeting this very evening. I just might drop in.

* * *

"Vindicated!" Maureen Macgregor burst through the doors of the Emporium the moment I flipped the sign to open, almost knocking me senseless.

"Good morning," I said.

"Without you doing a thing, which means I'm not in your debt, so there. I've always said, you aren't as smart as everyone says you are."

So not smart was I, I didn't have a clue what she was talking about. "What happened?" I asked.

"The police came around to my apartment last night. And what do you suppose they found there?"

"Maureen, I have no idea."

"They found me! At home."

I finally began to get it. Maureen was not a suspect in the death of Elizabeth; therefore the police were dismissing her as a suspect in the death of Kathy. Because, like me, they believed the two cases were linked.

"I'm glad for you."

"Not that I was pleased to see them at midnight, hammering on my door, waking up the neighbors."

Two women arrived; they edged around Maureen to get into the Emporium. "Welcome," I said. "Let me know if you need any help." I backed into the shop, hoping she'd get the hint and leave. No such luck, Maureen didn't *get* hints. She followed me.

"They were satisfied with my alibi." She didn't bother to lower her voice. "Do you want to know why?"

"No. If the police were okay with it, that's good enough for me."

"Because my apartment was full of company. My sister and her family are visiting the Cape for a week. I told her I don't have room for her, that lazy husband of hers, and those three bratty children, but did she listen to me? Of course not. She never listens to me. *'Hotels are so expensive,'* she whined. *'You won't even know we're there.'* I have to put up with comings and goings at all hours, meals for six, picnic lunches, smelly beach towels, sand tracked across my clean carpets. At least they left that ghastly dog at home." Moriarty purred his approval. He lay on the center table, draped across a display of puzzles, playing cards, and games, his chin propped on the box containing The Sherlock Holmes Puzzle Case.

"I was at the store until closing at nine last night, and I went straight home. My sister remembered what time I came in because they had just started watching some stupid sports program on TV. Bags of chips everywhere, dishes piled in the sink, children sleeping on the couch. My sister and her husband told the police I didn't go out again. Meaning, I was not sneaking around to Elizabeth Dumont's house to murder her in her bed."

"I'm glad to hear it," I said. "Have a nice day."

"I suppose I should thank you for trying to help me," she muttered. "Not that you did anything."

She left.

"You're welcome," I called after her. "Any time."

Moriarty returned to his bed under the table for a nap.

"Do you have this in blue?" the customer asked, holding up a Sherlock teacup.

"No," I said. "I mean, sorry, but no, we don't."

Now that Maureen had been cleared of police suspicion, I had no reason to continue to be involved in the case. But I am a curious sort, and the fates of Kathy and Elizabeth had aroused my curiosity. On the other hand, I had my relationship with Ryan Ashburton to consider. If we still had a relationship, that is. I'd ruined the police dog's attempt to track the killer, and Ryan had stormed out of Elizabeth's kitchen, beyond furious. His career was important to him, as it should be, and he was good at it. I dreaded what the police chief might have had to say about my activities last night. Ryan might be forced to choose between his job and me.

Regardless of how he chose, things would never be the same between us again.

As well as not having a retail business to interfere in the pursuit of his cases, or customers to interrupt his thinking, Sherlock Holmes hadn't been trying to have a love life either.

Ashleigh arrived for work ten minutes early. Today she was all ruffles and ribbons and bows sewn onto a plain black tunic. A pink and white feathered fascinator was attached to her head with a band.

"What are you supposed to be?" I asked, grateful that she wasn't imitating me again today.

"I've been reading that book you loaned me—*A Conspiracy in Belgravia*. The dress on the cover is so gorgeous—I'd love to have something like that. But I don't, and even if I could get one, I wouldn't want to bother with bustles and corsets—that must be so hot and uncomfortable—so I made a modern version. Like it?"

"It's certainly interesting."

"Are you the unnamed hero of West London?" she asked as ribbons fluttered.

"The what?"

"I caught a bit of the police chief's statement while I was having breakfast. Apparently, some woman was killed last night, and a brave and civic-minded citizen interrupted the crime in progress and attempted to apprehend the killer."

"Why would you think that was me? Did he say my name?"

The feathers on the fascinator bobbed. "No, but a killing in West London. You. They go together."

I thought about that for a moment.

"The chief thanked this unnamed person for their efforts, but he reminded us that although West London is a low-crime town and a safe place to bring your family for their summer vacation—I was surprised he didn't start singing an advertising ditty—citizens are advised not to interfere in police matters."

Could there have been another killing in West London last night? I hadn't heard of anything, but I hadn't had the radio on or checked the local news.

"Speaking of the cops . . ." Ashleigh said as the bells over the door tinkled to admit Ryan Ashburton.

He looked at me. I looked at him.

"Time to get to work," Ashleigh said. "Do you want to leave those on the counter while you continue shopping?"

The customer handed her two Sherlock mugs, a Benedict Cumberbatch wall calendar, and a stuffed teddy bear with a deerstalker hat on his head and pipe in his mouth.

"Do you have time for lunch?" Ryan asked me.

"Yes."

"Why don't I get sandwiches from next door, and we can go down to the harbor and find a park bench?"

"I'd like that."

He was soon back, balancing a bulging paper bag and two takeout cups. We walked side by side, not talking, down Baker Street. I'm usually pretty good at picking up on nonverbal clues, but I didn't know what to think here. After last night, I'd have expected Ryan to, at best, never speak to me again. I snuck a peek at him as we walked. He didn't look angry.

It was another beautiful Cape Cod day, and Harbor Road was packed with tourists. Sailboats zipped across the calm waters of the ocean, and further out a huge white and blue, multistoried cruise ship crossed the horizon. The benches along the boardwalk were all taken, so we went to the West London Lighthouse and sat on the cool grass in the shade of the sturdy old building. The lighthouse was open for visitors, and people walked up the path to the entrance or around the building to study the strong, straight white walls. No one paid us any attention.

My heart pounded in my chest, and not from the limited amount of exercise on the walk here. Was Ryan planning to dump me? Unlikely he'd do so over a picnic lunch, but then again, he wasn't the sort to break up by text.

Was he going to order me to stay out of the police investigation? I don't take well to orders, but I'd decided I'd do what I had to do to keep our relationship going.

How long my resolve would last was another matter altogether, and Ryan knew me well enough to know that also.

"Sorry, I didn't think to bring a blanket," he said.

"This is fine." I ran my fingers through the soft grass.

He reached into the bag, pulled out two wrapped sandwiches, and handed me one. I said, "Thanks," and bent my head to open the package.

"I love you." He reached out and touched my hand.

I looked into his expressive blue eyes. The circles under those eyes were as dark as Estrada's had been, meaning he also hadn't slept last night.

"I love you too. Very much. I hope you know that," I said. "Although I have to ask what brought this on. I thought you were mad at me."

"I was." He took his hand away and opened his sandwich. "I bought one roast beef and one ham. Which do you want?"

"This will do." I hadn't checked to see which one I had.

"You messed up the K-9 unit mighty bad last night, but that was a long shot anyway. Chances were the killer simply got into a car and drove away." A smile tugged at the corners of his mouth. "Although the dog didn't know that. He was highly pleased with his night's work, and his trainer praised him to the skies."

"Glad someone was happy with me."

"More than someone. The chief was. I decided to take my direction from my chief and let what happened last night go. This time anyway."

"Why? I mean what did I do to make your chief happy?"

"If you and Jayne hadn't decided to pay a call, Elizabeth might not have been found for days. She told her husband not to come home. She cancelled all her meetings and lunch dates at the yacht club for the rest of the week and the dentist appointment she had for tomorrow afternoon. She has a full-time maid, but the woman doesn't live in, and she'd taken a week's vacation, starting yesterday. The gardener comes two times a week, but he says he often doesn't see Ms. Dumont, and he never goes into the house. In the chief's words, it was a good thing you arrived and discovered the body while the evidence was still fresh."

"Wow," I said. "I can't imagine Louise was pleased at hearing me praised."

"As I've told you before, Gemma, Louise is a good detective. She agreed with the chief."

I bit into my sandwich. I'd been given the ham. I'd have preferred roast beef. Nevertheless, I chewed happily.

"Although," Ryan said, "in light of what I said about loving you, I'd rather you didn't chase a suspected killer ever again. I assume you've been thinking about what happened last night. Can you think of anything identifiable about the person you scared off?"

"More about who it couldn't have been than who it could," I said. "It was dark, they wore loose dark clothes, and they were quite a distance ahead of me. We didn't run far, so they didn't have to be a serious runner. Not that I am either. They ran fast and easily, so it had to be someone young or an older person in moderately good shape. Definitely not Sharon Musgrave, who's too short and stocky and was short of breath when she walked across the barn."

Robyn Kirkpatrick looked like a woman who regularly visited the gym. Dan Lamb would have been capable of a run like that if he had the fear of discovery pushing him. And then there were the Lamb children, both in their thirties. Crystal regularly played tennis. Brad had a skinny, wiry frame. I doubted he was any sort of athlete, but he'd be able to run a quarter mile without crumbling to the ground, gasping for breath.

"What did you learn last night after we left?" I asked. "Any leads?"

"Nothing definite. The statue on the floor—I assume you unnoticed that?"

I gave him a look.

"Right. It was the murder weapon, and the base of it had been wiped down. As was an ornament we found on the patio, surrounded by shards of glass. We're acting on the assumption that Ms. Dumont knew her killer and admitted him or her to the house. That person was either not offered anything to eat or drink, or refused."

"Reasonable, considering Elizabeth was ready for bed and not in a position to be entertaining visitors. She was a heavy smoker, and ashtrays and cigarettes butts were everywhere. Were all the cigarettes in the house the same brand?"

"They were. The same as the partially used pack we found in her purse and the unopened ones in the kitchen cupboard. I've sent the ends found in the living room for analysis, to see if we can find traces that aren't hers, but I'm not hopeful."

"Meaning our killer doesn't smoke or didn't have time to indulge. What about Dan Lamb?"

"Does he smoke? No. Must have been tough living with a partner who went through more than a pack a day. And Elizabeth didn't have any rules like no smoking in the car or the house. She wasn't always respectful of other people's boundaries either, people have told us."

"Worth knowing, but I meant, is he under suspicion?"

"The first suspect, as you know, is always the husband. Mr. Lamb is in the unfortunate position of being current or ex-husband to two recently murdered women. I interviewed him last night. His alibi is his son, Bradley. They say they left the funeral home together around seven thirty."

I nodded. "I saw them there, and the visitation was about to end."

"As Elizabeth had told Dan he wasn't to come home, and his daughter, Crystal, didn't want him in Kathy's apartment, where she and her brother are staying, he and Brad went to the West London Hotel, where they checked in at five to eight. They took only one room, and both Dan and Brad were in the room when we arrived."

"You called ahead to say you were coming?"

"Unfortunately, I had to. I didn't know where to find him. I arrived about ten minutes after calling, but yes, if he wasn't far away, I gave him a chance to get back to his room and set up an alibi. He told me he hadn't gone out again after checking in. Brad confirmed that story. The hotel desk clerk didn't see either of them again, but that means nothing."

I knew the West London Hotel; it had several exits.

"A son isn't a reliable alibi," Ryan said, "but I believed Dan. I hadn't told him on the phone why we were coming around. I led him to believe it was further questions about Kathy, and he appeared totally shocked by the news of Elizabeth's death. His legs gave way, and he collapsed onto the bed."

"What was Brad's reaction?"

"Surprise, but not shock. In fact, he laughed, and Dan told him to have some respect. Brad replied that didn't respect the woman in life, so he saw no reason to do so in death. He also made a crack about Dan now being a rich man."

"That would fit my impression of Brad. He and his sister were firmly on Kathy's side in the divorce. The daughter openly hates Dan, and the son's only marginally better, although Kathy was Brad's stepmother, not his biological mother,"

"Charming family," Ryan said.

"Any chance Dan hired someone to whack his wife?"

"Is that an English phrase?"

"Americanisms must be rubbing off on me."

"Anything's possible. Dan stands to inherit a great deal of money. I haven't seen Elizabeth's will yet, but I will later today."

"If he did hire a killer, he acted mighty fast. Elizabeth only threatened to divorce him a few hours before she died."

"Locating and hiring a contract killer," Ryan said, "arranging the hit, and making the preliminary payoff takes longer than a couple of hours."

"I must ask someday how one arranges that."

He grinned at me. "I wouldn't want you for an enemy, Gemma Doyle."

I leaned over and kissed him lightly on the lips. He tasted of hot spicy mustard.

"One thing does occur to me," I said when we separated.

"Go ahead."

"We've decided it's not worth considering that Elizabeth and Kathy were murdered in unrelated attacks, but it is possible there were two killers. I thought Elizabeth had murdered Kathy, although I have no evidence to that effect. Is it possible someone else came to the same conclusion and killed Elizabeth in an act of revenge?"

"Anything's possible. Which is why this case is such a darned mess."

"Maureen believes she's no longer under suspicion."

"That's correct. She has a rock-solid alibi for last night." He grinned. "Far from lying to protect her, I got the impression Maureen's sister, who we spoke to, would have loved to get Maureen in trouble if she had the slightest opportunity. Maureen had neglected to tell us that a couple of months ago, she'd been in a public alter-cation with Kathy Lamb over a bumped shopping cart in a parking lot. Keeping information from the police always makes us suspicious, but in this case, Louise and I agreed that Maureen was only trying to make herself look clean."

"Her past history—"

"Has nothing to do with this case," Ryan said, firmly closing the door on my weak attempt at getting the information out of him. He yawned.

"You need to go to bed."

He gave me a sad smile. "If I wasn't so tired, I'd take you up on that."

I laughed and started on the chocolate brownie Ryan had bought for my dessert.

As we finished our lunch and wrapped up our trash, I told him my thoughts. "I'd like to go to the museum this evening, check things out. Other than Dan's family, the only person I can find who Elizabeth and Kathy both knew is Robyn Kirkpatrick."

"Do that," he said. "But remember, no foot chases down dark streets."

Chapter Seventeen

Tonight's meeting of the museum board would be held on the grounds of the old house, as the building itself was unusable. The meeting would be open to museum volunteers and other interested people. Attendees were asked to bring their own chairs and something to share for dessert.

A chair and dessert. I could manage that.

At twenty-two minutes to four, I cleared my throat.

"Partners' meeting, back in twenty minutes. Carry on without you. Call you if needed. Got it," Ashleigh said.

I wondered if eventually we'd be able to get through an entire day without speaking to each other, like a longtime married couple.

Jayne was seated at the window alcove when I came into Mrs. Hudson's, talking on her phone. A few tables were still occupied, and Jocelyn was bringing one of them a fresh pot of tea while Fiona tidied up behind the counter.

I eyed the sparse remains. "I don't suppose there are any more brownies in the back?"

"We ran out of those long ago, Gemma," Fiona said.

"I'll take everything else then."

"Everything?"

"Yes, please."

Fiona put three raspberry and two blueberry tarts, a slice of carrot cake, two pecan squares, and three coconut cupcakes into a box.

"Thanks," I said.

I carried the box to our table and sat down. Jayne smiled at me and pointed to her phone. "That would be nice," she said. "Seven it is."

Jocelyn arrived with a pot of tea, a pitcher of milk, two cups, and a plate of small sandwiches. "No pastries today," she said. "Someone bought the last of them."

"Bye," Jayne said. "See you soon." She slipped her phone into her pocket.

"What are you smiling at?" I asked.

"I'm not allowed to smile on a nice day over a cup of tea?"

"Not with that self-satisfied look about you," I said. "Date with Jack tonight?"

"If you must know, yes. We're going out for dinner."

"I have a better offer."

Her eyes narrowed. "I don't want to hear it."

"Sure you do. It'll be boring, no dead bodies involved. I'm bringing dessert." I pointed to the bakery box.

"Why would I want to go to a boring event to eat my own baking, when I can have a pleasant dinner with a handsome man?"

"The Scarlet House board is meeting tonight at seven. Potluck desserts."

Jayne sighed. "And you're going. Fiona told me Ryan came in at lunchtime and bought two sandwiches, which he took into the Emporium. I assumed he was here to tear a strip off you." She eyed me. "You look remarkably unscathed."

"Not only unscathed but continuing to stick my nose where some might say it doesn't belong."

"Thus we're going to the board meeting."

I grinned. "That we are."

She sighed heavily. "Someone has to keep you out of trouble. Might as well be me. I'll call Jack back."

* * *

When we arrived at Scarlet House, each of us with a folding chair and me carrying the bakery box, the parking lot was almost full. Most of the cars were new and pretty high end, but I didn't see Robyn's Lexus. I parked next to a nifty little white Mercedes SLK.

As we got out of the Miata, I studied the main house. The warren of scaffolding was still in place, plywood nailed over the windows, and "Keep out" signs posted on all the doors, but much of the detritus of an active construction site was gone. Work had stopped, I assumed, pending the finding of further funds, although the lawn had recently been cut and the flowerbeds freshly weeded. That would likely be the work of unpaid volunteers.

We followed the buzz of conversation to the back of the main house. The building loomed over the meeting area, wrapped in shadows. Lights were on in the barn, and from it came the sounds of shuffling animals settling down for the night. A piglet squealed, and its mother grunted in reply.

Arrivals were placing their chairs in straight rows next to a neatly hedged section of well-maintained garden. "Unusual plants," I said to Jayne.

"That's our physick garden," a woman said to me. "One of the highlights of the museum. All the plants growing there would have been used in some form or another in the seventeenth century to treat illnesses."

"Interesting." I made a mental note to come back at a later time to give it a closer look. Many things that can be used to treat the sick can be used in higher concentrations to kill.

The woman pointed to another section of hedge-outlined garden. "We also have a kitchen garden where we grow a variety of vegetables that would have been known to the earliest settlers."

"No broccolini then," Jayne said.

She laughed. "Certainly not. You're Jayne from the tearoom, and Gemma from the bookshop. I saw you both at the auction. I'm Lacy Montgomery."

"Pleased to meet you," Jayne and I chorused.

"You maintain the gardens yourself," I said. "That must be a lot of work."

"How did you . . . ?" Lacy laughed again and lifted her hands. "It's my passion. I never can get all the dirt out. I wear gloves most of the time, but on occasion I can't resist getting my fingers down and dirty." Black soil was trapped in the deeper crevices around her cuticles, and her rings needed a good scrubbing, but it was the pride in her voice when she mentioned the gardens, and the affectionate look she gave them as she talked that told me.

"I see you brought something from the bakery for our potluck," Lacy said. "Why don't you put it on the table and grab yourself some refreshments before we begin?"

"Thank you," I said. "We will."

Lacy went to greet more new arrivals, and I set up my chair at the back of the slowly forming rows.

"Don't we want to be nearer the front?" Jayne said.

"I need to see everyone." I handed her the box and wandered into the crowd. To show their support of Scarlet House, many people wore something red or had the scarlet badge of the museum pinned to their shirt. A long table had been set up on the lawn, facing the rows of chairs. Sharon Musgrave put a stack of papers on the table and placed a rock on top to keep them from blowing away in the wind. She was dressed in her historical costume, and I wondered if that was because she hadn't had time to change after her shift of making inedible cookies or because she took every opportunity she could to wear it. She bustled over to the refreshments table and began pouring glasses of tea or lemonade. At that signal the attendees surged forward and dug into the plentiful dessert buffet. Most of the offerings were bakery bought, but some, such as a huge deep-dish apple pie and a platter of oatmeal cookies, looked homemade. A plate of rocks, aka Sharon's pioneer baking, went untouched.

I recognized many of these people from the auction. Several of them knew me and extended greetings; those who didn't smiled politely, searching their memory banks for where they'd seen me before.

"Probably the last person I'd expect to find here," Grant Thompson said. "Are you joining the board?"

"Just curious."

He mock-slapped his forehead. "You're still interested in the death of Kathy Lamb."

I lifted my finger to my lips, and he gave me a grin. I smiled and said nothing. "Anyone you want me to introduce you to?" he asked.

"What's on the agenda?"

"Electing a new chair is first and foremost, and then we're going to talk about raising money to continue with repairs to the house."

I glanced around the lawn. Thirty-four people were here, chatting to friends and enjoying the refreshments. Sharon scurried about, pouring drinks, handing out napkins, trying to press her cookies on the unwary, while the edges of her stack of papers fluttered in the breeze blowing in off the sea. A man in a Boston Red Sox ball cap walked past with half of one of Jayne's coconut cupcakes in his hand, a smear of icing on his lips, and a look of pure bliss on his face.

"Who are the candidates for chair of the board?" I asked.

"As far as I know, only one," Grant said. "That's her arriving now."

I turned to see Robyn Kirkpatrick crossing the lawn, her sharp heels digging into the grass. She was dressed in a red linen jacket worn over a white blouse and white trousers with dark red—scarlet—pumps. She greeted everyone with a quick word, a kiss on both cheeks, and a hug, looking like a politician at a fundraiser. Everyone seemed happy to see her; they all smiled and accepted her air kisses and hugs.

"She seems popular," I said.

"They're just happy someone's prepared to step in and take over. Means they won't be asked to do it," Grant said.

"Sounds like every nonprofit I've ever been involved in."

"Got that right."

"What about Kathy's friends and allies? How do they feel about it?"

"The same, I guess," he said. "Kathy hadn't been chair for long, meaning she hadn't made much of an impact." He lowered his voice. "This is a well-meaning volunteer group, people proud of West London and interested in its history. No one wanted to find themselves forced to take sides in a power struggle. Tell you the truth, I don't get the feeling many members are all that bothered about Kathy's death. All that unpleasantness can be forgotten, and everything can go back to where it should be. Excuse me, Gemma. I see someone I want to talk to. She's interested in acquiring a first edition copy of the *Moonstone*, but she's dragging her decision out, hoping I'll think she's unsure and thus drop the price. Not a chance."

He pasted on his professional smile and approached an elderly woman with a helmet of slate-gray hair, wearing a ferocious frown and a powder-blue suit that was fashionable in the days of shoulder pads. When she spotted Grant heading her way, her frown disappeared, and a look of sheer girlish pleasure crossed her face. I laughed to myself. She wasn't dragging out her decision about the book in an attempt to haggle over the price. She wanted the company of a handsome, charming young man. And Grant was all of that.

"How nice to see you, Gemma." Ben Alderson joined me, clutching a glass of lemonade and a plate of treats. "Thank you for coming."

"Wouldn't miss it," I said.

"You've decided to join us—that's wonderful. You English people have an appreciation for history. I hope you don't take it too personally that we kicked you out back in seventy-six." He laughed heartily.

I smiled politely. "I haven't decided."

He ignored me. "Being a small-business owner, you must have a good eye for detail. We need someone to coordinate the purchasing efforts. We're going to need a lot of furniture and household goods to replace what was lost in the fire. We'd prefer originals, of course, but the expense might run to more than we can afford. You and your team can take charge of that."

"My team?"

He finished his piece of apple pie and picked up a raspberry tart. "Once we get the board reorganized and the matter of financing out of the way, then we can start working on the subcommittees. I'll send you a list of interested folks, and you can give them a call in a day or two, form your committee, and start developing your plan." He stopped talking long enough to take a bite of the tart.

"Committee? My plan?" I said weakly.

"Oh good. Peter came. I was worried he wouldn't make it because of his leg. Talk to you later, Gemma." He tossed the last piece of tart into his mouth and hurried away. I blinked and watched him cross the lawn. With one quick movement of his arm, he threw one of Sharon's cookies into an heirloom rose bush.

Jayne's mother, Leslie, had arrived, and they were chatting at the edge of the crowd. I went up to them. "A word to the wise. Don't get trapped into conversation by

Ben Alderson. You'll end up being assigned to do all the catering for the work crew."

Jayne blanched.

"That's Ben," Leslie said.

Sharon slipped out from behind the refreshments table and headed for the barn. I decided to check on the piglets.

The barn was as neat and tidy as it had been on my last visit, the floor so clean you could eat off it, if you were so inclined. I doubted that was faithful to the condition of most seventeenth- or eighteenth-century barns. Heck, it wasn't the condition of most seventeenth- or eighteenth-century homes. The animals were all in their pens, the goats standing on their hind legs, forelegs on the fence, interested in what Sharon was up to. The scent of fresh straw and clean animals filled the air.

Sharon picked two lanterns off a makeshift kitchen cabinet and turned. She let out a small scream and lifted one hand to her chest. The lamp was iron and old-fashioned, with a large base, hourglass body, and flip handle, but battery operated. "My goodness, you frightened me."

"Sorry," I said. "Didn't mean to. I love the atmosphere in an old barn as dusk settles, don't you?" Not that I'd ever been in a barn, at dusk or any other time, before this week.

Her face beamed with the same intensity as the lights in her hands. "Oh my gosh, yes. Everything settling down for the night. All's right with the world." She patted her mouth, but I caught the scent of something strong and sweet on her breath. Homemade rose-hip wine was my guess. I glanced at the cabinet. The doors were closed, secured with a piece of wood through a loop. As well as coming in for the lanterns, Sharon had taken the opportunity to fortify herself for the meeting.

I waved in the vague direction of the gathering outside. "Everything seems all right in the museum world as well. Are things getting back on track?"

"Slowly."

"It hasn't been long since you lost your board chair."

Sharon shrugged. "I don't mean to speak ill of the dead, but we're better off without her. The priority right now has to be to get the house useable. Robyn's much better at fund-raising than Kathy ever was."

"You think Robyn's going to be voted in as board chair?"

"It's a foregone conclusion," she said.

"You'll stay on as bookkeeper?"

Her eyes narrowed. "That's never been in doubt, not with Robyn."

Fortune favors the brave, or so they say. Sometimes the only way to get an honest answer to your question is to out-and-out ask it. "But not under Kathy?"

Sharon stiffened and her brow darkened. "Kathy had some foolish ideas about making changes that everyone knew weren't needed. I told her she'd never get anyone as good as me, as dedicated to the museum, at the wages they were able to pay."

"You must love it here a great deal."

Her face softened. "It's the center of my life," she said quietly.

The arson investigator's report concluded that the fire at the museum house had been an accident. A candle left unnoticed when the docent locked up for the night, an open window, a sudden gust of wind. The volunteer hadn't been mentioned by name. The report only said that when questioned she'd been extremely upset about what had happened.

This person was, I knew, Sharon Musgrave. If Kathy had threatened to fire Sharon from her paying job as the bookkeeper, she would likely have also threatened Sharon's volunteer position. It can be difficult to fire a volunteer if she's good at her tasks, but it can be done. Causing the house to burn down would be cause enough.

Which meant Sharon Musgrave had reason to want Kathy Lamb dead. But Elizabeth?

"Did you hear about the murder in town last night?" I put on my best gossipy voice.

Her eyes opened wide. "Oh my gosh, yes. It was on the radio this morning. I can't imagine what West London's coming to."

"Did you know her? Elizabeth Dumont."

Sharon shook her head. "She came to the auction, didn't she? I saw her there, but I didn't speak to her, and I'd never met her before. She never came here. She was married to Kathy's ex-husband." She lowered her voice. "You don't suppose he did it, do you? Killed them both? They say the husband is always the first suspect."

"I have no idea. I'm sure the police will get to the bottom of it in due course."

"Ladies and gentlemen, take your seats, please," called a voice from outside.

Sharon lifted her lamps. "I need to get these out there—the meeting's about to begin." She pushed her way past me. The goats watched her go. Her voice had been steady, and her hands didn't shake. She hadn't had much of the wine, perhaps no more than a quick mouth-ful. If she needed a small tipple to get her through the meeting, I wasn't going to judge her.

I followed her and took my seat next to Jayne. The meeting got underway when Ben led a moment of silence in memory of Kathy Lamb, and a few people stood and paid tribute to her. While that was going on, I couldn't stop myself from studying the people around me and speculating on their life stories. That man three seats over, the one in the handmade Italian loafers and Armani shirt, had spent some time in prison. The woman next to him, his third, or maybe fourth, wife didn't know about that.

Robyn Kirkpatrick had taken a seat in the front row. Members of the board, plus Sharon who was taking the minutes, sat behind the head table, leaving the cen-ter chair vacant. A wooden gavel rested on the table in front of the empty space.

Ben announced that the slate of candidates for interim chair of the board would now be voted on. The "slate" consisted of one name: Robyn Kirkpatrick. Every hand was lifted, and blushing and smiling, Robyn got to her feet and took her place at the center of the head table.

"First order of business," she said, after shaking Ben's hand and thanking everyone for putting their trust in her, "is a plan for the rebuilding and refurnish-ing of the house we all love so much." Another round of enthusiastic applause.

Discussion then began on the best way to raise the needed funds. Sharon passed around a sheet of paper containing budget numbers and another with the quote from the construction firm and prices of both original and reproduction Colonial-era furniture. I glanced at the numbers and my eyes watered.

Some people wanted to have another auction. Several thought that would be in extremely poor taste. Someone said Kathy would want them to do what was best for the museum. I was close to dozing off when the words *Cape Cod Yacht Club* caught my attention.

Robyn had let everyone speak, and then she casually mentioned that the Cape Cod Yacht Club had offered the museum free space in their banqueting room and catering at cost to host a fund-raising dinner. Perhaps dinner and dancing and a scaled-down silent auction?

A man stood up. "We can't go there! Kathy was a member of the West London Club. Everyone knows the two clubs hate each other."

"Sit down, Ralph, you old fool," a woman said. "West London hasn't offered us anything."

"We can ask them," Ralph said. "Ask them to do it in honor of Kathy."

Another man rose. "The West London Yacht Club wouldn't offer free mustard on their hotdogs to a group of Boy Scouts. Not as long as that Jock O'Callaghan's commodore. The most miserly man who ever lived, Jock is."

"Enough of his virtues," someone called out. "Let's talk about his faults." Everyone laughed, pleased at the chance to do something to break the tension of the beginning of an argument.

Robyn hammered on the table with her gavel. "Noreen Westaway is right. West London hasn't offered us anything, but Cape Cod has."

"I wonder when this offer came in," I whispered to the man beside me. A beefy, florid-faced chap, he'd been at the auction. "Seems rather premature, wouldn't you agree?"

"Good question," he replied. He stood up. "When did Cape Cod offer to host us anyway? We haven't even discussed going back to Mrs. Hudson's and continuing with the auction."

Robyn's face tightened. She might have pretended not to hear the question, but Ben nodded. He opened his mouth to reply, but Robyn was quick to speak first. "I see Leslie and Jayne Wilson are here. I don't think we've properly thanked Jayne for providing the auction tea. The tea was a huge success, I think you'll all agree, although tragically the auction had to be abandoned."

"Huge success," the man next to me muttered, "if you forget a woman died."

Robyn applauded politely, and everyone followed her lead. Jayne blushed.

"We couldn't possibly ask Mrs. Hudson's Tearoom to host another function free of charge." Robyn raised a hand, although neither Jayne nor I had started to protest. Not that we had any intention of doing so. The shops on Baker Street and citizens of West London had got their auction donations back and might thus be expected to contribute next time. Mrs. Hudson's Tearoom had done its bit.

"Now," Robyn continued, "if there are no more objections, I'll let the Cape Cod Yacht Club know we're interested in working with them. Next item of business?"

"I gave up a dinner date for that?" Jayne said to me as the meeting broke up. "It would have been more exciting to stay at home and watch paint dry."

"You can watch paint dry anytime," I said. "Give me a minute, will you?"

I approached the crowd around Robyn. People welcomed her back and offered her their congratulations. Some said they'd be happy to work with her on the event committee. Sharon stood behind her, slightly to one side, holding a lantern in either hand like a footman assisting gowned ladies into their carriages. Night had fallen, and the lights, even though they were electric, cast a warm glow over Robyn and her circle.

I waited patiently, and eventually people moved on, back to their cars and homes.

"A productive meeting," I said to Robyn.

"Gemma. Nice to see you. Are you joining our Scarlet House family?"

"It would be interesting," I said. "I was at the Cape Cod Yacht Club the other day."

"Are you a member there? Someone told me your uncle's an excellent sailor."

"To put it mildly," I replied. "I talked to Elizabeth Dumont."

"Poor Elizabeth. Most unfortunate what happened to her. They say her husband did it because she threatened to leave him." She shook her head sadly. "If you'll excuse me . . ."

"She didn't say anything to me about helping the museum," I said.

"Elizabeth could be quite flirtatious." Robyn's smile was stiff. "She liked to dangle the offer of money in front of people and then whip it away. She married riches, and it went straight to her head." Realizing what she was saying, Robyn forced herself to relax. "But she always did the right thing in the end. She was very generous with what she'd been given."

"You knew her well." It was a question, but I made it sound like a statement of fact.

"We were friends in our youth. But as often happens, we went our separate ways after school, even though we continued to live in the same area. I hadn't spoken to her in years. She called me the other day, right out of the blue, to say she'd heard about the fire at the museum and wanted to help. She'd gone to the auction—wasn't that nice of her? But when the auction proved to be . . . unsuccessful, she had an idea about hosting something at the yacht club. So thoughtful. Her death is such a tragedy. We only spoke on the phone that once, but she said she'd see that everything was put in motion for our gala evening." She pulled a tissue out of her purse and dabbed at her eyes. "I'm heartbroken that we never got the chance to meet up again."

Chapter Eighteen

"Did you learn anything?" Jayne cradled her glass of wine in her hands.

"I learned that Robyn Kirkpatrick is keeping secrets."

"Really? I thought she did a good job running that meeting."

"She did an excellent job, kept everything on track and on focus. The museum's lucky she agreed to come back."

"But—"

I popped a piece of calamari into my mouth. After we left the museum, I suggested we go for a drink and something to eat, and Jayne eagerly agreed. We were at the Blue Water Café, our favorite restaurant. The café is not only our favorite place but that of a great many others, both residents and visitors. The deck jutting into the harbor was packed full when we arrived, and we had to take seats inside at a small table against the back wall.

"Robyn told me she hadn't seen Elizabeth for years," I said. "That was a lie. She was at the yacht club Tuesday. I saw her."

"Maybe she didn't run into Elizabeth?"

"Robyn wasn't on a casual visit or head to the bar for a drink. She was there to see someone, and she was either late or angry. Maybe both. Elizabeth wasn't in an office or a private room; she was running a meeting on the main veranda."

"Why would Robyn lie about something so easy to check? Other people would have seen her with Elizabeth."

"Probably because she didn't think she'd ever need to mention it, and when I brought it up, she denied it without thinking. No one else has connected her with Elizabeth."

I sipped my own glass of wine. A family had the table next to us. The baby was getting fractious, trying to climb out of his highchair, and the toddler was building to a full-scale temper tantrum because the ketchup on his fries had touched his burger. The father had one hand on the baby's diaper, holding him in place. The parents drank their beer and ate their meals and talked about her brother, who was, for some reason I didn't catch, not seeing reason, while trying to ignore the children. The wife was younger than her husband by about twenty years, and the look on his face clearly said this late-in-life new family had turned out not to be such a good idea.

"Jayne and Gemma, nice to see you." Andy White-hall, owner and head chef, stood next to our table. He gave me a quick smile and Jayne, a full-faced grin.

"Hi," I said. "Care to join us?"

Andy glanced quickly around. We were wedged up against the wall at a table for two. The baby was turning beet red, and the toddler yelled, "Nooooooo!"

"Sorry about the table," Andy said. "Let me find you something better."

"We're okay," I said. "If we get a better table, then you have to put someone else here."

"We don't mind," Jayne said. "We come for the food." She toasted him with a calamari dripping with seafood sauce. "The food, and in hopes of seeing you."

The tips of Andy's ears turned bright pink.

I considered making sudden excuses and fleeing into the night. Andy adored Jayne, although to her they were just good friends. I thought they'd make the perfect couple, but for some reason, my hints to that effect were not having an impact on her.

"I wanted to say hi," he said. "I can't stay and visit. We're backed up in the kitchen. I don't know why we're so busy this late on a Thursday night."

"Because you're the best restaurant in town," Jayne said. "Maybe in the entire Cape."

"If not the Eastern Seaboard," I said.

"Thanks," Andy said.

"I hear Scarlet House's putting on a gala at the Cape Cod Yacht Club," I said. "Going to be very swanky, I bet. You should go, Andy. Take Jayne with you."

Jayne threw me a look. Andy said, "That would be—"

I never did find out what it would be because, at that moment, a waiter dropped a tray piled high with glasses and plates. Cutlery crashed to the floor, crockery smashed, glassware shattered. Two patrons leapt out of the way, and the waiter swore. Andy disappeared in a flash.

"Gemma," Jayne said, "that's going to be an expensive evening. You can't tell Andy to take me. Suppose he can't afford it."

"Your birthday's coming up. It'll be my gift to you."

"My birthday's not for months yet."

"January sixth."

"You only remember that because it's the same day as Sherlock Holmes's."

She was right about that, but I didn't want to admit it. I wasn't entirely sure why January sixth had been settled on as the date of the birth of the Great Detective because he wasn't a real person and thus had not been born, but Sherlockians accepted it as such. The shop often featured special events that week, and I was sometimes invited to parties by Uncle Arthur and Donald Morris.

"Okay, so let's say your guess is right," Jayne said.

I gave Jayne a look.

"Yes, I know. You never guess. So what if Robyn went to the yacht club and met with Elizabeth? Robyn and Elizabeth know a lot of people. It's not much of a stretch that they might know each other."

"Agreed. But what's of interest to me is that they had a common enemy."

"Kathy?"

"Kathy was the new chair of the board, having pushed Robyn out. Judging by the reaction at the meeting tonight, Robyn's still popular. I wouldn't be surprised if Robyn had been plotting her return, but when disaster struck and the house burned, Robyn's plans were dealt a severe setback. Kathy leapt into action and organized the auction. If the auction had been a success, Kathy's role at the head of the board would have been secure. If—and I'm only speculating here—Robyn killed Kathy in an attempt to sabotage the auction, she might have then approached her old pal Elizabeth and asked for money for the restoration. Robyn could then return to the board, triumphant."

"But Robyn wasn't in the tearoom for the auction."

"And that presents a problem, I'll agree. She was, however, lurking outside. Sharon, her own position threatened by Kathy, was inside. Maybe they were in it together."

"Why kill Elizabeth, the benefactor?"

"Robyn said Elizabeth liked to tease people by offering money and then pulling it back. She tried to make it sound like a joke, but there was real anger in her voice. It's possible that's what happened in this case. Elizabeth offered money, or the free use of the club, which is much the same thing, to Robyn and then rescinded the offer. Robyn tried to argue with her on Tuesday, but Elizabeth stood firm. Don't forget that Elizabeth was furious with her husband at the time Robyn arrived at the yacht club. She wouldn't have wanted to be bothered by Robyn and her concerns. It's possible Robyn went to Elizabeth before Kathy died, and Elizabeth said she'd never give any money to any organization with Kathy at its head. Thus, Kathy had to be gotten rid of."

"Gemma, you've overthought this. People don't kill over a place on a volunteer board of a small history museum."

"People kill for a lot of reasons. Some of which make no sense to the rest of us."

"What was it you said about the death of Sir Nigel Bellingham? Someone's razor?"

"Occam's razor."

"Right. The theory that the simplest solution is usually the best one. Ryan agreed with you then. This time, you're twisting everything into knots."

"But there's no simple solution here, Jayne. Someone killed Elizabeth and Kathy, and the only person I can see who had reason to want them both gone is Robyn Kirkpatrick."

"There you are," a voice boomed down at us.

Jayne and I looked up. She smiled. I did not. Jack Templeton, grinning broadly, stood next to our table. He wore slim jeans and a close-fitting black T-shirt under a distressed denim jacket. His bare feet were stuffed into Italian loafers. He was freshly shaven, and he smelled of expensive soap and shampoo. "Great idea, Jayne. Thanks for calling. Let me grab a chair."

I looked at Jayne. She ducked her head and mumbled, "I called Jack when you went to the restroom and suggested he join us for a drink. I knew you wouldn't mind."

Jack found a chair and pulled it up to our table. Before sitting, he held his hand out to me. "I don't think we've met. Jack Templeton. Jayne and I went to school together. I've been away for a while, but now I'm back. You must be Gemma."

"I am." I took his hand in mine. He gripped it firmly. I gripped his more firmly.

He winced. "I love your store. It's such a great concept."

"Not at all pretentious?"

His smile cracked. "Uh . . . no. Why would you think that?" He turned to the waiter. "Yeah, a beer, thanks. Whatever you have on tap. Jayne, would you like another?"

"Thanks," she said.

Jack nodded to the waiter. The waiter glanced at me. I considered staying for another drink, just to be difficult, but I shook my head and stood up. "I have to run. See you tomorrow, Jayne."

"Sure," she said.

"Nice meeting you," Jack said.

"Your friend looks vaguely familiar," Jack said as I walked away.

"She has one of those faces," Jayne replied.

* * *

I heard via the branch of the West London grapevine that flows through Mrs. Hudson's Tearoom into the Emporium that Dan Lamb had left his hotel, and he and his son had returned to Elizabeth's house. Which presumably was now Dan's house. More than a few people around town were saying it was mighty suspicious that Dan had lost an ex-wife and a current wife in the space of less than a week. He'd been ordered by the police not to leave town, but it was unlikely he'd venture out onto the streets until the rumors died down.

I wanted to pay a call on Dan and considered doing it under the pretext of dropping off a book for him. But I decided to hold off on that for a while.

When I'd gotten home last night, I'd called Ryan to report on the happenings at the museum meeting. I outlined my thoughts about Robyn, Kathy, and Elizabeth, and threw Sharon's name into the mix for good measure.

Like Jayne, he'd been skeptical. "It's a heck of a stretch, Gemma. And with no physical evidence, it's also useless."

"Have you spoken to Robyn Kirkpatrick?"

"I have no reason to, Gemma, other than that you say you saw her going into the Cape Cod Yacht Club one afternoon."

"Ask at the club if anyone saw her talking to Elizabeth. If they did, then you have enough of a connection to question Robyn. Find out if she has an alibi for the time of Elizabeth's murder."

He sighed. "Okay, I'll go back to the club. We've interviewed many of the members at length. Plenty of people told us Elizabeth was not an easy woman to work with. They say she seemed to think of the place as her own private club and bossed everyone around accordingly. If it matters, there was never the slightest hint that she might be sneaking around behind Dan's back or that he was doing so to her. Despite that, some of the women said Elizabeth could be extremely jealous. About a month ago, she publicly accused one of the club's longtime members of having designs on Dan. The woman quit the club in a rage. Before you ask, that woman is not a suspect in the killing of Elizabeth. She's in Europe at the moment."

"Elizabeth didn't seem to be popular anywhere." I thought back to the auction and the first time I'd seen her. "Jock O'Callaghan."

"What about him?"

"He was at the auction. Made a big deal about having important things to do so he couldn't stay to answer police questions. He was with his mother."

"I know who you mean. You think he has something to do with this?"

"He had no reason to kill Kathy that I know of, so I never gave him any thought. But he hated Elizabeth, and that was clearly no secret. He's with the West London Yacht Club, and he was friends with Elizabeth's first husband, Edward Dumont. Mr. Dumont has been dead for seven years, and Elizabeth out of the WLYC, but the animosity between the two seems to be as strong as ever. Was as strong as ever, I should say. They squared off at the auction tea and threw insults at each other."

"You're thinking this O'Callaghan finally got his revenge for the killing of Edward? Unlikely he'd act after all this time, Gemma."

"Unless he's an exceedingly patient man who's been biding his time. I overheard him say to her that one of these days she'd get what was coming to her. Is it possible," I thought out loud, "that Jock, or someone else, decided they could get rid of Elizabeth right after Kathy's death so the police would think the same person had committed both crimes?"

Ryan groaned. "You're muddying the waters, Gemma."

"I'll agree that does seem to be happening in this case."

"I can look into O'Callaghan, but I'll have to be discreet about it. He's an important man in these parts. Old family money and lots of influence."

"Thanks," I said. I, on the other hand, never had to worry about being discreet.

"Good night," I said.

"Sweet dreams," he said.

* * *

While I waited for Ashleigh to come into work and debated what to do about visiting Dan Lamb, I placed a call to Donald Morris. I was always a bit wary of involving Donald in any of my queries. Being a lifelong dedicated Sherlockian, he wanted nothing more than to be the Watson to what he considered my Holmes, but he couldn't help thinking of it as a game.

I had considered visiting the WLYC in disguise, as I earlier had the CCYC, but I decided it would be easier and simpler to take a page out of Jayne's book and simply ask what I wanted to know. Donald Morris was the only "in" I had at the WLYC, and so I reluctantly made the call. It crossed my mind that I might suggest Uncle Arthur join every club in town, just in case I needed to drop in sometime to question a suspect, but that would get rather expensive.

"You talked to Jock O'Callaghan at the charity auction. How well do you know him?" I asked Donald when he answered the phone.

"Well enough to say hello or have a drink at the bar with. Why are you asking, Gemma? Is he on your suspect list?"

"I don't have a list," I said, "but I would like to talk to him."

"About Elizabeth Dumont, no doubt. Everyone's talking about it and wondering when the police are going to make an arrest. It's not looking good for the WLPD, Gemma: two killings in a week and no arrests. You'll be pleased to know I haven't revealed your secret to anyone."

I didn't want to ask, but I did anyway. "What secret is that?"

"That you're investigating. Like you did those other times."

"I don't investigate, Donald. I just ask a few questions." Although that did sound a lot like investigating.

"If you say so, my dear. Now, how can I help you? If you need to know about the death of Edward Dumont,

I'm afraid I can't help you. I was living in Boston at the time of that unfortunate incident. My father talked about it, but I have to admit I didn't pay much attention. I was busy with my own law practice in those days."

"The police investigated Elizabeth, but she had a solid alibi, and there was never any evidence she hired anyone to do it for her. But Jock O'Callaghan still seems to think Elizabeth killed her husband. Did other people at the club think the same?"

"From what little I remember, Gemma, it was more a matter that people didn't like Elizabeth and thus were quick to accuse her."

"Why didn't they like her?"

I could almost hear his shrug come down the phone. "Some people said reverse snobbery, that she didn't like rich people as a matter of principle. I considered it to be more a case of her not pretending to like people she didn't. She never made any attempt to fit in and didn't seem to care what people thought of her."

I remembered her lack of attention to her appearance and her off-the-discount-rack clothes. "I'd like to talk to Jock O'Callaghan. I looked him up in the phone book but can't find a number. Do you know it?"

"No, but I can take you to meet him," Donald said.

"That would be good. When can we do that? I don't want to wait too long."

"This afternoon. I don't go to the club often, Gemma." He coughed in embarrassment. I assumed he didn't go because he couldn't afford the prices. When the elder Mr. Morris died and Donald inherited his parents' small estate, he gave up his family law practice in order to devote himself to a study of the Great Detective and his creator. Being a Sherlockian isn't at all lucrative, not in the monetary sense, but Donald Morris was a happy man. "I'm occasionally invited to a dinner or a celebration at the club by people who were friends of my parents. I was last there in the spring for an anniversary party, and much of the talk was of the roster for the upcoming tennis season. Jock O'Callaghan was present, and he mentioned that he's on the mixed doubles team that plays every Tuesday and Friday afternoon at two."

"That's great. Thanks, Donald."

"I'll pick you up at two thirty, shall I?"

"You don't need to do that. I can go by myself."

"Jock will likely go to the bar after his game. The members' bar isn't open to the general public, Gemma. You need me to get you in."

"Oh," I said.

"Two thirty it is." He hung up.

* * *

At promptly one minute before two thirty Donald pulled into the loading zone in front of the Emporium. I dashed out and opened the passenger door. Before getting in, I noticed several years' supply of the *Sherlock Holmes Journal*, some back issues of *Strand* magazine, a copy of *The Sign of Four* nibbled around the edges by what creature I did not want to contemplate, and a couple of guidebooks to London on the back seat.

"Thinking of going to England?" I said, fastening my seatbelt.

Donald drove a 2001 Toyota Corolla held together by luck and rust. He spun the wheel and edged into the traffic, inch by painful inch.

"There's a major conference being held in London in January. I've been saving all year and am excited about going. You should consider coming too, Gemma."

"Why?"

"One of the streams is on Holmes and his effect on popular culture. You can look into what's forthcoming that you might want to stock in the Emporium, and maybe give a talk on what you're finding popular."

"January's not the best time of the year to go to London," I said. "It gets dark early and rains a lot. You could have made that light in plenty of time, you know."

"Better safe than sorry," he said as we drifted to a halt to the accompaniment of the screaming horn of the car behind us.

"I'll mention your name to the conference organizing committee," Donald said.

"You do that," I said. "Tell me about Jock O'Callaghan before we arrive. Has he been at the yacht club for long?"

"Forever. His baptism party was probably held there. His parents were members. The WLYC has a lot of legacy members, unlike the Cape Cod club, which is much newer."

"He has family money?"

"Oh yes. Quite a bit of it. Jock's grandfather founded a hotel chain, I believe. Don't know much about it—sorry."

"At the auction tea, Elizabeth made a crack about his wife not being with him. You know anything about that?"

"You met his mother, right?"

"I wasn't introduced to her, but I noticed her."

"She makes sure she's noticed everywhere she goes. Iris O'Callaghan's her name. A formidable woman in her day. They say Jock's father would have drunk and gambled his father's fortune away, but Iris took charge of the company and the money. She still has firm control, much to Jock's dismay. Or so they say."

"What about Jock's wife?"

"I don't remember her name." Donald drove with his hands in the approved ten-to-two position, his head forward and his eyes fixed firmly on the road. "I don't like to repeat gossip, Gemma."

"That's why we're going on this outing, to dig for dirt. Spill."

"Only in the interests of discovering the truth. His wife is from one of the richest families in New York, and it was most likely more a marriage of money than of love, but despite that, they seemed happy together. My father loved nothing more than gossip, particularly among the great and the good, which he disguised as an interest in maintaining the moral fiber of the club community. So I know more about some of these people than I'd like. Apparently, Jock and his wife—she has some sort of flower name—had a reasonably successful marriage for many years, but then, as I suppose often happens, they drifted apart. Since then, rumor and innuendo has linked his name with the wives of other members over the years, and the lady members pretend to be scandalized by her behavior."

"Her behavior being?"

"It's said that Mrs. O'Callaghan, who is the same age as her husband, late fifties, is . . . uh . . . enjoys the company of younger men. Much younger men."

"Does she now? That would explain Elizabeth's dig. All worth knowing, Donald. I don't suppose you know if Jock, his wife, or his mother have anything to do with Scarlet House?"

"That I can't say. I know nothing at all about them outside of the club. It's likely Jock only attended the auction at the insistence of his mother, who's a stalwart of many worthy organizations. He, on the other hand, is not known for his charitable activities."

For reasons unknown to me, the Cape Cod Yacht Club is in West London, and the West London Yacht Club is not, being located twenty miles up the coast. It took us about forty minutes to get there, although traffic was light. That is to say, traffic in front of us was light. Behind us, it was a stream of tooting horns, anxious drivers, and cars edging up to our bumper, trying to get past on the narrow, winding road.

"We should have taken a hansom cab," I said as the sign to the club came into sight at last.

"Wouldn't that have been great fun," Donald said.

"We might have made it in time." If Jock's tennis game had been short and his drink quick, he might have left by now.

We pulled into the farthest corner of the almost deserted parking lot and got out of the car. Donald had dressed in well-worn beige chinos, a white shirt in desperate need of the attentions of an iron, an excessively rumpled white linen jacket, and a large blue bow tie. I hadn't gone home to change, thinking that my new blue and green dress was perfect for drinks at the yacht club.

The West London Yacht Club is older than the Cape Cod one, and it pretty much screams history, money, and influence. We walked up the sweeping crushed-gravel driveway, past immaculate lawns, ancient trees, and flowerbeds bursting with color, to the main building. The building itself had been built to impress, and it did. Mid-nineteenth century, perhaps a private home at one time. It was all weathered stone, large chimneys, and ivy-covered walls. Dormer windows dotted the third level, and a green and white awning hung over the entrance. We climbed the wide stone steps. A man dressed in a white uniform, with the intertwined letters WLYC on the breast pocket, greeted us and held open the door. "Good afternoon, Mr. Morris," he said. "Madam."

"Good afternoon, Albert," Donald said. "I hope the family is well."

"Very well, sir," Albert replied.

"Geez, Donald," I whispered, "you sound like Mycroft Holmes arriving at the Diogenes Club."

We walked in, and I let out a low whistle. The resemblance to ancient London men's clubs continued inside. High ceilings, a huge chandelier at either end of the room, brown leather chairs and couches, low tables, rich red rugs, wide windows, and an enormous fireplace.

I turned to see Donald grinning at me. "Impressed?" he asked.

"I am."

"You're supposed to be."

"What do the fees for this place run?"

"I have no idea, Gemma. I don't pay any. My great-grandfather was a founding member, and one of the conditions was that the eldest male heir be granted membership in perpetuity. Sadly, it looks as though the legacy will die with me."

"How could Kathy Lamb possibly have afforded this place?"

He lowered his voice. "She couldn't. After Dan left her, and all their money went to lawyers, she would have had to leave at the end of this year."

"The prospect of that must have been humiliating." Kathy had plenty of reasons to hate Elizabeth. Destruction of her pride, perhaps most of all. If Kathy hadn't died first, she'd be top of the list for the murder of the woman who'd taken everything from her.

"Let's track the path of our prey into the bar," Donald said.

"You start the conversation, as you know Jock," I said, "Make pleasantries and introduce a passing comment about Elizabeth, but then sit back and leave the rest up to me."

He gave me a wink I didn't like one little bit. Now that we were here, I could think of no way to get rid of Donald. We walked through the main room. A few people nodded politely to my companion. He stopped abruptly in front of a line of portraits of distinguished-looking gentlemen down through the years. "Club Commodores," he said. He pointed to the first painting, thick layers of oil paint in an ornate gilded frame. "My great-grandfather." Muttonchop whiskers, formidable mustache curling at the ends, bushy white eyebrows, chubby cheeks, small eyes, red nose, tweed suit, and choking necktie. Exactly the sort of man who might be found knocking at the door of 221B Baker Street one fog-wrapped morning, needing to hire a consulting detective on a sensitive matter.

"You don't look much like him," I said to Donald, bearer of a face that was all bones and sharp angles.

"I take after my mother's side of the family," he said. "Let's go in."

I guessed that there must have been one heck of a battle over recent renovations to the members' bar. Modern was the word that came to mind. That wouldn't have sat well with some of the older, more traditional members. One wall was all glass, and everything else was chrome, steel, and cement accented by splashes of bright red in the abstract paintings on the walls and the leather stools at the bar.

The windows looked out over the spacious lawns and down to the harbor. Rows of masts and furled sails, blue water and fluffy clouds.

A handful of people, singles or in groups, were scattered around the large room. More were sitting outside on the deck. The man I was after sat alone in a far corner, nursing a crystal glass containing an inch of amber liquid. His phone was on the table in front of him, but he wasn't using it. He stared off into space, and his expression indicated he was wrapped in thought, and those thoughts made him sad.

"This room and the ladies' writing room are the only ones in the main building in which one is allowed to access electronic devices," Donald said.

"There's a ladies' writing room?"

"Used these days primarily for small-group functions such as meetings of the fund-raising committee."

"You open the conversation about Elizabeth," I said, "so I can gauge his reaction. But be subtle. Don't accuse him of anything."

"Furtive will be my movements." Donald marched across the room. "Jock," he bellowed in a voice that was not only far too loud for the room but also totally out of character for the quiet, timid man I knew.

Jock looked up with a start. He blinked. His eyes might have been wet; then again it might have been the effect of sunlight pouring in and bouncing off all that spotless chrome.

"Fancy meeting you here," Donald said. "Mind if we join you?" He dropped into a chair without waiting for permission to be given.

I smiled at Jock apologetically, so sorry to interrupt. He shrugged and the sadness behind his eyes vanished. "Please," he said, "do have a seat." He pushed a button to close the image on his phone, but not before I got a quick glimpse of the picture on it. A woman, not young, staring out to sea with a dreamy smile on her face. He stuffed the phone into his jacket pocket.

"Thanks," I said.

Jock sat on a cushioned bench against the wall, and Donald and I took chairs at a solid metal block of a table that allowed barely enough room for me to squeeze my legs in.

A waiter hurried over.

"Get you another, Jock?" Donald asked.

"Thank you."

"Gemma?"

"A glass of Sauvignon Blanc, please."

"It's early in the day for whiskey," Donald said. "A Nantucket Grey Lady, please. Have a good game?"

Jock was dressed in street clothes, and he didn't look to have recently emerged from the locker room showers. "Didn't play. Had to cancel the match. But I enjoy my afternoons at the club, having a *private* drink, so I came anyway."

"How's your lovely lady? Uh . . . ?"

"Rose. She's well, thank you."

Donald spoke to me. "Rose is Jock's wife. Marvelous woman."

Jock grimaced into his glass.

We made small talk while waiting for our drinks. I said something complimentary about the view and the building, and Jock told me some of the history of the club.

The waiter placed cocktail napkins, a bowl of mixed nuts (no cheap peanuts), and our drinks in front of us.

"Cheers," Donald said, and we clinked glasses.

Once we'd tasted our drinks, Donald said, "Terrible news about Elizabeth Dumont."

Jock's face clouded over. "Yes."

I sipped my wine.

Donald crunched his face up as though he was thinking hard. "Wasn't she a member here at one time? Wasn't there some business about the suspicious death of her husband? I was in Boston then, so I didn't follow the story, but I remember my father talking about it."

"That was a long time ago," Jock said. "Edward Dumont. No one ever called him by a diminutive of his name. He was always Edward. Good man. Close friend of mine." He lifted his head and stared directly at Donald and then at me. He blinked and dropped his eyes. "I didn't know her at all well."

"But you thought she killed him," I said.

"Pardon me, miss, but I don't know that that's any of your business."

"Just making conversation. Surely murder in our community is everyone's business. Some people are wondering if Elizabeth finally got justice for the killing of her husband."

He stared into the depths of the smoky liquid in his glass. Donald popped a handful of nuts into his mouth.

"After all this time? Unlikely." Jock lifted his head again. A small tick started in the corner of his right eye. He spoke rapidly, the words tumbling all over themselves as if he was in a desperate hurry to spit them out. "Can't say I'm all that upset about it. She had it coming. She killed Edward, or had him killed. Same thing. I, for one, won't be mourning her death." He finished his drink in one swallow. "Excuse me—I have an appointment I can't be late for." He raised his hand. "Jason. I'm ready to leave. Bring me my crutches."

"Certainly, Mr. O'Callaghan," the waiter replied.

Crutches?

The waiter hurried over, a pair of crutches in hand. He gripped Jock under the arm and helped him stand. Jock's face grimaced in pain and discomfort, and he balanced awkwardly to fit the crutches under his arms.

"Good heavens, what have you done to yourself, Jock?" Donald said.

I hadn't seen Jock's legs behind the solid block of the table. I saw them now. Jock O'Callaghan's right leg below the knee was encased in a gray boot cast. "Broke my blasted ankle at tennis on Tuesday," he said.

"Gave us all a fright when the ambulance arrived," the waiter said.

"Thanks for the drink." Jock limped away, watched over by the hovering waiter.

I dropped back into my seat. The person I'd chased across Elizabeth Dumont's lawn on Wednesday night, the one who had almost certainly killed her, had not been Jock O'Callaghan.

"A wasted trip," Donald said. "We didn't learn anything of significance."

"Wasted?" I replied. "Not at all. Jock didn't murder Elizabeth Dumont, but that's not the only killing we're talking about here."

Chapter Nineteen

D onald dropped me back at the Emporium at six
o'clock, in time for Ashleigh to take her dinner
break.

I'd decided that I had to try to talk to Dan Lamb.
Even if he knew nothing about the deaths of Elizabeth
and Kathy, he might be able to tell me if Elizabeth had
enemies. Maybe someone had been bothering her lately
about the death of her first husband. On the way to the
West London Yacht Club, Donald and I had driven past
Elizabeth's house. The gates, I couldn't help but notice,
had been secured with a thick chain and shiny new
padlock. Clearly, Dan didn't want any impromptu visitors. I didn't have his cell number, and a quick look at
411.com failed to turn up a number for the house.
Which didn't come as a total surprise, as I hadn't seen a
landline phone when I'd been in the house.

No point in calling Ryan to try to get Dan's number. He'd never give it to me.

Then I remembered. About a year ago, Dan had
wanted a copy of *The Art of Detection* by Laurie R. King,
a rather clever book in which King managed to introduce Sherlock Holmes into a twenty-first-century San
Francisco detective novel. I hadn't had the book in

stock, so I took his number and phoned him when it came in.

I called up the store's contact list, and there it was. I gave him a call.

A hesitant voice answered. "Hello?"

"Hi, Dan. It's Gemma Doyle here. How are you?"

"Fine."

"Glad to hear it. I haven't seen you in the store for some time, and I understand that you're probably busy these days, so I thought I'd drop off a book for you. My treat. Something came in recently I know you'll enjoy. It's the newest one by—"

"That's kind of you. You can leave it in the mailbox."

"I suppose I could do that, but—"

"I'm not receiving visitors. Thank you for understanding, Gemma." He hung up.

That closed that line of inquiry.

* * *

It opened again at six thirty when Crystal Lamb came into the shop. She was dressed well but causally in ankle-length trousers, pink shirt, linen jacket, and flat sandals. She didn't see me at first, and I watched her from the reading nook where I'd gone to pick up a discarded book. She glanced around the shop to get her bearings, as any first-time customer might do. Her eyes passed over the merchandise and settled on the Pastiche shelf. She stepped up to it and began scanning titles.

"Good evening," I said. "Can I help you find anything?"

She turned to me with a smile, and I could tell the moment she recognized me, which meant she had not come in looking for me. "Oh, hi. You were at my mother's visitation."

"Yes, I was. This is my shop."

"It's lovely and so original. I finished the books I brought with me and need to find something else."

I liked the sound of that—books. Plural. "You're staying in West London longer than you expected?"

"I can't really afford to take more time away from the office, but my mom's funeral has been put back a couple of days because of . . . developments in my father's life. As long as I'm here, I'd like to apologize for what happened on Tuesday evening. My father and I have our differences, but that's no excuse. I shouldn't have allowed myself to air our family laundry in public."

"Funerals are emotional times."

"That they are. And now I seem to be airing our laundry again. Sorry. What would you suggest? I love a good historical mystery."

We chatted about books for a few minutes, and she eventually chose *A Treacherous Curse* by Deanna Raybourn and *Let Darkness Bury the Dead* by Maureen Jennings. She carried her purchases over to the counter, and I rang them up.

"Your father's a frequent shopper here," I said. "Did you know that?"

She shook her head.

"Although he hasn't been in for several months."

She let out a soft chuckle. "Families, you can't escape them. Maybe I inherited something from my father after all. Do you do mail order?"

"Happy to," I said.

"I love your store, but it's unlikely I'll be back in West London for a long time. If ever. I grew up here and I love it, but without Mom to visit, and my father's situation . . ."

It was absolutely none of my business, but given an open door, I'll always step through it. "Situation?"

"People are saying my father killed my mom and Elizabeth. We might not get on all that well—we never really did, and the divorce reinforced the divide—but I know my father is no killer. He and Mom were going through a rough patch when he met Elizabeth and fell under the spell of all that money. Easy to do, I suspect." She laughed without mirth. "My brother, the so-called musician, is always looking for someone to be his sugar momma. I suspect that's the only reason he still went with Mom to her yacht club. It wasn't because he liked the people there. You'd think he'd have learned from Dad's example."

"In what way?"

"I'm beginning to think Dad regrets leaving us. Leaving Mom, I mean. He had absolutely no reason to kill her. The divorce was over, and they'd both moved on. As for Elizabeth . . ." Crystal shrugged. "She wasn't a nice person, and Dad was pretty darn unhappy in that marriage. He'd have left her soon enough—no need to get rid of her."

"You don't have to explain to me," I said.

"People can be mean once gossip and rumors start." Crystal let out a long sigh. "Poor Dad. Poor Brad. My mom loved us both equally, but Brad never believed that. He always thought I was the favorite." She accepted the package of books I handed her. "If Brad, who grew up with a chip on his shoulder, wants to let the past go, I should be able to. He wants me to make up with Dad. Maybe he's right; maybe it's time."

"For what it's worth," I said. "I don't think your father killed either of them. Certainly not your mother."

"Why do you say that?"

"I agree with you. He had no motive. Yes, people sometimes kill without what would look to others like a sensible reason, but when that happens, they're driven by sudden passion or rage. To do it calmly and lay a path of escape and not be detected requires some degree of presence of mind."

"You've spent some time thinking about this."

"I get curious sometimes. It means nothing."

She gave me a look I couldn't decipher. "Thanks for this. I'll drop by again before I leave."

On her way out, she passed Ashleigh coming back from dinner.

The shop was busy for the rest of the evening. I thought over what Crystal had said, but I couldn't see anything of relevance. If Dan Lamb did reconcile with his children, at least one good thing would come out of the two deaths. Quite often, families that had fallen out came together again in the face of tragedy.

I'd told Crystal I didn't think her father had killed either woman, and that was true. I shouldn't judge his character, having only met the man a handful of times, but I could see no reason for him to have murdered Kathy, the ex-wife, who was no threat to him. If he had, it would have been noisy and messy, the result of an argument out of control, not quiet and stealthy.

But Elizabeth? Yes, Dan might have killed Elizabeth and then run off into the night with me in pursuit. Maybe he thought, as I had, that Elizabeth had killed Kathy, and he wanted revenge.

"Basil Rathbone," Ashleigh said.

I blinked and returned to the here and now. "What about him?"

"Are we getting any more of those Basil Rathbone DVDs? The customer wants two sets for Christmas presents, and only one's on the shelf."

"Oh yes. Sorry. I have them on order. Should be in by Monday."

I forced my mind back to the running of my business and went to help a woman dithering over the young adult selection.

* * *

Ashleigh finished work at eight thirty, but before she left, she said, "I've had a great idea."

I tried not to groan. Ashleigh seemed to enjoy working here, and that was good. She was enthusiastic about our stock and keen to learn more about Sherlock Holmes and the books we sold, and that was also good. She had ideas for improving the business, some of which were not good—or at least not things I wanted to do. Such as open a second location or offer franchise opportunities.

I smiled at her. "What idea is that?"

"Have you considered stocking children's books?"

"We have children's books. Ones that suit the theme of our store."

"Those are YA—young adults. I mean real children's books, like with the alphabet and primary colors and lots of pictures. I know it's not what we're about, but those women just now were looking for gifts for a baby shower. They're hardly going to buy a biography of Sir Arthur Conan Doyle or *The Complete Sherlock Holmes*, volumes one and two, for a newborn."

I opened my mouth to say that wasn't our business, but shut it again.

I didn't think there was a Sherlock Holmes alphabet book, although just about everything else that could feature the Great Detective did. People came into a bookshop looking for books. If I could offer them board books for infants, maybe they'd pick up something for themselves as well. "That might be worth considering."

Ashleigh grinned.

"Do we have the space for another line of stock?"

"If you moved that shelf further down the wall, we could fit in a low rack. Get in a few books to start and see how they do."

"Let me think about your idea. On Sunday, I'll have some time to check out children's book catalogs."

She bade me a cheerful good night and left.

It had been a good day. A steady stream of people had come through our doors, and most of them bought. Some bought a lot.

Great-Uncle Arthur might not be much of a businessman, but he'd accidently hit on a great idea when he'd opened this store. If there was anything like a sure bet in this world, the continued popularity of Sherlock Holmes was it. After a hundred and thirty years, the craze showed no signs of dying down. If anything, it kept getting stronger.

At nine o'clock on the dot, I locked the door and flipped the sign to "Closed. I took most of the day's cash and receipt slips out of the register, switched off all the lights except for the ones behind the sales counter and in the display window, and climbed the seventeen steps to my office. Before going home, I needed to place orders for books we were running low on. Moriarty followed me upstairs. Not because he liked my company, but because my last task of the day was always to fill his food bowl.

I didn't bother to turn the office light on. The last long traces of the setting sun lingered outside the windows, and that, combined with the glow from lamps on the street, gave me enough light to see by. I locked the money away, dropped behind my desk, and wiggled the mouse to bring the computer back to life. Moriarty leapt onto the desk and settled himself on the keyboard.

I pushed him off.

He came back.

I lifted him up and put him on the floor.

He returned.

"Enough of this," I said. "The sooner I get this work done, the sooner you'll be fed and I'll be out of your fur."

Very, very slowly, he stood, yawned mightily, stretched languorously, and leapt to the floor.

I opened my purchasing file.

From downstairs came the sound of breaking wood.

I stopped, my fingers poised over the keys. I glanced at Moriarty. He stared into the hallway, his ears up, his whiskers twitching, the long hairs along his back standing at attention.

I got slowly to my feet. I slipped off my shoes and silently crossed the floor. I pulled my phone out of my pocket and held it in my left hand.

I took care not to make a sound as I crept to the top of the staircase.

I heard nothing but the soft murmur of cars driving past on the street. I held my breath for a long time. All was quiet.

The building that houses the Emporium was once a house, before Baker Street became the main shopping area of West London. It was built at the beginning of the twentieth century and still has many of the original features, such as wide-planked floorboards and foot-high baseboards. Over the years, the old wood has shifted and settled and shifted again. Some of the floorboards are coming loose. The worst one is by the back door, behind the YA bookshelves. Step on it just so, and it makes a noise as though it's about to break right though.

It creaked now.

I breathed softly.

I should have called nine-one-one from the landline in my office. I wouldn't have to say anything: just keep the line open and they'd come. The same couldn't be said for my cell phone; I didn't know if they'd be able to trace its location fast enough. The intruder might be a common thief, thinking the shop was closed, everyone gone home, and this a good time to rifle the cash register. If so, I didn't want him to know I was here. He was welcome to the ninety-seven dollars and sixty-five cents in cash that I'd left.

It was also possible I'd stirred something with my questions about the deaths of Elizabeth Dumont and

Kathy Lamb, and if so, I wanted to know what I'd stirred. And, more importantly, whom.

I moved carefully, knowing the location of every creaky board on the steps. I didn't have anything at hand I could use as a weapon, but I was counting on my knowing how to move silently and being able to get around this building in the dark to outmaneuver my opponent.

I put my foot over the edge of the bottom step, intending to place it in exactly the right spot so as to avoid the squeak of old wood. The light shifted as something moved in front of the sales counter. If I could get a peek around the wall, I'd be able to see who was there. Then I'd go upstairs and call nine-one-one. Very loudly.

A high-pitched screech sounded behind me, and I leapt into the air with a startled cry. A ball of black fur flew past my head, and my foot missed the step. I slipped, fell the rest of the way, and hit the floor hard, landing solidly on my rear end. I let out a grunt of shock and pain. Someone yelled in surprise mixed with pain of their own. Moriarty screeched again, and the intruder's voice rose.

Bright white light washed the inside of the shop. I heard a muffled cry, running footsteps, protesting floorboards, and then legs streaked past me. Too late, I reached out, but I only grabbed the soft night air.

Light filled the room. "Gemma! Gemma! Where are you?" Ryan called.

"Here," I croaked, struggling to my feet.

Ryan had his flashlight in one hand and his gun in the other. He shone the light into my face. "Are you all right, Gemma?"

"Sore bum," I said, rubbing the offending part.

"Call nine-one-one." And he and his light were gone.

I made the call, switching on lights as I talked. I told the operator an officer needed assistance at 222 Baker Street. Moriarty sat on the sales counter, rubbing his paws together.

"I suppose you think you saved my life or something," I said. "Not so. I was totally in control of the situation. I wanted to identify him. Or her."

"Who are you talking to, madam?" the 911 operator asked.

"My cat," I said. "I'm hanging up now; a cruiser's arrived."

I put my phone away and went to greet the responding officers. The back door, I wasn't surprised to see, had been smashed in. I had a quick look at the floor, but could see no identifiable prints. It hadn't rained for several days, and the streets were dry.

"Are you okay, Gemma?" Officer Johnson asked me.

"I'm fine." I stepped back to let her in. I tried not to limp. I'd suffered a most humiliating injury.

Ryan arrived at a trot, putting his gun back into its holster. "Streets are too busy. He got away. Gemma, did you recognize him? Anything at all familiar?"

"I didn't see him." I said. "Nothing but a black shape and legs in loose dark trousers. It might have been a woman."

"Could it have been the person you chased from Elizabeth Dumont's house?"

"That's possible. Likely even. Hard to tell, but I think they were much the same shape and size."

"I'm taking you home."

"I need to look around first. They might have left identifiable traces behind. Tell your officers to keep away until I've checked everything out."

Stella Johnson's eyebrows rose.

"I'll do nothing of the sort," Ryan said. "I want you out of here. Now. I've called forensics, and the K-9 unit is on its way. I don't want the dog recognizing you as a person of interest. Let's go." He turned to Johnson. "Get Detective Estrada down here. I want this treated as more than a break-in. It's to do with our homicide investigation."

"You got it, Detective," she said.

"Let's go, Gemma," Ryan said.

"But—" I said.

He grabbed my arm. "No *buts*."

Ryan almost dragged me out of the shop and stuffed me into his car. We drove the few blocks to my house in silence, both of us needing to process what had happened.

I unlocked the back door, aware of Ryan with his hand on the butt of his gun and his eyes checking out every dark corner or patch of bushes. Violet greeted us in her usual manner, and Ryan said, "No walk for her tonight. Let her do her business in the yard. Once she's back inside and you've locked up, I need to get back to town."

I didn't argue. Instead, in true English fashion, I immediately filled the kettle. "Your arrival was timely."

"Pure dumb luck. I finished up for the day and thought I'd drop in and give you a lift home. Maybe invite you out for a drink." He rubbed the stubble on his jaw. "You can imagine what I thought when I saw the back door smashed in and a dark figure running away."

"I can imagine."

"You couldn't identify anything about the intruder?"

"No. They were gone before I got more than a fleeting glimpse."

"All I saw was a blur. I must have scared him off."

I touched Ryan's face. I wouldn't mention that Moriarty had done the scaring. Moriarty had, uncharacteristically, saved me from a potentially violent encounter. But he'd gotten rid of the intruder before I could identify him. I began to ask myself if that had been his intention, but then I remembered Moriarty was a cat.

Ryan reached up and took my hand. "Are you okay, Gemma? It's okay to be in shock, you know."

And then, suddenly, I was. My legs gave way, and I dropped into a chair. My stiff upper lip collapsed, and I cried in great heaving gulps. Ryan held me for a long time.

At last, I pulled away and dug in my pocket for a tissue. I blew my nose, wiped my eyes, and gathered my composure. "It might have been a thief, chancing his luck for tomorrow's float of ninety-seven dollars and sixty-five cents."

"Mustn't forget the sixty-five cents," Ryan said. "But far more likely to be someone wanting you out of the Lamb case."

"Someone who thinks I'm a lot closer to solving it than I am," I said.

"They're going to get their way. No more, Gemma. Stay out of it. Completely out. I mean it."

"Okay," I said.

He gave me a doubtful look.

"I'm getting nowhere, Ryan. Absolutely nowhere. There are too many people and too many threads to sort out. The museum, two yacht clubs, the family—never mind the ubiquitous person or persons unknown—and lingering suspicions about the death of Elizabeth's first husband." I had something to tell him about that, but decided it could wait. He had enough on his plate to deal with tonight. "Two dead women, both of whom were known by a great many people and weren't much liked by many of them.

"I'm good at reading people and observing details others don't see, but I don't have any of your resources. Solid, determined police work is the way to get to the bottom of this."

"And solid, determined police work is what I'm going back to do. If we're lucky, we'll find some forensic evidence, or the dog will pick up the trail. I want you to lock up, leave the outside lights on, and stay inside. Can you do that?"

I gave him a mock salute and was pleased to get a wry grin in return.

"You're on guard, Violet," he said. "Don't let me down."

She wagged her tail happily.

Chapter Twenty

I meant what I said when I said it, but try as I might, I couldn't stop thinking about what had happened. Clearly, I'd put a fright into someone, and they'd come to the shop intending to put a stop to my investigation. One way or another.

But who?

I took my cup of tea and book into the den and curled up in the wingback chair while Violet snoozed at my feet. I didn't get much reading done.

The line of suspects marched in front of my eyes. I tried to imagine each of them stealing across the wooden floors of the Emporium, wrapped in darkness, crossing in front of the faint lights, but nothing, and no one, became clear.

Breaking into my shop, presumably to do me harm, was a drastic step. Drastic steps were taken by desperate people.

That the guilty party thought I was getting close didn't mean I was. As the saying goes, *the guilty run when no one pursues*. But something, I thought, had to have happened to cause the killer to commit that desperate act tonight.

Two things of significance had happened today: my chat with Jock O'Callaghan at the West London Yacht Club and Crystal Lamb's visit to the Emporium.

Jock had not been the person in the shop tonight. Not with his broken ankle.

Was it broken? I made a mental note to ask Ryan to check on that tomorrow. It was possible Jock had pretended to break it at the tennis game and was carted off in full view of the members of the club, only to have a miraculous recovery. He'd been wearing a boot cast, but he might have access to one unofficially. He'd supposedly had the break Tuesday afternoon, the day before Elizabeth died.

Seemed like a lot of trouble to go to. He couldn't have known Jayne and I would show up only minutes after the murder and he'd have to run.

Crystal had pointed out that I'd been thinking about the case, but that wasn't any secret. I'd been asking a lot of questions of a lot of people, and it didn't have to be something that happened today that sparked the attempted attack on me.

I reminded myself that I was out of it. I'd mention the conversation with Crystal to Ryan in the morning, perhaps suggest he take a closer look into her background.

I closed my book, having not read a word, and called Violet to bed.

Before settling for the night, I checked the locks on all the doors and windows and made sure every outside light was switched on.

* * *

I arrived at the shop the following morning with some trepidation, fearing to see the place strung with yellow police tape, cruisers parked willy-nilly on the sidewalk, and crowds of gawkers standing outside.

Instead, everything looked normal. I let myself in by the sliding door that adjoined the tearoom, giving Fiona a wave, and walked through the clean, quiet shop to the back, wondering why Moriarty hadn't come out to give me my morning hiss of greeting. My phone rang as I was admiring the solid wood panels of my new back door.

"Morning, Gemma," Ryan said. "I'm guessing you aren't letting last night's business upset you enough to miss work."

"I'm at the shop now. I assume I have you to thank for the new door?"

"I'll drop off the keys later. I'm sorry to report we didn't find anything of significance. Your intruder didn't have time to get far into the shop or do much of anything. Oh, your cat's upstairs, locked in a closet. Officer Johnson's nursing some bad scratches, and the K-9 handler has a highly traumatized dog on his hands. Moriarty didn't like having the dog in his shop."

"Oops," I said, as a howl of indignation came from overhead. "Two things occurred to me last night while I was not thinking about the case. Jock O'Callaghan appears to have broken his ankle. That would exclude him from running from me at Elizabeth's and from breaking into the shop last night. Can you check with the hospital that it was a real break and not just a minor sprain? It happened Tuesday afternoon at the yacht club, and he was taken to hospital in an ambulance."

"Jock O'Callaghan? Yeah, I can check with the hospital. You said two things?"

"Crystal Lamb came into the shop yesterday evening. She talked to me about her father, said she doesn't believe he killed anyone."

"I paid a call on Dan Lamb first thing this morning. He didn't have an alibi for last night at nine, says he was home alone. But that doesn't mean anything. He's not exactly a popular guy around town these days."

"He was alone? By home, do you mean Elizabeth's house? I heard he'd moved back."

"Yes," Ryan said.

"Where was his son?"

"Out with friends, Dan said. He wasn't there this morning either."

"Crystal told me she's going to try to rebuild their relationship."

"Good for her. Families are important. Dan mentioned to me that he's planning to venture out in public later today and go sailing with Brad. I said that's a good idea; some of the best times my dad and I ever had were on his boat. You be careful, Gemma. We can't assume this person has been scared off."

"I will," I said.

It was Saturday, and Ashleigh and I were kept on the hop all day. At twenty-two minutes to four, I was looking forward to a cup of tea and a plate of leftover sandwiches.

"Got it," Ashleigh said, without so much as looking up from the shelf she was straightening.

"Got what?"

"You're going next door for your daily partners' meeting, aka gossip session, with Jayne."

"It is a partners' meeting. We're partners, and good business partners need to communicate regularly if they want to keep the business on sound footing."

"Whatever. Why'd you replace the back door?"

"The old one had a crack in it. As you surmised, I'm going next door."

"I hear the clock sounding the time."

"Most amusing." I considered asking Jayne if we could move our meeting time back by ten minutes. I didn't like to think I was getting too predictable.

The tearoom was busy, and the seats in the window alcove taken, so I went into the kitchen. Jocelyn was taking dishes out of the dishwasher, and Jayne was putting them away.

"Good day?" I asked.

"Run off our feet," Jayne said. "Did something happen last night at the bookstore? When I got here this morning, a police car was parked outside."

"Someone tried to break in," I said. "They were scared off."

"Can't imagine what they were after in your store," Jocelyn said. "I don't think books do all that well on the black market, do they?"

"The sort of books I sell don't, but that's something I hadn't considered. Someone might have heard about *The Valley of Fear* being offered at the auction and thought the shop stocks items of that value."

"Yeah," Jocelyn said. "I saw it listed on the auction sheet. Hard to imagine someone paying twelve thousand bucks for an old book."

"As usual, you're overthinking it," Jayne said to me. "It's more likely someone broke in looking for cash. Some druggie needing a fix."

"Sad," Jocelyn said. "They'd be better off breaking in here, getting themselves something to eat."

"Please don't make that suggestion publicly," Jayne said.

"Sorry."

"I'm starving," I said. "I don't see so much as the makings of a cup of tea in here."

"Busy day," Jayne said. "But I'm sure we can find you something."

"Speaking of selling things," Jocelyn said, "that reminds me. I totally forgot. A woman came in this morning and asked if we had any more of those hanging teacup chains. She saw them when she was here for the auction, didn't buy it because of what happened and then the place being locked down, and now she'd like to get one."

Jayne suppressed a shudder. "We had only the one left, and I threw it away. I won't be ordering any more, but I can give you the name of the woman who makes them if she'd like to order directly."

"Why'd you throw it away?" Jocelyn said. "I thought they were nice."

"Bad vibes," Jayne said.

"Okay, I guess," Jocelyn said. "What about the one Kathy Lamb was going to buy? It might still be around somewhere."

That was news to me. "What was Kathy going to buy?"

"One of those teacup chains." Dishwasher empty, Jocelyn began wiping down the counters. "When the auction was over. Obviously that didn't happen, so I thought if you still had it, we could sell it to someone else."

"How do you know Kathy wanted one?" I asked.

"She took it down off the wall and told me she'd settle up at the end of the event."

"When was this?" My heart began to speed up.

"It must have been only minutes before she died." Jocelyn shook her head. "So I guess I can see what you mean about bad vibes. When I passed her in the hall, she was taking that ugly painting of Maureen's into the back. She put the painting down for a second and took the chain off the hook. She said she loved its whimsy."

"What did she do with it?"

"She took it into the back with her, I think. We were busy—it was time to start serving. I didn't pay much attention."

"Jocelyn," I said, "did you tell the police this?"

"I told them I'd passed Kathy in the hall. I told you that too."

"Did you tell them specifically about the chain?"

Her face crinkled in thought. "I don't know. I might have. Maybe not."

"You didn't tell us," Jayne said.

"Does it matter?" Jocelyn asked. "It wasn't important. Just a brief word when I was so busy. I didn't even stop walking to talk to her."

"When the police ask you to tell them everything you remember, no matter how unimportant it might seem, they really do mean everything," I said.

"Oh," she said. "Sorry. Should I call them now?"

"I'll do it. Forget about my tea." I left the kitchen and broke into a run as I passed through the dining room.

Jayne caught up with me on the sidewalk, still wearing her apron. "It matters, doesn't it, that Kathy took a teacup chain into the back with her?"

"It matters a heck of a lot." I pulled out my phone. "I've been working on the assumption that the killer accessed the storage room from the hallway. That they grabbed the decoration off the wall as they passed. Meaning, they were a guest at the tea. If, as it now appears, Kathy had the thing with her, everything's up in the air again. The back door was left unlocked. Someone, anyone, could have come in with the intention of stealing something, surprised Kathy, and used the first thing that came to hand."

"The teacup chain."

"Yes. Ryan, it's Gemma," I spoke to voicemail. "I've learned something that might be significant in the death of Kathy Lamb. Call me."

Jayne and I stood on the sidewalk. Pedestrians walked around us. A couple checked the menu on the tearoom window, and the woman said, "They're closing soon. Let's come back tomorrow." A middle-aged couple trailed by a couple of scowling, slouching teenage boys passed us. One of the teens moaned, "You don't need to be so mean, Dad."

"I told you, we can't afford it."

"But all the kids . . ." The boy's grating voiced died away as the family continued on their way.

Another family group—mum, dad, grandparents, three cute little kids—went into the Emporium. The father reached down and tussled the dark curly hair on one child's head. The boy looked up at him and grinned.

Happy families. Cute kids. Surly, whining teenagers. How children change as they grow.

I headed down Baker Street, walking fast.

Jayne followed. "Where are you going?"

"I've an idea."

"Are you going to tell me what that idea is?"

"Occam's razor."

"Meaning?"

"Meaning, Jayne, you're right. I've been complicating this case far too much. The death of Kathy Lamb was nothing more than a robbery interrupted and a panicked thief."

"Meaning it might have been anyone?"

"Yes. Except for the subsequent murder of Elizabeth Dumont. Once one has killed, and apparently gotten away with it, it becomes a great deal easier to kill a second time. The death of Kathy might not have been intended, but the murder of Elizabeth was. And it was done by the same person." I broke into a run as we reached Harbor Road. Jayne ran along beside me.

"Do you know who this person is?" she asked.

"Yes."

"Are you going to tell me?"

"Not yet."

"Are you going to at least tell me where we're going?"

"Not far."

"Why are we going there? Wherever 'there' is."

"Now that I know what questions to ask, I intend to ask them."

"Shouldn't we wait for Ryan to call you back?"

"I'm only going to ask a few subtle questions, Jayne. You don't have to come."

"'Subtle' is not your middle name. Someone has to keep you out of trouble. Might as well be me."

We ran past the stores lining the boardwalk, the harbor, and the fish pier, bobbing and weaving through crowds of holidaymakers. The shops and restaurants ended, and the houses began. Past my street, Blue Water Place, to the grounds of Scarlet House. Robyn Kirkpatrick and Sharon Musgrave were standing outside the house with a group of men in muddy construction boots and hard hats. Robyn held an iPad, and Sharon looked over her shoulder while one of the men pointed to the screen.

I kept going.

I darted across the street at the entrance to the Cape Cod Yacht Club to the accompaniment of honking horns. "Close one," Jayne said when she'd caught up to me.

It was shortly after four o'clock, and the sea was dotted with white sails. Many of them were heading toward the harbor ahead of the line of heavy dark clouds building on the horizon. We climbed the steps and went into the club building. People, in what passes for nautical attire among the well-heeled set, milled about, greeting friends and exchanging air kisses. The bar looked to be busy, and waiters were laying starched white cloths on tables in one of the conference rooms.

I spoke to Jayne. "You might want to take your apron off."

"Oh. Forgot I was wearing it." She untied the sash, slipped it off, and rolled it into a ball. "What am I going to do with it?"

I took it out of her hands and stuffed it into the base of a potted plant. I then went up to the reception desk and spoke to the young woman behind it. "Hi. I'm looking for Dan Lamb. He took his boat out earlier; do you know if he's come back yet?"

If he hadn't, I'd wait.

"I saw Mr. Lamb not more than a few minutes ago, going out to the veranda," she said helpfully. "The rain's about to hit, but much of the outdoor seating area is covered if you'd like to join him."

"Thank you."

I headed for the French doors leading outside. The veranda doubled as an open-air bar and restaurant, and it was almost full. I spotted Dan Lamb and his two children at a small table next to the railing. They sat stiffly in their chairs, Dan and Brad reasonably close together; but Crystal's chair was so far away, she was halfway to the next table. People seated nearby whispered across their wine glasses and beer bottles and threw the Lambs surreptitious glances.

"What's the plan of attack?" Jayne whispered.

"Attack, of course," I replied. I marched across the deck, Jayne scurrying along behind. I stopped at the Lamb table. Three sets of identical eyes looked up at me.

"Good afternoon," I said.

"Oh, Gemma," Crystal said. "Hello. I didn't know you were a member here."

"Just visiting. May we join you? Such a nice day." Without waiting for an answer, I dropped into the vacant chair.

"May I?" Jayne said to the people at the next table. Tendrils of her fair hair had come loose as we ran through town, and they moved in the strong wind coming off the sea.

"Help yourself," they said, and she pulled a chair up beside me. She gave Dan Lamb an awkward smile.

The veranda of the yacht club rests only a few yards from the closest dock. A wood and glass railing, a patch of perfectly maintained lawn, a line of flower beds, and then the dock itself. A motorboat pulled up, and a young man dressed in a T-shirt and shorts in the club's colors ran over and grabbed the rope thrown to him. He looped it loosely around a pillar while the three passengers cautiously disembarked.

A fishing charter slipped into the space behind it. It had three big engines attached to the back, with a line of fishing poles mounted on the roof. Four men in their late forties, tall and trim, with short gray hair and light tans disembarked. They had no fish with them, so I assumed they'd not had a good day. But it didn't seem to matter as they thanked the young man for his help, shook his hand—while passing on the tip—slapped each other on the backs, and headed for the bar. The young man secured the craft and then cracked open a beer and put his feet up.

I smiled at the Lamb family. "Lovely day, isn't it. You've been out on your boat, I hear. Did you enjoy it, Brad?"

"Uh, yeah. It's a really great boat, a thirty-footer, a heck of a lot better than the one Dad had to sell after the divorce." He added quickly, "It was nice to spend some time with my dad too."

"I'm sorry," Dan said, "but I'm enjoying some private time with my family. If you brought the book, you can leave it with me." He held out his hand. "I won't keep you."

"Book? Oh, that book. Sorry, forgot it. Crystal came into my shop yesterday evening."

"So I did," she said. "And I bought a book."

"Two books."

"Two books," she said. "I don't see what that has to do with anything."

"Did you pay a call on your family after?" I asked.

She exchanged glances with her father and brother. "What are you getting at? And perhaps more to the point, why is it any of your business?"

"Funny how these things work. I'd decided it was none of my business. The murders of Kathy Lamb and Elizabeth Dumont, that is. I was getting nowhere and realized it was time to leave it up to the police."

"Probably a good idea," Dan said. "What changed your mind?"

"I had a late-night visitor yesterday at my store. Someone who accessed the premises by breaking down the back door rather than politely ringing the bell, so I assume that person meant me no good."

I studied their faces. Dan looked surprised, but not much caring. Crystal appeared genuinely shocked. Bradley's eyes narrowed, and he sat closer to the edge of his chair. He drummed the fingers of his left hand on the table in a rapid rhythm. With his right hand, he lifted his beer bottle and took a long, deep slug.

"How'd you get that cut on your hand?" I asked.

He paled and looked at his right hand. "Don't know," he mumbled.

"It looks like a cat scratch to me. A bad one. Deep enough to draw blood. Recent too. My shop cat's got a foul temper, and he attacked the intruder. The police will be able to get DNA traces off his claws."

I hadn't been sure. Every conclusion I'd come to was nothing but speculation and, although I'd never admit it, guesses. But now, looking at Brad's face, watching the movement of his fingers, seeing the scratch on his hand (so similar to the ones Moriarty regularly gave me), I knew I was right.

"Crystal told you I'd been informally investigating your mother's murder, didn't she, Bradley?"

He shrugged, trying to look casual, but the twitching movements gave him away. "We talked about lot of things." He rubbed at his hand. "This cut, yeah, now I remember. I scratched my hand on a loose nail somewhere. I'm not submitting to any DNA test, if that's what you're suggesting. I know my rights. Where's that waiter? I need another beer."

"I went around to Elizabeth's house—Dad's house, I mean, after talking to you," Crystal said. "I thought it was time we had a family chat. My mom's dead, and nothing can bring her back, but we can try to honor her memory by being a family again. She'd want that. I gave Dad one of the books I'd bought, as a way of starting to clear the air between us. I might have mentioned to Dad and Brad what you told me. What of it?"

"You're a heavy smoker, Brad," I said. Signs informed me that smoking was not allowed on the veranda or anywhere in the club, but the heavy scent clung to Brad's clothes even after a day on the water.

"So are a lot of people," he said.

"Elizabeth, for one."

"I wanted her to quit," Dan said. "I told her she was taking years off her life, but Elizabeth didn't like to be told what to do."

"The scent of tobacco was so strong in her house, it was impossible for me to tell that another smoker had recently been there."

"When were you in her house?" Crystal asked.

I didn't answer her, as Brad had pushed his chair back and started to rise. "I'm outta here," he said.

"Sit down, Bradley," Dan said. "We're going to listen to what this woman has to say."

Brad hesitated, and then he dropped back down.

"Did your stepmother tell you what sort of things she got for the auction?" I asked Brad. "Or were you just trying your luck?"

"I've no idea what you're going on about," he said.

"The charity auction at Mrs. Hudson's Tearoom. The day your stepmother died. You went into the back room before the auction started. There's no point in denying it. It took awhile, but I managed to find someone who saw you in the alley."

"I wanted to say hi to Kathy." Brad looked everywhere but at the people seated at his table. "She was busy, so I left."

"You didn't tell me that," Dan said.

"Gee, Dad, you were kinda busy with your new wife."

"There were some valuable items in that room," I said. "Small portable things that could be fenced. Jewelry, rare books."

"I don't like what you're implying," Dan said.

"Implying?" I said. "I'm not *implying* anything. I'm saying that chronically short-of-funds Brad found out where some small expensive items could be had for the taking and came to the tearoom intending to steal something. Instead, Kathy arrived unexpectedly and found him there. Did she realize right away what you were up to, Brad?"

"You're dreaming, lady."

"The police found your fingerprints on one of the little teacups on the chain."

"They couldn't have. I wore—"

"Gloves?" I said. I let silence fall over the table. A range of emotions flew across Brad's face. Anger, defiance. Then, finally, sadness.

"I didn't mean it," he said, his voice very low. "Yeah, I came in. Figured I'd try my chances, like, and nab one of those pieces of jewelry before anyone saw me. I had a quick look in the front window, and everyone was getting ready for the fancy tea." He lifted his chin. "Bunch of rich people playing at being generous. If they wanted to give something away, they might as well give it to me, right? I needed it more than that stupid museum."

"Oh, Brad," Crystal said. Dan had slumped forward, his face in his hands.

"Kathy came in. She was already flaming mad about something, and she started in on me. Called me a loser, a liar. She threatened to call the cops. I told her to calm down. She just got madder. She was always on my case, always comparing me to her precious daughter. Nothing I did was ever good enough for her."

"That's not true. Mom—" Crystal began. Dan put his hand on her arm.

"She started waving that stupid piece of rope around and those small teacups were making a racket. I grabbed her hands, to get her to be quiet, to stop the noise, to put a stop to her constant nagging. Somehow . . . I don't know, I got hold of it and . . . then she was on the floor. Not moving. So I ran outta there."

Dan groaned.

"You aren't going to tell anyone, are you, Dad, Crystal? You don't want me to go to jail. It was an accident. No one will believe what this woman says. I'll deny it."

"Deny it if you want," I said. "I do believe you didn't intend to kill Kathy. It was sad, it was tragic, but not your intent, and you'll have to live with that. Elizabeth, however, was a different story, wasn't she?"

Dan lifted his head. "What about Elizabeth?" he said slowly. All the color had drained from his face.

"When Detective Ashburton phoned you after the discovery of Elizabeth's body, Dan, he didn't know where you were staying, so he couldn't pop in unannounced, as he would have preferred to. He wouldn't have told you on the phone why he wanted to talk to you. But Brad already knew, didn't he? Thus he needed to set up an alibi."

Dan looked at his son. "You said the cops were determined to pin Kathy's death on me. That it would be easier if we said we'd been together that night, in case they said they saw someone burying evidence or something. Maybe they were planning to frame me, to get the case over with, you said. So that's what I told them, when they asked, that you were with me all evening. I was in such shock when they said Elizabeth was dead, I didn't realize the obvious. In providing me with an alibi, you ensured that I gave you one."

"Bradley," Crystal said, "is this true?"

"Of course not. This woman's off her rocker."

A man walked onto the deck. His hair was mussed, his face ruddy with exercise, his boat shoes wet. Jack Templeton. He glanced around the room, spotted Jayne, and his face broke into a huge smile. He headed our way.

Not a good time for company.

Deep in my pocket, my phone sounded the tune I'd set for Ryan's calls. I didn't answer, but said to Jayne without looking at her, "Would you try that number I couldn't get earlier. Thanks."

"You needed money," Crystal said to her brother. "You came to me last week, begging for a loan. Another loan. Another chance to get your failure of a band back together, and this time you were sure to hit the big time. Finally, I said no. I've given you plenty over the years, and I'm finished with your promises and your wild schemes. And so your greed killed my mother. But that wasn't enough, was it? You went after Elizabeth too. Did you ask her for money and get mad when she laughed in your face?"

"You're not listening to her, are you?" Brad grabbed his beer and sucked at the empty bottle. "She's crazy."

"We're at the Cape Cod Yacht Club," Jayne said quietly into her phone. "I think you'd better get down here."

Dan stood up. Crystal started to cry.

"Hi, Jayne," Jack said. "This is a surprise. What brings you here?"

"Uh," she said.

"The police are on their way," I said. "Why don't we all wait here?"

"Police?" Concern crossed Jack's handsome face. "Is there a problem?"

"No problem," I said. "But Jayne needs a drink. Why don't you get the waiter?"

Everything I'd said to Brad about physical evidence was a lie. I had nothing but my observations of his mannerisms and guesses as to his character, but he was jumpy and inclined to take action without thinking things over first. I was counting on that. It worked better than I expected.

He leapt to his feet, knocking his chair over. With a yell of rage, he threw the bottle of beer at my head. Fortunately, I read his movements in time and ducked. It hit the floor behind me and shattered. Dan shouted, Crystal screamed, Jayne jumped up, and heads at nearby tables began to turn.

"Hey!" Jack lifted his hands, and Brad punched him full in the face. Jack went down hard.

Brad vaulted over the railing separating the veranda from the grass and took off toward the dock. With slightly less agility, I clambered over the barrier and jumped. A stab of pain in my hip reminded me that I'd suffered a minor injury last night, but I was able to ignore it, and I ran after him. I heard a soft grunt as Jayne hit the ground behind me.

Two boats were parked at the dock. One of them was the fishing boat. The man with the beer had finished his drink, untied his boat, and was perched on the gunwales, preparing to shove off. Before he knew what was happening, Brad had vaulted into the craft and was on him. The guy went over the side with a yell and a splash. He must have left the keys in the ignition, as a moment later the boat started with a roar and pulled away from the dock, going much too fast and barely missing the bow of a smaller boat heading in.

A party had finished disembarking from a Sea Ray Sundancer, a sports cruiser, brilliant white with black trim, diving platform at the back, comfortable seats, and plenty of room below for relaxing, cooking, sleeping. The valet got in, ready to take it to mooring. I scrambled on board. "Follow that boat."

"What the heck?"

"West London Police!" I shouted. I then continued in a lower voice, "They're on their way. We have to follow him."

"You got it, ma'am," he said.

I hadn't stated that I was with the police. I'd merely made a statement of fact. If he chose to interpret my words that way in the heat of the moment, who was I to argue?

I didn't want Jayne to come, but she was stranded half on and half off the boat. If we pulled away, she'd end up in the water. I grabbed her arm and pulled her aboard. "Tell Ryan what's happening. Tell him we're in pursuit and to get a police launch out there to intercept."

We leapt over the wake left by Brad's boat and roared through the rows of docks to the mouth of the harbor. I glanced back to see people on shore waving their arms and jumping up and down, yelling. I toppled over as we made a sharp turn. "Sorry," I called to the frightened group in the sailboat we'd almost collided with. A paunchy, red-faced man in a too-small swimming costume shook his fist in reply.

"Your people had better be quick," my captain said.

"Why?"

"That's a Fountain Bluewater; they're built for speed. It's a faster boat than ours for one thing, but mainly because this one's almost out of gas. I was taking it to fill it up."

Brad roared out of the harbor. We were close behind, but the distance between us was widening.

"Just keep him in sight until the police or Coast Guard can get in position. I'm Gemma, by the way, and that's Jayne."

"He wants to talk to you." Jayne tried to hand me her phone.

"Probably not a good time," I said.

"Dave," said my pilot. "I can't wait to tell my buddies about this." He shouted into the wind.

We were heading straight out to sea. "I don't like the look of those clouds," Dave said.

"No kidding," Jayne said. A dark boiling mass filled the horizon directly in front of us. It was a lot closer than it had appeared from the comfort of the sunny veranda of the Cape Cod Yacht Club.

"A minor disturbance," I said, as drops of rain began to fall. "It'll soon pass."

"I guess you English people know all about the ways of the sea," Dave said.

"Don't you?" Jayne asked.

"Heck no. I'm from Kansas. This is my first summer in West London. I've been working at the yacht club for two weeks. Haven't been out of the harbor before."

"Perhaps you should try to get Uncle Arthur on the line, Jayne," I said. "In case we need some nautical advice."

"Advice like not to steer directly into a storm?"

A helicopter flew low overhead. I waved at it and pointed to the boat in front of us.

"It is okay, right, that I took this boat out without the owner's permission?" Dave said. "You're going to tell them you impounded it, right?"

"We're not—" Jayne said.

"Sure," I said as the rain began to fall harder.

"Where do you suppose he thinks he's going?" Jayne said. "This isn't exactly the Caribbean, with thousands of tiny uninhabited islands to hide in where he can live off coconuts and rainwater."

"He's not thinking," I said. "He's panicked and running blindly."

"What'd he do?" Dave asked.

I didn't answer. With the rain came wind and high waves. Brad's boat raced over the seas, and ours followed. I braced myself against the railing. Jayne's face was turning green. She lowered herself into a seat, phone gripped in her hand. I glanced anxiously around for the police or Coast Guard, but all I could see was moving clouds and darkening seas.

I'd chased after Brad without thinking things through. That might have been a mistake. He couldn't get away, but who knows what he might do if he found himself cornered.

"Back off," I said. "Give it up."

"What?" Dave said.

"The authorities have been notified. They're on their way."

"Aren't you the cops?" The engine coughed. "Moot point anyway. We're outta gas." Our boat began to slow.

"There!" Jayne yelled.

A Coast Guard cutter was coming in fast from the east. Another moved on us from the north. They were on a path to intercept Brad. The helicopter reappeared and circled low overhead.

Our boat slowed to a stop. The three of us stood in the bow, watching. The wind whipped at my hair, and salt spray stung my face.

We could see activity on the deck of the Coast Guard ships as they approached Brad's boat. He maneuvered to his right, searching for an escape route. But he couldn't outrun his bigger, faster pursuers, and he knew it. His boat gradually lost speed and drifted to a halt. The smaller of the Coast Guard ships came alongside.

"We have company." Dave turned and pointed behind us.

A much smaller WLPD launch was approaching. Ryan Ashburton stood in the bow. He was not smiling.

They came alongside. An officer threw a rope, and Dave caught it and tied it on. The boats shifted and buckled in the wind, but the rain was already moving on, the wind dropping, the waves dying. The moment the boats touched, Ryan leapt nimbly aboard.

"Hi," Jayne said.

"I'm glad you decided to stay out of it, Gemma," Ryan said. "Otherwise, who knows what trouble you might find yourself in."

"That was exciting," Dave said to me. "Anytime you need help, Officer, I'm your man."

"Uh . . ." I said.

Chapter
Twenty-One

"Occam's razor. In the end, it was all pretty simple. Brad didn't intend to kill Kathy, but they'd always had a difficult relationship, stepmother and stepson, and he resented what he thought was her preference for her own daughter. Crystal maintains that Kathy loved both children equally, but it was getting difficult not to favor one over the other as the children grew up. Crystal had a successful career; Brad was down and out, desperately wanting to start yet another band." I rubbed Violet's head. "Kathy must have been beyond furious when she came across him intending to steal from her museum fund-raiser. She was angry enough after the altercation with Maureen and not inclined to back down a second time. She told him what she thought of him, and he pulled the teacup chain out of her hands and used it to stop her talking. On purpose or not, she died. Then, when he seemed to be getting away with it, and he was presented with another obstacle, killing a second time wasn't so difficult."

"The obstacle being Elizabeth?" Jayne selected a sandwich from the picnic basket.

To the casual observer, we would have appeared to be a cheerful group of friends enjoying a picnic lunch on the lawn of the West London Lighthouse on a pleasant Sunday afternoon. The casual observer would not have guessed we were discussing murder and motives.

Ryan had not exactly been happy with me yesterday after the boat chase and the arrest of Bradley Lamb. I'm sure he briefly considering letting me be arrested for stealing a boat, kidnapping its pilot, and impersonating a police officer. But after our disabled craft was towed to shore, he gritted his teeth and managed to convince the boat's owner that I'd been attempting to make a citizen's arrest. Fortunately, the boat itself had not been damaged, and the owner was a big fan of vintage TV cop shows. "Like being in an episode of *Miami Vice*," I heard him say to Ryan.

"What's a Miami vice?" Jayne whispered to me.

Ryan walked away, without another word, to follow the car taking Brad into town, and left Jayne and me to be escorted to the police station by Louise Estrada. Jack Templeton, streaks of blood on his shirt and his eye turning all sorts of colors, tried to intervene, but Estrada barked at him to back off.

"I'll explain later," Jayne said, giving him a huge smile. Jack had been injured simply because he'd been in Brad's way, but no doubt the incident would soon loom large in Jack's mind as a valiant attempt to save her.

Ryan had not joined Estrada for our interrogation, and I thought that was not a good sign.

But he'd called me as I was opening the store the next day and suggested an impromptu late picnic lunch with anyone who might be interested in the case. Shortly before the appointed time, I left Ashleigh to mind the store and went home to get Violet, knowing she'd enjoy the company and the outing.

While I'd been debating over asking Andy to join us, Jayne had called Jack, and he arrived at the tearoom as I was leaving. I had to admit, his face looked pretty bad, bruised and swollen, but he carried his injuries like a badge of honor, and Jayne kept throwing him radiant smiles.

Once again, my plans for Jayne's love life had been dealt a setback.

At home, I grabbed a couple of blankets to provide seating, and Violet and I walked back to town. As well as Jayne and Jack and an overflowing picnic basket, I found Grant, Irene, and Donald waiting at the lighthouse. I laid out the blankets, and we sat down. Grant stretched his long legs out on the grass with a contented sigh, and Donald instantly reached for the basket. Jayne slapped his hand. "We're waiting for Ryan. Here they come now."

To my considerable surprise Louise Estrada was with Ryan. She greeted the others warmly, even Violet to whom she gave a tap on the head. Then she looked at me and said in a low voice, "Nicely done." It was an effort, I thought, for her to get the words out, and I smiled my thanks.

And so we were now gathered on the sunny lawn of the West London Lighthouse around a picnic hamper full of Mrs. Hudson's goodies. When Jayne nodded to Donald, he opened the basket and began handing around wrapped sandwiches and bottles of lemonade or iced tea. He was wearing his favorite T-shirt today, the one that said, "You know my methods." The shirt was starting to look worn, and a small tear had appeared at the hem.

I accepted a sandwich but didn't open it. "The obstacle being Elizabeth," I said in answer to Jayne's question. "Again, the simplest and most obvious of motives: money. And of suspects: the victim's nearest and, although not in this case, dearest. Elizabeth was going to divorce Dan. She wanted nothing from him but total devotion, and he couldn't give it because he regretted leaving Kathy. Elizabeth knew that now Kathy was dead, she'd only loom larger, and ever more perfect, in Dan's mind. Dan and Kathy pretty much wiped themselves out financially, fighting their divorce. Kathy had to sell her house and move into a small apartment, and was about to lose her membership at the yacht club because she could no longer afford the fees. Dan found himself penniless and financially dependent on Elizabeth. Dan and Elizabeth hadn't been married long; if she divorced him, he'd be left with pretty much nothing. Brad didn't want that to happen."

"So he killed Elizabeth," Grant said.

"He's probably going to argue that it was an accident." I glanced at Ryan. He nodded but said nothing. "But I've no doubt he went to her house that night intending to kill her. Elizabeth would never have given him any money, and he had to have known that. Before she could begin divorce proceedings or write Dan out of her will, Bradley had to get rid of her. Ironically, Dan will probably now inherit everything, but Brad won't be around to enjoy it."

Ryan shook his head, "You took a heck of a risk once again, Gemma. Why didn't you just tell me all of this and let me handle it?"

"Because, as you always tell me, you need physical evidence. Whereas all I need is a suspicion. I thought Brad was more likely to fall apart and confess in front of his father and sister and a couple of strangers than in interview room number one in the West London Police Station. And now, thanks to my tip, you have your physical evidence. Beneath Moriarty's claws."

"And wasn't that a nightmare getting it. The forensics officer is going to have to take time off work to recover. We'll be running the DNA tests soon."

"It'll match," I said.

"I hate it when I know these things and can't use them in the paper," Irene said.

"You can write your story ahead of time," I said.

"No, you can't." Estrada took a hearty bite of her salami sandwich. "Things will change when they come out in court."

Irene grumbled, but she knew how the game was played.

"The DNA evidence will only prove that Brad broke into the shop," Jayne said. "Not that he killed anyone. What's he saying?"

"He's saying," Ryan said, "that Gemma's a nut case and he has no idea what she's talking about. Running looks pretty bad, and we can hold him on theft of the boat and reckless endangerment while we're building our case."

"Cases," Estrada said. "One thing leads to another, and they soon start falling like dominoes."

"I feel sorry for Dan Lamb," Jayne said. "Two dead wives and a son in jail. Poor guy."

Violet nuzzled my hand, telling me to hurry up and open my sandwich. I dug in my pocket for a dog treat and handed it to her.

"Tragic all around," Ryan said. "It's brought him and his daughter close again, so I suppose that's something. I called this morning, and they were together at his house, making plans for Kathy's funeral. Elizabeth's will be a few days after."

"What I don't understand," Jack said, twisting open the cap on his iced tea, "is how you got involved in this, Jayne."

"Because she's friends with a nutty English woman," I said.

"Huh?" Jack said.

Jayne glared at me.

"So all this had nothing to do with the people at the museum or at the yacht club?" Grant asked. "Both yacht clubs?"

"Nope," I said. "But we can't forget that some of those people were around at the time of one other murder."

"You don't mean Edward Dumont?" Donald said. "That was years ago, long before Dan Lamb met Elizabeth. Wasn't it?"

"That case is still open," Irene said. "What do you know, Gemma?"

"Dan and Kathy would have known Elizabeth and Edward when they were all at West London," I said. "Elizabeth left the club after Edward's death, and she and Dan met up again years later at a wedding. I don't believe Dan had anything at all to do with Edward's death."

Ryan raised one eyebrow. I gave him a small nod and unwrapped my sandwich. "Oh, goodie. I got the roast beef. My favorite."

Donald peered into the basket. "Anything for dessert?" He was not to be disappointed.

"Speaking of the museum," Grant said. "It turns out that Elizabeth did put the wheels in motion to have the museum gala at the Cape Cod Yacht Club. Robyn went to the club on Tuesday to discuss the details, which is when Gemma saw her there. She says Elizabeth was highly distracted, furious about something, so she simply ordered the function coordinator to give Robyn everything she needed and to put it on her account."

"They're going ahead with it then?" Jayne asked.

"Apparently so. Robyn and Sharon Musgrave have thrown themselves into organizing every little detail. They're planning a formal dinner at the club, with a scaled-down silent auction." Grant coughed lightly. "Do you think Arthur will be donating *The Valley of Fear* again?"

Donald froze, a piece of shortbread halfway to his mouth.

"I heard from him last night," I said. "He's in Madrid and will be catching a flight home tonight. You can ask him yourself."

We went on to talk about other things, and enjoyed our picnic. I'd tied Violet to a nearby tree, and, all the food gone, she wandered around its base, inspecting the scents before setting down for a nap, chin in my lap.

Eventually, Estrada began checking her watch, Jayne started gathering up the debris, and Jack leapt to his feet to help. As did Violet, hoping something had been overlooked.

"I'd better get back to work. Coming, Gemma?" Jayne asked.

I gave her a quick jerk of my head that encompassed Grant, Donald, Irene, and Jack.

Jayne wiggled her eyebrows in acknowledgment and pushed herself to her feet. "I need a strong man to carry the basket. Jack, that's you. Grant, you can bring Gemma's blankets. Donald, I'd love to hear more about *The Valley of Fear*. I'm not familiar with that book. Is it a later one?"

"Written in 1914," Donald said. "*The Valley of Fear* is generally regarded as . . ."

Irene put her hands behind her head and stretched out on the grass. She'd earlier kicked off her sandals, and now she wiggled her bare toes.

"Let's go, Irene," Jayne said.

"I'm fine here."

"No, you're not. Aren't you interested in the back-story of *The Valley of Fear*?"

"Not particularly, but if I must." She groaned and struggled to her feet. "Catch you later, Gemma. And remember, Ryan, when you're ready to speak to the press, I expect the exclusive."

Louise Estrada also made a move to get up, but I said, "Stay, Detective. A few minutes."

She sat back down. "I thought you were getting rid of everyone so you two could have a romantic moment."

"Gemma wants to talk about the third murder," Ryan said. "Which I assume is that of Edward Dumont."

"Is that what passes for a romantic moment for you two?" she asked.

I didn't dignify that comment with a reply. Instead, I rubbed Violet's ears, and she settled her chin deeper into my lap. The sun was hot, the boardwalk crowded with tourists. A couple of young girls, pigtails bouncing, chased each other across the lighthouse lawn. No one paid us any attention. "Jock O'Callaghan killed Edward Dumont."

"What?" Ryan said.

"What makes you think that?" Estrada said.

"He was in love with Elizabeth Dumont."

"I have to admit," Estrada said, "you did some good thinking as regards Bradley Lamb and his movements, although we would have arrived at that conclusion ourselves eventually without your help, but now you're stretching. By all accounts, they hated each other."

"In this case," I said, "I'm doing exactly what Ryan always tells me to do. I'm presenting my observations and deductions and leaving it up to you to find the evidence. Hear me out. When I went to the WLYC on Friday to speak to Jock, it was because I thought it possible he'd killed Elizabeth in revenge for her murdering her husband seven years ago. Instead, I found him genuinely grieving. He was looking at an old picture of her on his phone—if you can get a warrant for his phone, you might want to ask why he carries a picture of someone he supposedly hated so much—and he quickly closed it when he saw me looking. His grief was genuine when he thought he was unobserved. As soon as we started talking about Elizabeth, he verbally turned on her, as he'd done before, but his entire demeanor didn't work for me. He was lying and almost choking himself on his lies."

"He publicly accused Elizabeth of killing her husband. He had her kicked out of the yacht club," Ryan said.

"I believe Jock killed Edward, expecting Elizabeth would then agree to marry him. Donald told me that Jock's marriage, which had apparently been a good one, suddenly fell apart around the time of Edward's death, at the same time as it was rumored around the club that Elizabeth was having affairs. I think she was having one affair, and it was with Jock O'Callaghan. Jock asked Elizabeth to divorce Edward. Elizabeth said no. Perhaps because she didn't love Jock, but that doesn't matter. She told Jock she couldn't divorce Edward because he'd cut her off without a cent. Whether or not that was true also doesn't matter. Jock's mother, Iris, according to club gossip, still controls their family money, and his wife, Rose—he must be thoroughly sick of flower names—has a great deal of money in her own right. If Jock and Elizabeth divorced their respective partners and married each other, they'd have seen a substantial reduction in their circumstances."

"I'm not saying I buy this, Gemma," Ryan said, "but let's pretend I do. Jock arranged a boating accident for Edward. It worked, and then what happened?"

"Elizabeth told him she wasn't going to marry him. I think she told him in pretty blunt terms something like it had been fun while it lasted, but now it was time for him to get lost. She might have even suspected Jock killed Edward—that I don't know. All of Jock's subsequent anger at Elizabeth, lasting right up to last week when they met at the auction tea, indicates a scorned and humiliated lover. He had to have her kicked out of the

West London Yacht Club because he couldn't bear seeing her every day, knowing that not only could he not have her, but she no longer wanted him. Jock then went on to have a string of affairs, and his wife, probably shocked at the change in him, found solace elsewhere."

"That's incredibly far-fetched," Estrada said.

"I'll admit," I said, "I'm sure of only one fact: Jock O'Callaghan loved Elizabeth Dumont, he loves her still, and the agony of unrequited love haunts him. All the rest is conjecture from that point."

Ryan and Estrada exchanged glances. "What can it hurt?" she said.

"I'll ask to have another look at the files," he said.

I brushed grass off my jeans. "I have to take Violet home and get back to the shop. Anyone want to walk with us?"

"I think I'll pass," Estrada said. "Some of us have work to do."

Ryan smiled at me. I smiled at him. Violet wiggled her way between us.

Chapter Twenty-Two

Two weeks later, Ryan invited himself to dinner at my house. Fortunately for Ryan, Uncle Arthur was home, and he'd put the traditional English Sunday joint of beef—to be served along with roast potatoes, Yorkshire pudding, and two veg—into the oven while I was at the shop. A sherry trifle for dessert rested on the countertop.

Ryan arrived at the door, bearing a bottle of wine and a satisfied grin.

"What's up?" I said, accepting the bottle while Violet danced her excitement.

"I have some news. Where's Arthur?"

"He went out. Donald stopped by earlier to see *The Valley of Fear*, and then they went to the pub."

"I thought that book was donated to the auction for the Scarlet House restoration fund?"

"It was. Uncle Arthur escorted Mrs. Johnston to the gala at the yacht club. When the bidding began, he had second thoughts and bought it back. Essentially, he paid fifteen thousand dollars for his own book."

"Sounds like your uncle Arthur, all right."

"He said not to wait dinner for him." I got out the corkscrew and set to work on the bottle, with a determined frown. I'm a big fan of screw-top wine bottles. "What's your news?"

"We've arrested James Cameron O'Callaghan for the murder of Edward Dumont."

The cork came out with a pop. "I assume that's Jock's full name. Is the charge going to stick?"

"Probably not. But O'Callaghan didn't like being taken away in the early hours in handcuffs. A picture of that scene will likely grace the front page of the *West London Star* tomorrow. Irene Talbot got an anonymous tip."

I handed Ryan a glass of wine. "Let's have a seat in the living room, and you can tell me what you found."

We settled ourselves comfortably on the sofa. Ryan leaned against the cushions, and I tucked my bare legs onto his lap. Violet smiled approvingly from the floor.

"Cheers." Ryan lifted his glass. I touched it with mine. "The lead detective on the case was an old guy by the name of Patrick Brown. He was close to retirement and not looking forward to it. Twice divorced, estranged from his kids, a couple of black marks on his record, and known to be a heavy drinker."

"That you're telling me the detective's life story leads me to suspect what happened."

"Yup. On the day he died, Edward Dumont arrived at the yacht club early in the morning, which was his regular routine. He was alone when he greeted one of the gardeners, a man he knew well, and then made his way down to his slip. The gardener watched him go but then went around the side of the building. No one saw Dumont again. It was, remember, very early in the morning.

"Detective Brown took early retirement six months later. He bought a place in Florida and moved down there to enjoy his retirement years."

"A nice place?"

"Very. He didn't enjoy it for long as he died of a heart attack less than a year later. His kids decided to keep the place for a vacation home. They found some papers he'd left, boxed them up, and stuck them into a closet." He sipped his wine. His blue eyes sparkled. He was enjoying dragging the story out.

"He concealed evidence that implicated Jock?"

"Yes. I had nothing to go on other than your suspicions, but I managed to make the Florida cops think I'd found fresh evidence while investigating the murder of Dumont's widow, and I needed to see if the original detective had kept anything I could use. They went through his papers and found what we were looking for soon enough. Brown was, apparently, guilt-stricken at subverting the law."

"But not enough to confess to what he'd done."

"No. He left his papers with instructions to his heirs to hand them over to the police after his death. His kids didn't care enough to even read the note, and everything was stuffed away to look at another day. We're lucky they didn't throw it all out. O'Callaghan had been a witness to a robbery in a liquor store a few weeks before Dumont's death. Brown had been the investigating officer, and he interviewed the witnesses. He'd noticed Callaghan had on an expensive designer blue blazer, which he was wearing as he'd just left the yacht club. A torn scrap of cloth matching that jacket was found caught on a loose piece of wood in Dumont's boat. Brown simply lifted the evidence and paid a call on O'Callaghan by himself, without telling anyone. He asked to see the jacket, and O'Callaghan couldn't produce it."

"Because he realized it was torn and had thrown it away."

"Brown could have ordered a search of the trash from O'Callaghan's neighborhood, but he didn't. He said he'd get rid of the fibers for a hundred thousand dollars."

"And so Jock got off scot-free."

"Until you began looking into Elizabeth's death and read his mind."

"If you want to put it like that."

Ryan grinned. "Any reasonably competent lawyer will try to get O'Callaghan off on the grounds that all we have is Brown's letter, which means almost nothing in a court of law, and a torn scrap of cloth he'd included with the note that we have absolutely nothing to match against."

"Maybe questioning him will have the domino effect Louise talked about earlier, and he'll fold."

Ryan raised his glass. "Here's to smart beautiful women who don't know how to mind their own business."

I saluted him with my own drink. Violet barked her approval. Ryan put down his glass and reached for me. He plucked my drink out of my hand and put it on the table next to his. "I hope that roast will keep."

"It won't," I said.

"Too bad."

The front door opened. "The problem with *The Valley of Fear*, Arthur," Donald Morris said, "is that—"

"Never mind." Ryan kissed the top of my head. "I've always wanted to know what the problem is with *The Valley of Fear*."

I leaned back and lifted my fingers to caress his face. "In that case, you've come to the right place. From now on, all my detecting will be between the pages of a good book."

I meant it. People don't often get second chances, and I was extremely lucky Ryan had come back into my life. From now on, I'd focus on building our relationship.

No more detecting for me.

Not until the next time, anyway.

Acknowledgments

It's getting difficult to think up cute and clever Sherlock-related titles for the books in this series. So this time I used a team: Mary Jane Maffini, Linda Wiken, Robin Harlick, Barbara Fradkin, Cheryl Freedman, Melodie Campbell, and Jenny Chen. The final decision was mine, but I thank them all for their input.

I'd also like to thank Cheryl Freedman for her keen editor's eye and Melodie Campbell for helpful advice on boats. As I know nothing at all about boats, any mistakes are strictly mine.

Read an excerpt from

THERE'S A MURDER AFOOT

the next

SHERLOCK HOLMES BOOKSHOP
MYSTERY

by VICKI DELANY

available soon in hardcover from
Crooked Lane Books

CROOKED
LANE

NEW YORK

Chapter One

My sister Phillipa Doyle is a minor functionary in the British government. What that means I'm not entirely sure, and she has never bothered to enlighten me.

Pippa is seven years older than I am, and we have never been close. People tell me I'm smart, but I am—although I'd never admit it—the slow one in my family.

I'd hoped Ryan and Pippa wouldn't meet on this trip, but such was not to be.

She extended her long thin fingers toward him, and for a moment he looked as though he scarcely knew what do to with them. Then he recovered his wits, took her hand in his, and pumped it enthusiastically. "Pleased to meet you," he said.

"Charmed," she drawled.

She wasn't going to make this easy.

When Pippa had come into the hotel bar, where we were gathering for predinner drinks, we'd exchanged air kisses and muttered insincerities. I hadn't seen my sister for five years, not since I'd moved to West London, Massachusetts. She never visited me there, and when I'd come to London to visit my parents, Pippa had been out of town. Or so she'd said.

As a child she'd been overweight and, tired of the snickering of her peers, had set out to change that with the single-minded determination characteristic of the way she does everything. By the time she'd gone to Cambridge, she'd been thin to the point of emaciated. Now, I thought, she'd lost weight since I'd last seen her. She'd probably come straight from her office, dressed in a gray skirt suit that cost in the hundreds, if not thousands, of pounds, a pink silk blouse with a bow at the neck, gray pumps—Manolo Blahnik, possibly—with four-inch heels, and small, but perfect, pearl earrings. Her brown hair, highlighted with streaks of caramel, was perfectly arranged to come to a sleek bob at her chin, and her manicure was fresh.

In contrast, I'd been on a plane all night, and although my friends and I arrived at Heathrow on time, my suitcase had not. I'd had to run out to the shops to buy what I could so I didn't have to go to dinner with my family wearing my traveling jeans, comfortable cardigan, and well-worn trainers. Greeting Pippa, I felt like a country bumpkin in my new black-and-white dress under a black shrug, black leggings, and practical shoes.

My friends had all stood when I had, and I made the introductions. As well as Ryan Ashburton, I'd come with Jayne Wilson, baker and business partner; Grant Thompson, rare-book dealer; and Donald Morris, retired lawyer and active Sherlockian.

Pippa told everyone how *absolutely* delighted she was to meet them and took the chair Grant offered her with a warm smile.

Ryan found my hand under the table and gave it a squeeze. I gave him a grateful smile in return. Our on-again, off-again, on-again romantic relationship was at the moment on again, and I was determined to keep it that way.

I hadn't told him I was nervous about seeing my sister, but I never could fool Ryan. Which was a good part of the reason our relationship was sometimes in the off phase.

"Are you a Sherlock aficionado, Ms. Doyle?" Donald Morris asked Pippa.

She turned to him with a smile. "I greatly enjoyed the Jeremy Brett TV program and some of the modern interpretations, although I wouldn't say I'm an aficionado. It is a passion of my great-uncle Arthur, whom I believe you know."

"Fabulous man, Arthur," Donald said. "His knowledge of the Canon is unparalleled."

"Has Gemma told you about our most famous relative?" she said.

I let out a breath, squeezed Ryan's hand, and then released it. So Pippa had decided to play nicely tonight. That came as an enormous relief.

Donald's eyes grew wide beneath his thick spectacles. "You mean Sir Arthur?" He turned to me. "Gemma, you always said that wasn't true. That you aren't related to the great man himself. The creator of Sherlock Holmes."

"Opinions on that differ," I said.

Pippa had instantly taken Donald's measure and decided to play along. Great-Uncle Arthur insisted that Sir Arthur Conan Doyle was a distant relative of ours. My father maintained there wasn't the slightest bit of evidence to support that.

Although, I suppose if you go back far enough, most everyone is related in some way or another, particularly those who share a name.

Pippa had never shown any interest at all in the tales of Sherlock Holmes, and I assumed she was pretending to in order to be polite to Donald. That Donald was a devotee of the Great Detective was obvious. Not only was he here in London the night before a Holmes conference, but he wore a pin attached to his jacket indicating he was a member of a Sherlockian society. His ulster was tossed over the back of his chair. That type of garment—a calf-length coat with a small cape—had last been fashionable around the time Holmes and Watson were dashing through the fog-shrouded streets of London hunting for the origins of the goose that swallowed a priceless jewel.

The waiter placed another small bowl of nuts and wasabi peas onto the table. "Can I get you something from the bar, madam?"

"A soda water, please," Pippa said. "With a slice of lemon."

"Good beer, this," Grant Thompson said. "I've missed a good English beer."

Pippa turned her smile on him, and this time genuine interest flashed in her eyes. "You're obviously an American, but you've spent time in England. How marvelous. Oxford would be my guess."

"I did my PhD in English lit there, yes," Grant said.

A middle-aged couple came into the bar, and I leapt to my feet. "Here they are now." I ran across the room and gathered the newcomers into a deep hug.

My mother hugged me in return and then stepped away so my dad could shake me with enough enthusiasm to make my teeth rattle. "Gemma," he said when we finally separated. "Here you are. Gosh, but I've missed you."

"I missed you too, Dad. Come and meet my friends." I led my parents to our table. "Everyone, this is Mum and Dad. Anne and Henry Doyle."

We were having drinks in the downstairs bar of the Bentley Hotel in Kensington. My American friends and I were in London for the weekend-long Sherlock Holmes in the Modern World conference being held at a big convention hotel a few doors down the street.

I'd come because I was giving a talk on Holmes's influence on popular culture, Grant because he was on the lookout for rare books at a good price, and Donald because Sherlock Holmes was his life. Jayne was here for the vacation, and Ryan had come because he was Ryan.

I noticed my mother glancing between Ryan and Grant, sizing them both up, wondering which one was with me. They were similar in age, and both extremely handsome. Ryan, all six foot three of him, had the look of his Black Irish ancestors, with warm blue eyes and thick dark hair cut very short. Grant was slightly shorter but also fit and lean, with brown hair curling around his collar and hazel eyes containing flakes of green that danced when he smiled.

Greetings over and introductions made, my parents took their seats. We occupied a large round table in a corner with enough space for us all. A plush banquette, covered in red silk with a pattern of tigers and cheetahs etched in gold thread, was tucked into an alcove, and the chairs around the table were upholstered in green and gold velvet. Paintings of big cats hung on the walls, and the doorways and alcoves were trimmed in gilt. Being in the basement, the room had no windows; a soft golden light, the type that makes everyone look good, came from lamps and the candles on each table.

This time, it was my turn to give Ryan's hand a squeeze. He was anything but the nervous sort, but he'd been nervous at meeting my parents for the first time. Earlier, he'd called me down to his room to help him choose what to wear. He didn't want to look too formal, as though he were trying to impress anyone, or too casual, as though he couldn't be bothered to make the effort. I'd told him to take off the suit and tie and wear jeans and a leather jacket and just be himself. He looked so good tonight.

Of course, he looked good all the time.

I gave him a smile and his blue eyes twinkled in response. My mother noticed and she nodded in approval.

The waiter brought Pippa's drink and asked what the newcomers would have. Mum ordered a Kir Royale and Dad a single-malt scotch. My mother had come straight from court and was dressed in her regular uniform of black suit with white blouse and black shoes with low heels. Dad, recently retired, wore neatly pressed beige trousers and an oatmeal sweater. In contrast, Donald looked like an unmade bed—which he was, as he still wore the clothes he'd slept in on the plane—in many-times-washed jeans and a rumpled T-shirt under his equally rumpled sports jacket. Jayne looked lovely, as she always did no matter how jet-lagged she might be, in a navy-blue dress with a thin white belt. Grant, like Ryan, had dressed suitably for a casual dinner.

When the waiter left to fetch the drinks, Dad asked Donald if this was his first time in London, and Donald erupted with enthusiasm. "I can't believe I've never been to England before. Imagine, I'm treading the very streets frequented by Sherlock Holmes and Dr. John Watson."

"You do know they weren't real people, don't you, Donald?" I teased. Donald knew, but his enthusiasm got the better of him sometimes.

"Imaginatively speaking, of course," he said. "But Sir Arthur himself trod these ancient cobblestones." Donald's eyes shone, and I thought of the construction work we'd had to detour around on the approach to the hotel. Not many ancient cobblestones left in Kensington.

"On the cab ride here," he continued, "we drove right past Gloucester Road station. I couldn't believe it! The very place where, in *The Bruce-Partington Plans*, Holmes himself walked along the rails, intent on a mission of the utmost national importance, to ascertain if the houses backing onto the rail track had windows looking over it. I was so excited to see more, I didn't take the time to unpack but rushed off to have a closer look." He leaned over and pulled a leather briefcase off the floor. "Would you like to see my pictures?"

"Of Gloucester Road station?" Mum said. "Perhaps not right now."

Undeterred, Donald pulled a small compact camera out of his case and switched it on. He leaned closer to Jayne and held the camera in front of her face. He flicked happily through it. "I particularly loved the flower seller. QUEEN OF GLOUCESTER ROAD spelled out in flowers. Isn't that clever?"

"Very clever," Jayne agreed, suppressing a yawn. London time is five hours ahead of Massachusetts, and we'd been on a late flight last night. I should probably have put dinner with the family off for another day, but the conference began tomorrow and we'd be busy over the weekend.

"What time's your talk, Gemma?" Dad asked.

"Two thirty tomorrow."

"We'll be there," he said.

"You don't have to come if you don't want to," I replied. "It's not going to be very exciting."

"A lecture on Sherlock Holmes pastiche," Pippa said. "What could possibly be more thrilling?"

Donald didn't catch my sister's sarcasm. "I totally agree! Gemma is going to be fascinating, and her talk will be about far more than just books. I printed out the schedule for the weekend, and I've marked off the lectures and panels I'm planning to attend." He rummaged around inside his bag. "Would you like to see?"

"No, thank you," she said.

He pulled the sheets of paper out anyway. "The weekend will be all about the conference, but on Monday I'll be free to visit Baker Street and the Sherlock Holmes Museum. I'm scheduled for a walking tour of Holmes's London on Monday afternoon."

I sipped my glass of prosecco. "I assume you're too busy to come and hear me speak, Pippa."

"I wouldn't miss it," she replied.

Jayne glanced between us.

"And you, Grant," Pippa said. "Will you be speaking also?"

"Not me," he said. "I'm here to check out the books for sale. I'm a rare-book dealer, and I specialize in Victorian and Edwardian crime fiction. I have several clients at home who might be interested in some of the items on offer this weekend."

"Book collecting must be *so* interesting," she said.

He straightened in his chair and adjusted his shoulders. "I find it so."

Pippa was seated on the other side of the table from me. Too far away for me to give her a solid kick in the shins. Instead I gave her a warning look. She smiled in return before turning back to Grant. "Do tell me about your time at Oxford. I myself went to Cambridge."

"We're rivals, then," he said.

"So we are."

"Did you remember to get us banquet tickets, dear?" my mother asked.

"I did, and it's a good thing, because they told me they're almost sold out. Are you sure you want to come? I can probably sell the tickets back to the organizers."

"Of course we want to come," Dad said. "Arthur is being honored."

My great-uncle Arthur Doyle had opened the Sherlock Holmes Bookshop and Emporium at 222 Baker Street, West London, Massachusetts. A few years later, I'd joined him in the business, and I was now the manager and co-owner. He was being given an award at the conference's Saturday night banquet for helping to spread the love of Sherlock Holmes beyond Britain's shores. Actually, I was being given the award and would be saying a few words of thanks in his place. Arthur had considered attending the conference until he heard he'd be expected to give a speech, so he'd suggested I (more like forced me to) come instead.

"I reserved us a table at a place not far from here." My father scooped up a handful of nuts and popped them into his mouth.

"Thanks," I said. "Jayne had a nap when we checked in, but we'll all want an early night."

Jayne attempted, and failed, to smother another yawn.

Pippa flirted with Grant, and Grant flirted back. Mum asked Jayne if she had plans for the visit apart from the conference. Dad asked Ryan what he did for a living, and my father, a retired officer in the Metropolitan Police, was absolutely delighted to hear that Ryan was a West London police detective.

It was early, just after five, but the bar was filling up. I caught quite a few American accents and wondered if those people were here for the conference.

A burst of loud laugher came from the stairwell and a group of men came in. They were a mixture of nationalities—American, English, French, a Scotsman—but they had one thing in common: they weren't here for their first drink of the day.

They grabbed a table in the center of the room and, with much shouting and laughing, pulled up chairs.

"Do you live nearby, Mrs. Doyle?" Jayne asked.

"Call me Anne, please. We're not far at all. The location of this conference of yours turned out to be very convenient for us."

"Things have changed a lot on the force since my day," Dad said to Ryan. "Even though that wasn't long ago."

"What do you do, Pippa?" Grant asked.

"A minor clerical position with the Department for Transport," Pippa said with a light laugh. "I'm basically just a pencil pusher." She ran her hands across her glass as she talked. She was, I knew, keeping them busy and out of the nut dish.

I sipped my prosecco and glanced around the room. The waiter had brought tall glasses of beer and bowls of nuts for the newcomers at the center table. The men lifted their glasses, clinked, and said, "Cheers," before taking a hearty swig. One of them did not join the others in the toast. Instead, he stared intently at our table. He caught me watching but did not turn away.

I leaned across Ryan and spoke to my dad in a low voice. "Center table. Big guy in a blue shirt. He seems to be watching you."

Beside me, I felt Ryan stiffen. Dad stretched his shoulders with a groan. He leaned over to speak to Jayne, which, not at all incidentally, gave him a view of the room behind him.

Shock, followed by anger, crossed his face.

The big man in the blue shirt grinned.

My dad turned back to our table. He picked up his glass and finished his drink. "Time to be off. The restaurant won't hold our place much longer."

"Excellent," Donald said. "I'm starving. Perhaps we could go to a genuine English pub one night?"

"I know the perfect place," I said.

"Is something the matter?" my mother said to my father.

"No." He got to his feet, his face set in tight, angry lines.

Ryan jumped up, ready to follow him.

"The walking tour should be fascinating," Donald said to Jayne. "I hope it doesn't rain."

The man at the center table watched us gather our coats and bags. The waiter hurried over with our bill. I grabbed it. "I'll sign for it." If Donald had to calculate his share of the bill, determine the exchange rate, work out a suitable tip, and then examine every pound note and coin in his wallet, we'd never get out of here.

Dad stepped back and allowed Mum and Jayne to precede him. Mum was telling Jayne she must visit the food hall at Harrods, which was within easy walking distance of our hotel.

"What's wrong?" Pippa asked in a low voice. "Why the sudden rush?"

"Nothing's wrong," Dad said. "I'm hungry. Let's go."

I gestured to Grant and Ryan to go with Pippa, Jayne, Mum, and Donald. Dad and I followed. As we passed the big table in the center of the room, the man in the blue shirt stood up. "Henry Doyle."

"Randolph." Dad's voice contained not a touch of warmth. "What brings you to this part of town?"

"Business, what else?" Randolph studied me, his hand resting on his chin, his head cocked slightly to one side. "It's been a while, Henry. Don't tell me this is sweet little Phillipa, all grown up."

"I'm not Phillipa." I took my cues from Dad. He was not at all friendly with this man, so I wouldn't be either.

"You must be her sister, then. You look very much like your mother when she was your age. Anne's as beautiful as I remember, although *you've* aged a lot, Henry. Nice to see you two are still together. And they said it wouldn't last." A small smile touched the edges of Randolph's mouth. He was about the same age as my parents, late fifties, well groomed and casually yet expensively dressed. His companions' conversation died as they looked between us and their friend in confusion. One of the men wore a Baker Street Irregulars lapel pin. So he, at least, was here for the conference. Which might mean this Randolph, whoever he might be, was as well.

Ryan and Pippa hadn't left the room with the others. They stood in the doorway, watching.

"Anne didn't recognize me," Randolph said. "I guess I've changed a lot over the years. But you knew me right off, Henry."

"I've seen your mug shots," Dad said.

Randolph laughed heartily. "I bet you made a point of searching for them. Oh, yes, I've followed your career too. Now that we've run into each other, let's keep in touch." He opened his wallet and took out a business card. He held it out, but my father didn't accept it.

"If you'll excuse us," Dad said. "I'm going to dinner with my family." He walked away. I followed. I couldn't resist glancing over my shoulder as I passed through the doorway.

Randolph had picked up his beer, but he hadn't taken his seat. He lifted his glass in a toast and gave me a broad wink.

I grabbed Dad's arm at the bottom of the stairs and spoke in a low voice. "What was that about?"

"Best not mention this to your mother," he said.

"Why not? Who was that?"

"An old case," he said.

"No it wasn't. He knew Mum and he knew your children's names, Pippa anyway. He said I look like Mum, but he looks more like her than I do. The same accent, the same eyes and chin. They even have the same mannerisms, that way of cocking the head to one side when studying something."

Dad grinned at me. "I see living in America hasn't dulled your wits any. Which one of those young men is your boyfriend? The police officer, I suspect. A good choice. The other was clearly smitten by your sister, yet you didn't seem to mind overly much."

"Dad. Tell me what's going on. Those men Randolph is with are here for the conference, so I suspect he is too."

My father hesitated for a moment before he said, "That, my dear, is your uncle Randolph. The family called him Randy."

"I have an uncle named Randolph? Why have I never heard of him before?"

"He's your mother's younger brother. The black sheep of the Denhaugh family. He and I never did like each other much. I haven't seen Randy since the night he stole the Constable your grandfather had put away to provide him and your grandmother with some much-needed income for their old age. Shall we join the others?"